AZULA

AN EXTREMELY TABOO NOVEL
seven rue

Copyright © 2021 by Seven Rue.
All rights reserved.

No part of this book may be reproduced, scanned, or distributed in any printed or electronic form without permission. Please do not participate in or encourage piracy of copyrighted materials in violation of the author's rights. Thank you for respecting the hard work of this author.

This is a work of fiction. Names, characters, places, and incidents either are the product of the author's imagination or are used fictitiously, and any resemblance to locales, events, business establishments, or actual persons—living or dead—is entirely coincidental.

Editor: Jennifer Marie
Cover design: Seven Rue
Formatting: Seven Rue

Trigger warning.
This book includes incest.
Meaning that the main character is related to the five men she has sex with, which are her dad, uncle, two brothers, and cousin. Yes, full-on blood-related, and if this is something that triggers you, do NOT read this.
If you do choose to go ahead and read this book while knowing that you won't like it, I am not responsible for whatever you end up feeling.
If you're open-minded and want to experience fiction differently, enjoy!

Sexual scenes in this book contain:
Watersports (piss play), dominance, group sex, voyeurism, slapping and spanking, anal, double penetration.

Since this book is only available on my website, leaving a review on the Zon is impossible.
But you can write a review on your Instagram, Blog, Goodreads or whatever website/socials you're on.

Thank you!

To myself, for not caring what others think.
Because let's face it...writing a book like this and putting it out there for like-minded people to enjoy but also for a whole bunch of haters to send me (insanely rude) messages about how disgusting it is to write such books takes a whole lot of courage.

one

AZULA

"He wants to fuck you."

I looked at the can of soda in my hand to avoid Dustin's stare from across the beach, which was essentially just a small patch of sand by the lake.

The trailer park had one hang-out spot, and that was the beach where every night from spring to fall, we'd all hang out.

It's where I grew up, and the only place I liked to be other than my bedroom.

"He's a senior," I muttered, squeezing my half-empty can in my fist.

"So? He obviously wants to fuck you. He's been staring ever since he arrived and his gaze has already stripped and clothed you multiple times by now," Bonnie stated, laughing softly.

"And am I dressed or naked right now?"

She turned her head to look at me, and with a stupid grin on her face, she replied, "Naked."

I rolled my eyes at my best friend, and when I lifted my gaze, his eyes were on mine again.

"I don't think I even like him that way," I admitted, taking a sip of my soda, then placing it on the empty tree trunk next to me.

"No one dislikes Dustin. And you damn well know that this is your only chance to let him fuck you."

"What's he even doing here?" I asked, frowning at the fire in front of us.

"No idea. But he obviously came to see you. And I don't think he'll move unless you talk to him. Tonight's boring anyway. It's still too early for everyone to come out here to hang."

Yesterday, only a few of our neighbors came to drink a beer and talk to each other, but I had hoped for more people to show up tonight.

Excluding Dustin.

"Thane and Wesson will be here soon. They went to get some groceries and Dad's closing up the garage."

"And what about your cousin?" Bonnie asked.

I shrugged. "I haven't seen Reuben today. He wasn't at breakfast but Warren didn't say anything about why he wasn't there this morning."

Uncle Warren and cousin Reuben lived in the trailer next to ours, and being Dad's brother, Warren came over a lot to spend time with us.

Not only that.

Dad and Warren owned a car repair shop, and since my brothers and Reuben didn't attend college, they all worked for them.

Whatever money came in from their work, they'd share it, and therefore we ate breakfast and dinner together most evenings.

"Well, anyway. He's still staring. And if you don't go over there now, I will."

I looked at Dustin again, and seeing his determination in his eyes, I decided that I couldn't just let him stand there all on his own any longer.

He came here for a reason, and I should show some hospitality.

"Don't bother," I sighed, standing up.

"Go get him," Bonnie said with a grin, and once I started walking, I began to wonder why he came.

I had never really talked to him at school, and we've only ever crossed paths in the hallways.

I really had no clue why he'd wanna fuck me, as Bonnie said.

Dustin was handsome and popular, and I was the redhead who lived in a dirty trailer in the town's worst area.

But hey, there was obviously something that attracted him to me if he came all the way here on his own.

"Thought you'd leave me standing here until that fire dies down," he said once I stopped in front of him, and with my arms crossed, I smiled tightly.

"Bonnie pushed me to come talk to you. Why are you here?" I asked, eyeing him carefully.

"Am I not welcome?"

I shrugged again.

"Usually, no one who's not part of the trailer park comes to the bonfires."

"So I needed an invitation?"

I shook my head. "We don't invite people who don't live in the trailer park to come hang out with us."

He chuckled. "Right. Forgot this is a gated community. Although it is quite the shithole."

Raising a brow at him, I punched his arm with my fist. "Don't talk shit about the trailer park. It's my home, and I can kick you out quicker than you came here."

"All right, all right. I'm sorry I said this place is a shithole." As serious as his words were, his face wasn't.

"Why are you here, Dustin?"

"Hoping to finally get to know you a little better." His eyes wandered from my face down to my tits, legs, and back up to my eyes.

"You see me in school almost every day. That's a good place to get to know someone," I stated.

"School's crowded."

"School's got your friends around. You'd never talk to me there."

The corners of his mouth curled up. "Wouldn't be caught dead talking to you there, you're right. But that's because I wanna spare you all the jealous stares of other girls."

He reached out to wrap a strand of hair around his fingers, and while I kept my eyes on his face, he moved his back down.

"How about you grab that towel you were sitting on so we can sit down by the water further back? To talk without anyone near?" he suggested.

"To fuck."

"What?"

"To fuck without anyone near is what you wanted to say I presume?"

He chuckled and shrugged, then looked back into my eyes. "Whatever you want, babe."

I wanted to throw up.

He wasn't as smooth as he thought, and I had no clue how he got so many girls to fall to their knees and suck him dry when his personality was so goddamn awful.

"You don't have to pretend to like me to get your dick inside of me."

My words surprised me.

"I don't?"

God, what a fucking idiot.

"No. But you have to be honest. I don't like when guys act all innocent to get a girl naked. I don't need you to filter your words if you know exactly what you want from me."

Another chuckle left him. "Shit. Okay. So you'll let me fuck you?"

"Sure. Whatever."

He still looked unsure, but excitement soon washed over his face while his eyes were glued to my tits.

"Wait over there," I said, pointing to a more shaded spot on the beach.

The sun was going down, but with all the trees surrounding the beach, we'd be covered enough for others not to see.

Once he turned and walked away, I went back to the tree trunk I was sitting on and grabbed the towel that I left there the night before.

I wouldn't bother taking it back inside, seeing as we didn't get much rain around here, but after fucking on it, I would definitely take it inside for a wash.

"So?"

I looked up to see Bonnie walking over to me, and with a nod toward Dustin, I replied, "I'll be right back."

Bonnie laughed, then took a sip of her beer. "Have fun. Does he have condoms?"

"Didn't ask, but if he doesn't, I won't let him."

"Good girl. Now, go. I found Reuben. Gonna hang out with him until you're done."

I sighed and looked past her to see my cousin

standing next to the cooler, filling it with more beer.

"Don't tell him where I am."

"Do you really think I would ruin this moment for you? Your last time was six months ago. You need a dick or you'll dry out."

I didn't respond, and when I walked back to Dustin, I put the towel down in front of us.

"Okay," I said, letting him know that he was now allowed to initiate us fucking.

And he didn't waste any time.

His hands were on my hips, pulling me to him as his head tilted down to kiss me.

I wasn't much shorter than him, yet I pushed myself onto my tiptoes to stop him from arching my back so much.

He was leaning into me like the tower of Pisa, and I needed to somehow straighten us both to not feel awkward standing there kissing like in all the stupid rom-coms.

His lips moved against mine before his tongue pushed between them, almost stabbing my own.

Safe to say that Dustin wasn't as spectacular as most girls at school claimed him to be.

Yikes.

"Lay down," he mumbled into the kiss, and to hopefully reach a climax quickly and get this all over with, I broke the kiss to take off my shirt, then I laid down on the towel and watched as Dustin opened his pants while keeping his eyes on me the whole time.

"Suck my dick?" he asked, but I shook my head.

"No. Just fuck me."

But that wouldn't be as easy as I had thought, and I was shocked to say the least when he pulled down his shorts.

two

AZULA

His cock looked…sad.

No hardness whatsoever, and although it was a decent size for it not being erect, I was starting to question if he ever had sex before.

I looked up from his cock, raising an eyebrow at him. "Was looking at me not enough to get you at least semi-hard?" I asked.

He frowned, wrapping his fingers around his cock and rubbing it. "I didn't think you'd let me," he stated, then he got down on his knees with his eyes still locked on mine.

"Maybe if we kiss a little more it'll get hard," he suggested, but that just made me laugh.

Of course, it wasn't his fault if he couldn't get a boner while flirting with a girl and the intention of fucking in the back of his mind, but this was ridiculous.

"Please tell me you've had sex before."

"Shit, of course I have! Jesus, Azula, not every guy gets rock hard by just looking at a girl."

"'Course they fucking do. Put that larva back in your pants and get the hell out of here."

Wesson's voice was louder than appropriate, seeing as we weren't too far away from the fire.

I looked up at him, sighing and leaning back on my elbows while Dustin stood up fast.

He turned away as he pulled up his shorts, but that didn't stop Wesson from staring at his back.

"Shit," Dustin muttered, and when his pants were buttoned, he turned around but took a few steps back already. "Who the hell is that?"

"My brother," I said, nonchalantly.

"Shit," he repeated. "Sorry, man. She wanted me to fuck her. I wasn't going to without her consent."

"With that sorry excuse for a dick dangling between your legs?" Wesson asked, his brows raised high. "Fuck off."

I watched as Dustin left between the trees, and when I looked at Wesson again, he pushed my shirt lying in the sand closer to me with his foot.

"No fucking on the beach," he growled, and when he turned to walk away, I quickly reached for his leg and gripped his sock at his ankle, making him stop and look back down at me.

"You fucked that girl here too a few nights ago. You can't tell me what to do."

He shook off my hand and bent down to grab my wrist, then he pulled me up with his other hand fisting my shirt.

"Dad's not gonna be happy about this when I tell him."

I laughed. "You're telling Dad? What are you, four?"

"I'm your older brother and I don't want some cocksucker fucking my little sister on the beach with other people able to see. Shit, Zula. The fuck is wrong with you?"

He let go of my wrist and pulled my shirt over my head.

"Nobody would've seen us," I muttered, letting him dress me like he used to when we were younger.

At sixteen, I was the youngest in our family.

Wesson was twenty-three, and Thane twenty, and being seven and four years older than me, they always felt the need to protect me.

"The whole damn trailer park would've seen you let that idiot fuck you. Why the hell was he even here?" he asked.

I shrugged. "He came on his own."

"Good thing he knows not to come back anymore. He doesn't belong here. Go. Do some teenage-shit girls your age always do."

"Girls my age get fucked and drunk at parties," I stated, frowning at him.

"Then do the second thing out of those two options. No fucking."

I rolled my eyes and walked past him to get back to the bonfire where now more people were sitting around on the trunks, and I heard Wesson follow close behind.

"Go say hello to Dad," he told me, and when he was off my back, I stopped to look around and find my father.

My eyes met his as he took a sip of his beer, and when he waved at me, I walked around the fire to get to him.

"Hey, Dad," I greeted, letting him pull me against his side with one arm while he held the other out to get his can and cigarette far enough away from me.

"Hey, baby. Wesson bossing you around again?" he asked, kissing the top of my head.

I shrugged, not wanting to get into what happened just minutes ago. "How was your day at work?"

"Good. Rough. How's school? Any tests coming up?"

"Nope. Just boring stuff we're learning about. Where's Thane?"

Thane was definitely my favorite brother, just because he wasn't as bossy as Wesson.

We'd get angry at each other at times, but that's because we still shared a room and I hadn't gotten used to him playing video games until late at night.

At one point our fights had gotten so out of hand that I decided to just sit on my bed and watch him play until he was tired and went to sleep too.

Trailer homes weren't fancy, especially not the ones in our community, and sometimes you just had to accept things you weren't okay with.

"He went to grab some snacks and cigarettes at the gas station with Reuben and Bonnie. They'll be back soon."

"Didn't he go grocery shopping with Wesson before they came here?" I asked.

"Yeah, guess they forgot a few things."

We got interrupted as an old friend of his walked toward us, and I knew it was time for me to go.

"I'll go check on Warren," I whispered, kissing his jaw before stepping away from his side and walking up the small path to get to the street.

Our trailer park wasn't big with only twenty-three trailers, but that made this whole community so special.

Everyone knew each other, and no matter how scary it was to walk around at night, there was no reason for you to be scared.

Ever.

I walked up the two steps of Uncle Warren's trailer and knocked on the door before opening the door, knowing it would be unlocked.

"Ren? Are you coming to the beach?" I asked, looking around the living area and kitchen.

I heard steps coming from the back of the trailer, and when I closed the door behind me, he entered the living area with only his jeans on.

His blond hair was wet, dripping onto the carpet.

"Hey, Z. Did your father send you?" he asked.

Warren was handsome, but then…that gene flowed through our whole family, making my brothers, Dad, and cousin Reuben handsome.

I was average.

Well, I was the prettiest girl in this community, and I still had to become an adult, but there were much prettier girls in this town.

Not that I gave a fuck about them.

Or my looks.

I was happy with myself, and that's what mattered.

"No, but he's down there already. Are you coming?" I asked again, and this time, he answered.

"Yeah, just need a few minutes. Did you wear that to school today?" he asked, nodding to my shirt and skirt.

"Yes, why? Don't you like it?"

I looked down at myself, puckering my lips and trying to figure out what was wrong with my outfit.

I couldn't care less about the way I dressed, seeing as these clothes were only temporary.

I was still going through puberty, and my breasts had grown in the past year.

Not too much, but enough to make me go from an extra small to a small-sized shirt.

It was getting pretty tight up there.

"I love it. You know that shirt once belonged to me, right?" he asked with a grin.

"I thought it was Dad's. I took it out of his closet this morning."

It was fairly large on me, but I had tied a knot in the front and tucked the rest of the fabric into my skirt.

"I gave it to him one day at work because his was dirty. Guess he never gave it back."

"Do you want it back?" I asked, ready to take it off again.

He studied me for a moment, then shook his head. "Keep it. Looks better on you."

I smiled at his words.

Warren and I had always been close, and out of everyone in my family, he was the only one I could calm down with.

I was an agitated person, even when I was just sitting at my desk in class, but whenever Warren was around, I was able to relax.

My eyes moved from his face to his chest, then down to his stomach where his muscles were toned enough to show off a six-pack.

He didn't do fitness, and neither did Dad.

But my brothers and Reuben lifted some weights in

our backyard whenever they had the time to.

They weren't all ripped like bodybuilders, but they were defined enough to be on magazines.

When Warren let out a chuckle, I looked back into his eyes and smiled, then watched him walk back into his bedroom to get himself a shirt.

"Are many people at the beach?" he asked.

Warren was a more reserved guy, and although he got along with everyone, he liked being alone at times.

"When I first got there, not many were around. But before I left, more came," I explained, looking at my fingers while he got dressed.

He didn't respond, and when he came back, I smiled again and eyed his shirt.

"Cool shirt," I complimented. "Is it new?"

"I found it at the thrift store last week. I'll take you there soon so you can shop for new clothes."

"I'd love to."

My smile never faded when he was in my presence, and he damn well noticed my happiness whenever he saw my face.

Not even Dad had this effect on me, and I loved Dad like no other.

He was my hero, but sometimes even I needed a break from him.

Or Wesson.

And Thane.

And Reuben.

We were quiet again, eyeing each other while our thoughts stayed hidden inside our heads.

When he moved, I kept my eyes on him, making sure to follow every single one of his movements, and when he stopped in front of me, I tilted my head back to keep him in sight.

13

"Let's go," he whispered, lifting his hand and placing his forefinger underneath my chin, then brushing along it with his thumb.

"You look pretty today, Z."

My smile widened, and although my nose and cheeks were covered in freckles, he liked my face the way it was.

No makeup.

Nothing.

"Thanks," I replied, letting him caress my skin a little while longer before turning and opening the door to get outside.

"Come on! They're waiting on us," I told him as I walked backward, motioning for him to hurry up.

"I'm coming," he said, chuckling and following me.

He was happy, and in moments like these, I wished I knew what he was thinking.

I wondered if he was thinking the same that I was…

three

WARREN

"Brought you cigarettes, Dad," Reuben said as he walked around me to stand in front of me.

He was blocking my view from watching Azula dance on the other side of the fire, enjoying the music and not being bothered by anyone else around her.

She's never been ashamed of anything, and I loved watching her confidence grow each day.

I looked up at my son and grabbed the pack of cigarettes out of his hand, then I pushed him aside with the back of my hand pressing against the side of his leg.

I needed to get my eyes on her again.

"Thanks," I told him, now observing how Bonnie joined in on the dancing.

"What are you staring at?" he asked, sitting down next to me, but he answered his own question just seconds later. "Back off, old man. I got a thing going on with Bonnie already. She's not into older men."

"Don't care about your little girlfriend, son," I stated, leaving him quiet for a moment when he realized I've been staring at his cousin.

"Still acting like a possessive motherfucker? Zula's doing fine, Dad. She doesn't need protection."

As the only girl in our family, she had always been the one person all of us took the most care of.

Some differently than others, but it was important to us all that she grew up happy and protected.

"Should be you taking care of her the way I do. When's the last time you talked to her?" I asked.

My brother joined us, sitting down on the other side of me with two beers, handing me one and grabbing a cigarette out of his own pocket.

"What are you two grumbling on about?" Viggo asked.

Although he was three years older than me, he looked much younger than a fifty-three-year-old.

My hair was already starting to turn white at some parts, whereas his dark blond hair was shining like the ones from a fucking shampoo commercial.

Lucky fucker, but white hair was the least of my problems.

"Has she ever complained about anything?" I asked, nodding toward his daughter who was now trying to get Thane to dance with her and Bonnie.

Thane wasn't as grumpy as Wesson, but both could pull those sticks out of their asses and loosen up a bit.

"My baby doesn't complain about anything and you damn well know it. She's an angel. At times I wonder how I lucked out so damn much."

"Her mother was an angel too," I said.

"Yeah, look-wise. Aunt Bee was a witch," Reuben muttered, making me push my elbow against his ribs.

"He's right," Viggo laughed with a shake of his head. "After mourning her death for way too long, my boys made me realize how much of a waste of time she was becoming. Not saying I was happy she was taken from us, but now I am."

I had never understood how you could forget the love you felt for a person after only a few months, but my family was different than others.

Death was accepted differently here, and it took Azula and her brothers just about two days to get over their mother's death.

Could be them showing off how strong they were on the inside, but the more I studied them, the more I realized that they did, in fact, not give a single fuck about Bee not being around anymore.

Life came and went, so why not just fucking accept it?

"What do you think of Bonnie, Vig? Hot piece of ass, isn't she?" Reuben asked, but Viggo shrugged and kept his eyes on his daughter.

"As long as she makes my baby happy, I don't care what her ass looks like."

Age was nothing but a number in this community, and it showed.

Hell, even I had a thing for one of the neighbor's daughters one time when she was only nineteen, but she decided that this community wasn't her home and left.

Fucked her once, hell, maybe even twice, but then she was gone.

When Azula finally managed to get Thane to dance,

she stepped away to let Bonnie seduce him on the little dancefloor they created, and when her eyes met mine, she smiled and jogged over to us.

"You should come dance with us too," she suggested, sounding out of breath.

"You should sit down here with us and take it easy," I replied, nodding to my lap as I leaned back more into the camping chair.

"You're no fun. And Thane's taking Bonnie from you, by the way," she told Reuben.

"The hell he is. He's got no chance with her," Reuben spat, emptying his beer before standing up to head over to his cousin.

Thane was only a year younger than Reuben, and watching them grow up together was amusing as hell.

They were competitive, but in the end, nothing was breaking their bond.

"Come here," I nudged, hooking my foot around her ankle to pull her closer.

She came willingly, sitting down on my lap sideways with her arm around my shoulders.

"Warren said he'd take me to the thrift store soon," she told Viggo happily as I placed my left arm around her back and my right hand still holding the beer on her leg.

"Good for him. Hope he spoils you like he should every day," Viggo said in a teasing tone.

He knew I was the one bringing her cake and snacks almost every night after work, and I was also the one who took her to fast food places sometimes.

Not saying that Viggo never did, but he was often tired after work, and going out was not his thing.

I took another sip of my beer and watched as my son pulled Bonnie to him, leaving Thane standing there on his own but not looking too bothered.

He turned, searched for Wesson in the small crowd, and went over to talk to him and a few other guys from the neighborhood.

"Hungry?" I asked Azula, my eyes on hers again as she turned to look at me.

"Not really. I ate a sandwich before coming here, and today at lunch I went to grab some tacos with Bonnie," she told us.

"And that's enough?" I asked.

She shrugged, puckering her lips as her eyes moved to my bottle of beer. "I guess."

"Gotta eat, baby. We got food in the fridge and freezer," Viggo told her, taking a drag of his cigarette before throwing it into the sand.

"I'll eat something later," she promised, leaning into me a little more with her ass wiggling against my crotch.

I moved my left hand to her hip, pressing my fingers into it and making sure she wouldn't move anymore.

Her skirt had already ridden up too much, barely covering her thighs and almost showing off her panties.

Didn't need others to see it, but it had gotten dark quickly, and the fire was the only light source besides the moon hiding behind the clouds.

"Dad?" she asked, her hand now moving to my neck and into my hair at the back of my head.

"Yeah, baby?"

"Wesson didn't tell you about what happened before you arrived, did he?"

Viggo frowned, and at first, I had thought he'd say no. "'Course he did. And I didn't think you'd bring it back up. No fucking on the beach."

I raised a brow. "Who wanted to fuck you?"

Azula scowled at both of us. "Why does it matter? I'm sixteen. And I've had sex before."

"But not on this beach," Viggo muttered, taking a sip of his beer before looking at his daughter with a serious expression.

"That boy didn't belong here."

"So?"

"So I don't want people who don't belong here hanging around our properties."

Azula rolled her eyes, muttering under her breath. "You're not the king of the trailer park."

"Not what I need to be to make you do what I tell you. No boys."

"You can't stop me from dating them," she stated.

I put my bottle down and brushed back a long strand of hair, then tucked it behind her ear with a smile on my face.

"You don't need those fuckers, Z. You got your brothers and cousin. Don't need any more guys in your life right now."

She studied me for a while, then she smiled back and placed her hand on my chest, fisting my shirt in her hand.

"And I got you."

"That's right. And a grumpy old man who wants the best for you. Don't be so hard on your father."

She looked at Viggo who was chuckling at our conversation, and after he rubbed Azula's head with his large hand, he got up, leaned down to kiss her temple, then left to grab two more beers from the cooler.

"I don't understand why you all have to act like I'm a child. I'm not stupid, you know?"

"Not what I said," I told her, cupping her jaw and squeezing her cheeks until her lips puckered. "Just saying that boys can wait. And in the meantime, you have us to love and worry about."

"I can't love you the way I would love another boy," she told me, and at that point, it was best for me to keep my damn mouth shut.

Can't fuck your own damn niece, a voice in my head said, while another was just laughing like a crazy person.

"You can do whatever the hell you want, Zula, as long as your heart's happy."

Her eyes moved from mine to my lips, and while I continued to cup her jaw and squeeze her cheeks, she tried to smile which eventually resulted in an adorable frown.

"My heart's happy right now."

Without thinking much about it, she leaned in and pressed her lips onto mine, but as quickly as they touched mine, they were gone again.

"You're my favorite uncle, Ren," she told me with a grin, then pushed herself off my lap and grabbed my hand to pull on it.

"I'm your only uncle," I stated, laughing.

"Exactly, so you have to do what I want. And I want you to come dance with me and the others. Dad won't."

I was recovering from the tingles her lips left on mine, but I got up to not upset her.

When I looked to my right, Viggo was still standing by the cooler, his eyes narrowed.

He had seen Azula kiss me, although it was just a simple peck to show affection.

But instead of looking angry, he looked as if he was trying to figure something out.

As if he had been thinking about Z kissing him before, and now he was wondering why she hadn't done the same to him.

Maybe I could get her to kiss him too if that's what he wanted.

He's my brother, and sharing was never an issue for us, as long as we got the same thing.

four

VIGGO

Azula looked just like her mother.

Long legs, wide hips, a tight waist, beautiful tits.

She looked exactly like Bee when she was her age, and that long, fiery red hair shined as bright as ever.

Safe to say Bee had duplicated herself perfectly, without my genes getting in the way.

It was different with our boys.

Wesson had my same hair color and same dark blue eyes, while Thane's hair was strawberry blond with green eyes complimenting the color of his pale skin.

Thane was more a mix of Bee and myself, but as much as we all looked alike, our characteristics were far from the same.

I watched as Warren spun Azula around, making her laugh and fall into his arms while their hands were still clasped together.

At times, my brother was more of a father figure to her than I was, or at least that's how I saw it.

Seeing her kissing him just minutes ago made my stomach turn.

Not because it made me sick to my stomach watching my daughter kiss her uncle, but because I wanted to feel her lips on mine too.

I had always known my kids were different than others, and our family had always had a bond that not many would understand.

But that she'd go as far as kissing him right there in front of everyone was unexpected.

"You saw it too," Wesson stated, stopping next to me with a beer in his hand.

"Saw what?" I asked, keeping my eyes on my brother who was now trying to explain to Azula that he had done enough dancing for tonight.

"Zula kissing Warren. Think they've done it before?"

I should've been furious.

No matter how simple and innocent that kiss looked.

"Does it matter?"

Wesson chuckled and shrugged. "Seems like it doesn't to you. People get kicked out of towns for doing shit like that. He's her uncle."

"It was just a peck, kid. She adores him."

"Shit, I adore her too. Doesn't mean I wanna kiss her."

He didn't sound too sure about his own words, which almost made me laugh out loud.

"Just forget about it. As long as they don't do it again, I don't fucking care."

Wesson nodded and didn't add any more to this topic.

Instead, he looked straight ahead, sipping on his beer just like I did.

They were still dancing, Azula more than Warren, and she tried her best to keep him on the dancefloor while the music continued to blast through the speakers lying somewhere on the beach.

"Where's your brother?"

Wesson let out a heavy sigh, pushing his free hand into his front pocket. "Took Bonnie back to the trailer. Reuben's with them too."

"Shit," I muttered, letting out a low laugh. "They sharing her now?"

"Looks like it. Better that way than seeing them fight over some pussy. There's better pussy out there anyway."

"Yeah? How the hell do you know? All you do is work and sleep," I stated.

He didn't reply, knowing it was the truth.

Well, he did work out a lot with Thane and Reuben, but other than hanging out around the trailer park, he didn't get out much.

"Take the boys to a bar some time. Dance, or whatever people do to have fun," I suggested.

"Not much dancing going on at bars, I think. But I'll take them with me someday."

I nodded, ending the conversation silently and straightening my back as Azula walked toward us with a tired smile on her face.

"Enough dancing?" I asked when she was close enough, but she shook her head and pointed back at Warren who was following her.

"He's boring. We danced for like fifteen minutes and he wants to go home already."

I pulled her into my arms, turning her around so her back was pressed against my body. "Warren's getting old, you know? And we worked all day. Tomorrow we'll have to wake up early too," I told her, leaning in so my mouth was close to her ear.

She sighed and placed both her hands on my arms around her shoulders, and with her head tilted to the side, she looked up at me.

"Tomorrow's Friday. Promise me we'll stay out late tomorrow night?"

"Promise, baby."

Her smile grew. "Can't wait."

"So we're leaving?" Wesson asked, and I nodded.

"I'll find Bonnie and say goodnight," Azula announced, freeing herself from my embrace.

"She's gone home," Wesson told her.

"Already?"

"Yeah. Saw her leave earlier."

"Alone? Where's Thane? And Reuben?"

Wesson didn't reply this time, and I grabbed her hand to pull her toward the small path leading through the trees and onto the road. "Don't matter where they disappeared to. Let's go to bed."

She followed me without saying a word, and when we reached our trailer, she stopped to hug Warren.

"Goodnight, Ren. See you in the morning."

He hugged her tight, letting his hands move along her back and then resting them on her hips while she smiled up at him.

"Sweet dreams, Z." He pressed a kiss to her forehead, his eyes meeting mine.

Yeah, my damn brother's got a thing for my baby. It's as clear as day.

When he finally stepped back, I nodded at him, then pushed the door open to let Azula in.

"See you in the morning," I told him.

"All right. Night, kid," he said to Wesson before turning and walking over to his own trailer.

"And if Thane's in there, send him home," I called out.

I didn't get a response, so I waited for Wesson to enter our home before I did the same, leaving the door unlocked.

We didn't have to worry about people entering our trailers uninvited, seeing as they never got close to the community anyway.

People stayed away from us, which we didn't have a problem with anyway.

We were safe here.

While Azula was in the bathroom getting ready for bed and Wesson headed into his room to do the same, I went into the kitchen to look out the window directly at Warren's trailer.

The lights were on in the back where Reuben's room was, and the three shadows told me that they had snuck in there to have some fun.

Not one minute later, Thane stumbled into our trailer with his shirt only halfway on, and I turned to look at him with a raised brow.

"Had fun?"

A cocky grin spread on his lips, and with a shrug, he said, "Always fun fucking a girl like Bonnie."

Unlike Wesson, my middle tried the best he could to get laid at least three times a week, and it didn't matter if he had fucked that girl before.

As long as he got off, he was happy.

"Don't tell your sister," I warned, not wanting Zula to get upset.

"Why? You think she doesn't know about me fucking Bonnie? Wasn't the first time, you know?"

"Did Reuben know?"

He laughed and shrugged, obviously not caring about that. "We're all adults, right? Why hide who we fuck?"

That wasn't the point, but I wasn't going to argue with him any longer.

"Go to bed. You gotta help me with that old truck first thing in the morning."

"All right. Night, Dad."

"Goodnight."

I watched him head to the back where our three bedrooms were.

Having three grown men and one teenage daughter living in a trailer of this size together wasn't easy at times, and although I had initially planned for Azula to have her own bedroom, I knew Wesson wouldn't give up sleeping on his own.

I poured myself a glass of water, drank it, and headed to the back myself to get to my bedroom.

Wesson had already closed his door, and Thane was sitting on his bed, taking off his shirt again.

"Tell your sister to come tell me goodnight before she goes to sleep."

"Sure," he replied, putting his shirt away and then grabbing the remote for his TV.

"And keep it down."

"I won't play games," he told me.

"Still. Keep the TV down."

I walked into my bedroom and unbuttoned my jeans before pushing them down my legs and getting rid of them.

I did the same with my shirt, and after pulling back the covers, I sat down on the side of the bed.

Azula walked out of the bedroom, and after talking to Thane for a few seconds, she appeared in my doorway.

"Tired?" she asked with a smile.

She had changed into her pajamas, which was essentially just a large shirt Wesson didn't wear anymore.

I'd have to wash it soon. It had coffee and jam stains on it.

"A little. Come give me a kiss goodnight," I told her, watching as she quickly walked over to me to throw her arms around my shoulders and kissing my cheek by bending her head down.

"Tonight was fun," she told me, ready to step away again.

Before she could, I placed my hand on the back of her thigh and pulled her closer, making her stand up straight again with her hands propped on my shoulders now.

I looked up at her by tilting my head back, with her smiling down at me.

"Is that how you kiss your daddy goodnight?"

She frowned at first, then she leaned back down to kiss my cheek again. "Now you got two," she stated with a crooked grin, a hint of unsureness in her voice.

"That's not it," I told her, placing my other hand on the back of her thigh as well, inching her closer between my legs.

"What do you mean?" She was confused now.

"Don't you remember how you kissed me when you were a little girl?"

"No, I don't think I remember," she told me, her smile slowly reappearing.

"You kissed me right here," I said, moving my right hand up to tap the pad of my pointer finger against my bottom lip.

"I did?"

"'Course. Your brothers did too."

She studied my lips for a while, but she wasn't trying to figure out if that was okay.

She was trying to remember the time she was little.

"I wish I'd remember. That's a sweet gesture. Did I kiss Mom on the lips too before going to bed?"

"Sure did. But Momma ain't here, so you're gonna double the kisses you give me," I told her.

Her smile went wide, and by leaning down once again, she pressed her lips on mine, giving me a quick kiss before doing the same right afterward.

My dick jolted the second her lips touched mine, and even if it was just for a split second, I couldn't help myself from imagining Azula being Bee.

"There. Two goodnight kisses," she said proudly. "I'll remember this tomorrow night."

"Good. Now, go to bed. I'll see you in the morning."

She nodded and squeezed my shoulders, then left my room and headed into her own, closing the door behind her.

I needed a moment to process what I had made my daughter do, but instead of feeling sick and disturbed by my own words and actions, I felt good about the fact that now I was one kiss ahead of my brother.

But of course…I wasn't a competitive person at all.

five

THANE

"Mind if I keep the TV on for a little while?" I asked Zula as she got under her covers.

We had been sleeping in the same bed ever since she was little, and the older we got, the less we cared about sharing it or the bedroom.

"Uh, no. It's fine," she replied, laying down on her side facing me.

I was sitting on the bed, leaned against the headboard and with my legs stretched out in front of me.

"Where did you and Reuben go earlier?" she asked.

"Doesn't matter."

"It does to me. Bonnie was gone too."

"Put two and two together, Zula. You're not stupid," I muttered, and sure enough, a deep crease appeared between her brows.

"God," she murmured, looking at the remote in my hand. "You slept with her? Reuben too?"

I nodded without answering, because that wasn't needed.

"At the same time?"

I nodded again.

"Slut."

"Watch it, Z. Just because she let us both fuck her, doesn't mean she's a slut," I warned.

"It was a figure of speech," she replied, rolling her eyes at me. "She should've told me. I'd tell her too if I'd slept with her brother."

"Yeah, well, her brother's not around anymore. You're too young to have sex anyway."

She continued to look at me, her frown vanishing slowly. "Bonnie's sixteen too," she stated.

"Yeah, but Bonnie isn't my damn sister. Don't care about how old she is."

I met her eyes and grinned, knowing how much she hated not getting what she wanted.

It's always been that way when it came to adult stuff, but it wasn't said that my baby sister wasn't ready to have sex.

I just didn't like knowing about other guys fucking her, and Wesson didn't like that either.

"I've had sex before, you know?" She asked, sitting up and crossing her legs.

"Wish you wouldn't have had sex. You're too young."

"How old were you when you had your first time?"

I chuckled, looking back at the TV and trying to find a channel that was worth watching this late at night.

"Old enough."

"How old?"

"Jesus, Azula. I was old enough. Sleep and stop bothering me."

I watched her frown reappear out of the corner of my eye, and as serious as she looked, I couldn't help but grin and turn to look at her again.

"Stop looking at me like you hate me," I chuckled, hooking my arm around her neck and pulling her down to lay her head onto my lap.

"You know I could never hate you. I just wish you'd be as open with me as I am with you. You tell Wesson everything too," she said, sighing and looking up at me.

I placed my left hand on her waist and pushed my other into her hair, brushing back the bright red strands.

"I tell him everything because he's old enough to know about the things I do when I'm with girls. Don't wanna scare you off, you know?"

"Scare me off? I'm not a prude, Thane. Tell me. How old were you?"

She wouldn't let go of this, and to finally get her to shut up and sleep, I'd have to tell her.

I breathed in deeply and watched her frown turn into a grin as she realized I was about to tell her.

"I was fourteen. Did it with Kia."

Her eyes widened and her jaw dropped. "Kia Brock?"

"The one and only," I replied with a grin, thinking back to the time I was fourteen and Kia seventeen.

Shit was different around here, but no matter who found out about the things that went down in this community, you wouldn't be judged.

At least not from the people living here.

"Too bad she's not here anymore, huh?" she teased, reaching up to poke the side of my neck.

I grabbed her wrist and pushed it down on the bed above her head, and with my left hand, I started tickling her side.

"There's plenty more girls I can fuck."

She laughed, trying to free her hand from my grip and kicking her feet. "Stop!" she squealed, reaching for my hand with her free one to try and stop me.

"I'll stop when you start minding your own business. You should be sleeping by now. You've got school tomorrow."

I stopped tickling her and watched as her cheeks turned from red back to white while she calmed her breathing.

She didn't move away.

Instead, she pulled the covers over her body and cuddled up to me more, letting me stroke her hair.

"Thane?" she whispered with her eyes already closed.

"Hmm?"

"Why do you think Warren doesn't have a girlfriend?"

Not a question I had expected from her, but now that she had asked me that, I was wondering the same thing.

"Maybe he's not over Shayleen yet."

"You think? Wasn't he the one kicking her out?"

I looked back down to see her eyes open again. "He kicked her out in the hopes she'd return sober and clean. Guess she didn't feel the same way he did when she left. No reason for her to stay here."

"Reuben's a reason to stay. He's her son," she stated.

"Right. But Reuben doesn't give much of a fuck about his mother anymore. Maybe Warren's done with women, just like Dad is."

Ever since Mom died and Shayleen left, both Dad and Warren weren't on the lookout for new women.

"It's none of our business anyway, Azula. Sleep."

She sighed, then closed her eyes again.

***

I woke up with Zula sleeping in my arms and the smell of bacon moving up my nose.

We didn't have an alarm, other than Dad waking us up when it was time to get up, but I often woke up before that happened.

Most times, Azula was awake already too, but this morning it seemed as if she was comfortable than ever sleeping next to me.

I hugged her closer to my body with my left arm around her back, and by cupping the back of her head with my right hand, she nestled her face into the crook of my neck.

We'd still have a few minutes before Dad would call us to eat breakfast, and I wasn't hearing any voices coming from the kitchen, knowing Reuben and Warren weren't here yet either.

A sweet noise escaped Azula, and when I looked down, I watched as she turned her head to hide from the sun shining through our window.

We didn't have blinds or curtains, and now that summer was coming closer, we'd be up even earlier than usual.

"Gotta wake up, sleepyhead," I murmured, kissing the top of her head and moving my hand to the side of her neck, making her turn her head again.

"No."

I chuckled. "Yes. Don't wanna be late for school, hm?"

"A few more minutes," she mumbled, and I let her hide her face again.

I turned onto my back and pulled her with me, wondering what this would feel like when another girl was lying in my arms.

This was normal to us, and ever since we stopped fighting about the littlest things when I was still a teen too, we started cuddling.

Of course, I was going to protect my baby sister even when we were asleep.

Wesson would do the same thing.

I caressed the soft skin underneath her ear and stared up at the ceiling, listening in on Wesson and Dad talking now.

Two up, two more to go.

"They'll eat our breakfast if we don't head out there soon," I nudged, but she didn't seem to care.

"A few more minutes," she repeated, but as she heard the front door open and shut, she was awake in an instant.

"Jesus," I laughed, looking at her as she pushed herself up and uncovered herself. "What's gotten into you now?"

She looked at me with tired eyes, and after rubbing them with both her fists, she said, "Nothing. Warren and Reuben are here."

"You're weird as shit, Zula," I told her, still grinning at her. "Didn't you get enough of Warren last night while dancing with him?"

"I did. I just like seeing him before going to school," she replied, then she jumped out of bed and walked straight to the door.

My gaze dropped to her naked legs which had been linked with mine under the covers, and once I took them all in, I couldn't stop myself from looking at her ass.

Maybe the biggest reason why I didn't want her to have sex was because those men would touch her all over, and it would definitely make me jealous.

Not in a brotherly way.

More like a possessive and obsessive way.

And if she'd continue to insist that she was old enough to get fucked, I'd do her the favor and show her that no other guy could show her a good time like I could.

six

AZULA

"Morning!" I called out as I entered the living area where Reuben, Wesson, and Warren had already taken a seat at the table.

"Someone's in a good mood this morning," Wesson said with a grin, and I smiled at him before walking over to Dad and helping him with the food and setting the table.

"Fridays are always good days for good moods," I explained, turning my head to look at Uncle Warren who was already sipping on his coffee.

He had already showered and was dressed for work, just like Reuben.

Couldn't say the same thing about Wesson, who was sitting there in his boxer briefs and his hair all messy from sleep.

I always took a shower after breakfast, because Thane was hogging the bathroom anyway, and I didn't mind hanging out in my pajamas for a little while longer.

Warren liked to look at me when I was wearing just my shirt which barely covered my ass, and I liked the thought of his eyes staring at my legs while I tried to make myself taller to accidentally let my shirt ride up a little more.

"Go sit down," Dad told me as he gave me the plate with slices of bread on it.

I turned around and walked over to the table, watching Warren as his eyes followed my legs until he couldn't see them anymore when I sat down next to him.

"Bread?" I offered, holding out the plate and letting him grab two slices before I did the same.

"Something fun going on at school today?" he asked.

"Nope. I'm just excited to leave school again after lunch and come back home. That's what I look forward to when I wake up. Makes classes pass faster," I explained.

"Can't imagine sitting around and waiting for the time to pass is fun," Reuben said in a mocking tone, but I ignored his words and started to spread my favorite jam onto my bread.

"Has anybody seen my hat?" Thane called out from the bathroom.

He had already taken a shower, and that wasn't because he wanted to be ready for work quickly.

We didn't get warm water most of the time, so we kept our showers short.

"Come eat, Thane!" Dad replied, ignoring his question.

"I need my damn hat," Thane muttered as he walked up to the table, his hair damp and still dripping.

"Maybe you left it at Reuben's last night when you were fucking Bonnie."

Reuben's eyebrows raised after I finished my sentence, and when he looked at my brother, he sighed.

"You told her? Jesus, man, even Bonnie said not to tell her."

"She would've found out anyway," Thane told him with a shrug, then he sat down and grabbed himself a banana.

"Still. Zula doesn't need to know about every girl we fuck."

"Like there are so many that would let you," I teased, wanting to get on Reuben's nerves.

"Stop talking about fucking at the breakfast table," Wesson warned, giving us both a serious look as he took a bite of his food.

"Whatever. I'll have another one in my bed tonight," Reuben muttered.

Dad had heard enough of it, so he changed the subject when he sat down at the table as well.

"We got a few cars to take care of tonight. I need you all to work hard so we don't spend half of the evening at the garage like yesterday. Those cars need to get back to their owners, and I'm not up for any of the customers getting mad at us again."

As much as I cared about Dad and his business, my mind drifted off and only focused on Warren sitting next to me.

I was sitting on my chair with my left leg tucked underneath me and my knee touching his thigh, silently trying to get his attention on me.

He seemed invested in Dad's words, but while he kept his eyes on his brother, Warren's right hand touched my knee.

This would've been an innocent move if I hadn't kissed him last night and felt all those butterflies inside of me while dancing with him.

I looked down to see his fingers dig into my skin, and once he hooked his hand underneath my knee, he pulled my leg over his lap and moved his hand to my inner thigh.

My body tensed for a moment but then relaxed as he started to caress my skin.

I smiled but tried to hide it, knowing my cheeks would soon turn red.

"Azula," Dad said, making me look up at him with my lips pressed into a tight line.

"Hm?"

"I said Bonnie's at the door."

I turned to look at our front door, seeing my best friend standing there with a smug grin on her face.

"Someone's still in dreamland," she said, noticing my absence.

I cleared my throat and took the last bite, then placed my hand on Warren's and squeezed it gently before pulling my leg back and standing up.

"I'll go shower," I announced, making my way to the bathroom quickly.

I heard them all chuckle, and once Bonnie reached me, I frowned. "How long have you been standing there?"

She shrugged. "A minute? Maybe two? Long enough to see your face turn red while Warren did something to you underneath the table."

"He didn't do anything," I hissed, still feeling his touch on my thigh.

"Didn't seem like nothing to me. He was fully invested in whatever he was doing to you."

So the others noticed too?

At least they didn't say anything.

Not that it mattered anyway.

"I'll be ready in a few," I promised her, pushing past her to grab my clothes from my bedroom and then heading back into the bathroom to take a shower.

"You should tell me if something's going on with you and your uncle," Bonnie said as she leaned against the doorframe, looking at her nails.

"And you should've told me that you'd be fucking my brother and cousin last night. Thought I wouldn't find out, huh?"

I had already taken off my shirt and panties and was standing in the shower with the water turned on, and after quickly tying my hair into a bun, I stepped under the water.

"Shit," she murmured, then she sighed and tilted her head to the side. "They told you?"

"Thane did. But it should've been you enlightening me about your fun time with them."

She rolled her eyes and looked back at her nails. "It's just sex, Z."

"Exactly. Just sex. Yet, I've not had it in months and my brothers keep on ruining it for me."

"So then find other ways to get a dick inside of you. At school, maybe."

I shook my head. "That's the last place I'd wanna do it."

"In someone's car then?"

I sighed. "Honestly, as long as I'm far enough away from my family, I wouldn't mind getting fucked in a damn car."

"Good, then choose someone from school and tell them to take you to their car. Not that hard. They probably won't turn you down anyway."

They wouldn't.

Once I finished showering and put on my clothes for the day, I headed back to the front where the others were still sitting at the table, talking and finishing up their coffees.

"I'm off to school. I'll come by the garage afterward," I told them, but with my eyes on Dad.

"I'll text you later so you can get us a few things from the grocery store before you get there," he said. "Have a good day at school."

I nodded, looking at Warren before turning back around to leave the trailer.

Bonnie followed close behind, and once we were outside and walking down the street and out of the trailer park, she started laughing.

"What?"

"You got a thing for Warren. Z, you know that's dangerous, right?"

"What do you mean?"

She let out a heavy sigh and shrugged. "He's your uncle. I know our community doesn't give a shit, and I'd be the last to care whose cock you suck, but people talk, and I don't want you to be known as the girl who fucks her uncle."

"I'm not fucking my uncle."

"If you keep looking at him like that you soon will."

I waved a hand in her direction to push her words aside, but they started bugging me the more I tried to ignore them.

"People don't have to find out about what's going on in our community. And just because I look at someone with admiration in my eyes, doesn't mean I want to fuck them. I love him the same way I love my brothers, Reuben, and Dad."

She was quiet for a while, and to my luck, she changed the subject.

Well, kinda.

"Is it weird that most of our conversations are about sex? Girls our age care more about those stupid apps and new social media stars who do nothing but dance in front of a camera. Why aren't we obsessed with those people?"

I've never cared much about social media, knowing that most people who get famous nowadays had little to no brain cells.

"Because we don't need those things. Every girl in school is the same, and to fit in, you have to stoop to their level. It's a brainwashed society."

"The trailer park community is a society too. Does that mean we're brainwashed as well?"

I laughed. "Of course. But in the best way possible."

seven

REUBEN

Bonnie was the closest thing I could get to Azula.

Being her best friend, they shared a lot of stuff, but mostly their clothes and body sprays.

Ever since Bonnie bought herself the same spray Azula owned, I was starting to get obsessed with her.

Smelling that sweet scent of peaches and honey made my dick jolt just at the thought of it, and whenever I got Bonnie close, all I could think of was Azula sitting on my lap with her perfectly round ass pressing against my crotch.

I had always had a crush on Azula since we were little but being her cousin made things a little complicated.

We played a lot with each other, and whenever Thane and Wesson didn't want to play pretend with her, I always volunteered to be her husband when we were kids.

She loved to play family, reenacting her own mother and mine while they stood in the kitchen or cleaned our homes.

Azula was always fun to play with, but she'd never know that I wasn't just pretending to be her husband.

I wanted to be.

I wanted to love her the way my father loved my mother before he kicked her out and she never came back.

"Pass me the impact socket," Wesson said, holding out his hand from where he was standing in front of the lifted car's wheel.

I turned to grab it and hand it to him, then I got back to polishing the hook and pick set we found lying around in the back.

"The hell are you thinking about? Been quiet for almost fifteen minutes," he stated, not sounding as if he was actually interested in knowing what was on my mind.

Wesson and Thane were like brothers to me, but no matter how close we were, I'd never come clean about my feelings for their baby sister.

Wesson was a protective son of a bitch, and whoever got too close to Azula would quickly change their mind about their action.

Saw it happen with that fucker Dustin last night.

"Nothing. Just ready for the weekend," I told him, which I actually was.

"Then help me instead of standing there like an idiot. These wheels won't get screwed on their own."

I grabbed the second impact socket and walked under the car to get to the other side. "Where's Thane?"

"Helping Dad outside with that old truck. I told them it's hopeless to get that motor to run again. They should just fucking scrap it already."

They had been working on that old Ford pickup truck for weeks, in the hopes to get it back on the road, but the longer they worked on it, the less hope I had in them fixing it.

"They're stubborn. They'll hit the wall head first sooner or later."

Focusing on the car now, my thoughts drifted off to Azula again.

Knowing she'd soon be back from school to visit us at work motivated me to keep on working, and although I didn't give her much attention lately, I wanted to grab her and pull her into the back where we could be alone.

That was impossible though, not only because my dad was sitting in his office doing paperwork, but because Azula would find it strange if I'd show her the same affection her brothers showed her most days.

Especially Thane.

That lucky fucker slept in one bed with her every night, and I've seen them cuddle before.

Acting like a damn couple instead of siblings.

But even just the thought of them fucking turned me on, and me doing the same with her caused the same emotion inside of me.

I heard voices coming from the outside, and the high-pitched sounds told me that Bonnie had come here with Azula.

Guess she's enough for now.

I set my tools down and turned to look out the big windows, seeing Azula's fiery hair falling over her shoulders and back.

I wanted to grip that hair and tug on it, wrap it around my hand and fingers.

I had never seen a color like that in my life, no matter how close Thane's own hair color came to his sister's.

When both girls walked inside, I looked at Azula first before my eyes moved to Bonnie who was grinning at me.

Shit.

Was she here for me?

"Hi," Zula greeted, looking around the garage. "Where's Warren?"

I looked back at her and nodded to the back like an idiot. She obviously had a thing for my damn father, because no girl would ever look at her uncle the way she did.

I hated the thought of her and my dad doing things I wanted to do with her, but at least my father knew better than to give in.

I watched them this morning, and while Dad was quietly sitting next to her, Azula was squirming and turning red by him just being in her presence.

He wouldn't touch her, so I'll let her have some fun until she realizes she can't have him. And when that time would come, I'd be the one to hold and comfort her.

"Hey, Reuben," Bonnie said once Azula was in the back.

"Hey."

I turned back around to grab my impact driver and socket to get back to work, but I quickly changed my mind and set them back down.

"Wanna see something cool?" I asked, my voice almost bored and not interested at all.

"What is it?" she asked, sounding like one of those dumb girls who acted like they had zero brain cells to get what they desired.

Bonnie just wanted to fuck, and I'd give that to her to get what I wanted.

Her scent creeping up my nose while she sucked my dick and I imagined Azula being the one kneeling there.

I grabbed her hand and pulled her to the back, leaving Wesson to work on the car by himself and mutter a curse when he realized what I was about to do with Bonnie.

Not my fault he didn't get pussy.

He wasn't doing shit to attract women.

When we reached the back, we walked down the narrow hallway with her hand still in mine, and once we entered the bathroom, I turned to look back at the wide open office door.

Azula was standing next to my father with her hand on his shoulder and his head tilted back to look up at her.

He was leaned back in his chair, smiling and talking to her in a soft voice.

He sure knew how to make her think she'd have a chance with him, but in the meantime, I'd keep on dreaming about her unbuttoning my pants the way Bonnie was already doing.

I closed the door after looking at Azula's head one more time, and when I locked us inside the tiny bathroom, I leaned against the sink and let Bonnie do what she was good at.

"Take it all the way in like last night," I told her, and as soon as my boxer briefs hit the floor, her mouth was on my dick.

I closed my eyes and let my head fall back, and with my hand on the top of her head, I gripped her hair tightly.

The smell of peaches immediately hit my nose, and the honey followed close behind, and just seconds later, it was Azula whose lips were wrapped around my hardness instead of Bonnie's.

I groaned as she sucked harder, feeling the tip of my dick at the back of her throat, making it jolt and send electric shocks through my body.

My body tensed, and with my other hand cupping her jaw, I held her head in place and thrusted in and out of her with my hips moving fast.

"Fuuuck! That's it, baby," I hissed, keeping my eyes closed.

If I opened them, all of this wouldn't feel as perfect as it was at that moment.

I needed to keep Azula on my mind until I emptied myself in her mouth.

I felt her hands gripping my ass, somehow trying to get away but also get my dick deeper inside her mouth at the same time.

I wanted the second thing, and when she gagged, I only pushed inside deeper until no noises came out of her.

Another groan escaped me, and when I moved again, I heard her take in a deep breath.

There wasn't much time for her to do so though, as I pushed my shaft back inside her mouth.

"Gonna shoot my load right down your throat, baby. Don't move," I muttered, and it didn't take long until the first drop hit the back of her mouth.

She coughed, and with her tongue, she pushed up against my length, only making it feel better.

It also triggered me to come, and sure enough, her mouth was filled with my cum.

My body trembled if only for a short moment, because when I opened my eyes again and met hers, all the magic was gone.

I breathed heavily, letting go of her and watching as she leaned back to get my cock out of her mouth.

Strings of cum hung from my tip to her lips, and with her tongue, she licked them to get as much of my fluid as possible.

"Maybe next time you should slow down so you still have the strength to fuck me," she suggested.

"Get dressed," I replied, ignoring her words and pulling up my own pants.

Yeah, it was her making me come and not Azula, but it was the thought of her being the one doing it that made me come so easily.

Bonnie was hot and her tits were nice enough to jerk off to, but all those things didn't get me the same sensation as when I thought about Azula.

She was the one I wanted, and once she realized my father was not the man for her, I'd show her just how happy I could make her.

eight

WARREN

"Reuben seems to like Bonnie," I stated as I kept looking up at Azula who was standing next to me with her hand on my shoulder.

She shrugged, not very bothered by her best friend and cousin having sex in the bathroom down the hall.

My son's groans could be heard through the door, and although I was used to hearing him have sex in his bedroom, I didn't think it was appropriate to do it in the bathroom here at the garage.

He wasn't alone.

"How long do you have to work today?" Azula asked me, her hand caressing the back of my neck and playing with my hair.

"I have to finish some paperwork and then check on Viggo. He's been working on that truck for a few hours now."

My eyes moved from hers down to her shirt which was white and almost see-through.

"Are you allowed to wear that to school?" I asked, eyeing her bra underneath her shirt closely and placing my hand on the side of her thigh.

She shrugged. "Teachers don't care much," she told me, pushing her hand into my hair now.

I moved my eyes back up to meet hers, and after hearing another loud groan coming from the bathroom, I sighed and nodded toward the office door.

"Close the door," I said, watching as the corners of her mouth curled up into a small smirk.

She didn't hesitate, and after quickly walking to the door, she closed it and walked back to me.

I turned in my chair to welcome her between my legs, making her stand in front of me with her hands on my shoulders.

I placed mine on the back of her thighs, pulling her closer and making sure she wouldn't get away.

"What's on your mind?" I asked her.

She bit the inside of her cheek, then shrugged with another grin spreading across her lips.

"You, mostly."

I chuckled, brushing along her soft skin right underneath where her skirt ended.

"Sweet Azula's got a little crush on me," I said, my voice quieter.

With her gaze dropping to my lips, her grin disappeared.

"I think we both know that it's not gonna end well if you keep on crushing on me, Z."

"Why not?"

"Because I'm still your uncle, and as much as I like the thought of us, I don't think you could handle it."

She studied me for a moment, then her grin was back and her hands hid in my hair again.

"You have no idea how much I'm able to handle, Warren. I may be young…but I can make you feel better than Reuben while he's getting his dick sucked by my best friend."

Azula was full of surprises, and although I knew she'd always had a naughty side, the words she spoke to me took my breath away.

I stared at her, taking in her beauty as her words sunk in, and because I couldn't keep my hands off her anyway, I pulled her onto my lap to straddle me.

I placed my hands on her hips and crashed her crotch with mine, letting her feel my hardness already growing in my pants.

"Is that so? Because I've always wondered how that pretty mouth would feel covering my dick," I growled, surprising myself with my own words.

I had thought about the kiss she had given me last night all day long, and knowing me, I couldn't leave it to just one peck.

I had been quiet about my thoughts and the lust that was inside of me, but Azula had always been a tease, no matter if she tried to be or not.

Her eyes were slightly widened, looking slightly unsure about what was happening at that moment, but when she relaxed on my lap, she started to move her hips in small circles.

"This could be our secret," she whispered, her hands now tugging at my hair while her warmth pressed against my shaft.

I could smell her from up here.

I let out a low chuckle. "Don't think we have to keep this a secret, Z. Not that your father would care that his brother was fucking his daughter."

The way Viggo had looked at her last night at the fire was enough for me to realize that he'd wanna fuck his own daughter himself, and if he'd ask nicely, I would let him.

There was no need for an explanation as to why our

brains worked the way they did, and our preferences of the people we wanted to fuck was our business only.

What went on in our lives was for us to decide, and if I wanted to fuck my niece, then I would without thinking about it twice.

Soft moans escaped her as she continued to move on top of me, and I looked back at her see-through shirt to watch her tits jiggle with every circling of her hips.

"Fuck…" I hissed, pressing her pussy more against my dick. "Can you feel how hard I am? God, baby, keep going."

She lowered her head and put her lips on mine to muffle her sounds as if she wanted to listen to Reuben's groans instead of her own moans.

I brushed my tongue along her bottom lip and she granted me access to her mouth, letting her tongue move with mine.

I ran my hands to her ass, cupping and squeezing it tightly.

My dick was throbbing already, and with her sweet tongue swirling around mine, I deepened the kiss to get even more of her.

Her skirt had ridden up in the front and I pulled it up higher in the back to touch her soft skin with my fingers on my left hand hooked around her panties.

I wanted them off, but knowing she was getting close already with the heat between her thighs rising more and more, I just let her continue to rub her clit along my length until she exploded.

And who would've thought, she was perfectly timing her orgasm with my son's.

He was panting louder than before.

"Fuck! That's it, baby," we heard him groan, and after breaking the kiss to look at her again, I saw the tension in her face as the orgasm slowly hit her.

I continued to rock her on top of me, wanting this

wave to hit her harder than she'd hoped for.

"That's it. Listen to him come," I encouraged.

Azula threw her head back with her eyes closed and her lips parted, and to get one last taste before she'd leave my lap, I leaned in to lick her throat and kiss it while she started to shake on top of me uncontrollably.

"Oh, God!" she cried, digging her fingers into my shoulders now.

I let her calm down for a moment before she looked at me again, and with a grin, I brushed back her hair with one hand while I caressed her ass with my other.

"You like the thought of multiple men touching you, huh? Maybe I can get Reuben in on this next time."

She kept her eyes on me, trying to figure out if that's what she wanted.

But of course, I had read her right while she came listening to my son come.

"Only Reuben?" she asked, making me chuckle.

"Whoever you want. As long as you will give me the same attention you will give them."

"I promise I will." She was determined to please not only me but whoever would be in on the fun too.

I looked down at her lap, adjusting her skirt a little before placing my thumb on her clit over the fabric covering her.

In slow circles, I massaged that little nub and watched her body tense again as she had yet to come down from her high.

"Next time, I'll make you come with my tongue playing with this pussy. I wanna taste it," I whispered, meeting her eyes again.

"I want that too," she whispered back, her voice filled with hope and excitement.

"And would you let Reuben play with it too?"

She nodded without hesitating.

"And your brothers?"

She had to think about that for a second, but then she nodded her head.

"Yes, I would."

I continued to rub her clit with my thumb, and before I could ask her about her father sucking on that pussy, she beat me to the punch.

"And Dad too."

"You're a naughty little girl. Just how I like it."

She smiled brightly, then bit her bottom lip as her cheeks turned red and her gaze dropped to my hand.

"Can you make me come again?" she asked, but before I was able to reply, we heard Reuben walk down the hall with Bonnie following him.

"Another time. Go home. I'll see you after work," I promised her and kissed her lips before making her get off my lap.

"Azula?" Bonnie called out, and once she had straightened her skirt and shirt, she walked to the door to open it and find her friend standing there.

"Are you coming?" she asked, and Azula nodded.

"Be right there."

Bonnie walked away, and Azula turned to me with a sweet smile on her lips. "See you at home," she said.

I nodded, adjusting my pants and turning back to my desk. "See you there."

I felt good about what we did, and since Azula looked happy with it herself, I knew I didn't have to worry about anything.

She wanted it.

She wanted so much more.

And I knew exactly how to give her more with the help of my brother, son, and nephews.

nine

WESSON

If Reuben was getting head from Bonnie, then it had to be Warren making Azula come in the office.

I should've gone in there and pulled her out by her wrist, telling her how wrong it was to let her own uncle do shit like that to her, but I couldn't help but notice the tension inside of me growing with every moan that came from that room.

Not even Dad cared about hearing his daughter come, and Thane was just sitting there on the passenger seat with a stupid grin on his face.

We had left Dad and Warren behind with Reuben to finish work and close up the garage so we could drive down to the gas station and get some beer and cigarettes for tonight.

"Always knew she was a freak," Thane said, making me turn my head toward him.

"What do you mean?"

"When she's asleep, she always pushes her damn ass against my dick. She wants to feel it pressed against her, and at times she even tries to lay on top of me. Says it's much more comfortable sleeping like that."

I frowned at his words, looking back at the road.

"Ever touched her?" I asked.

"Not the way Warren did back at the garage."

"Do you want to?"

He was quiet for a moment, then he shrugged. "If that's what she wants, why not?"

"It's wrong," I stated, but the words even sounded wrong coming out of my mouth.

"It's wrong if it would happen in a normal society. No one gives a fuck at the trailer park, so why not just fuck your own sister? Azula's prettier than any other girl anyway."

She did have a pretty face, and her curves were getting nicer with each day that passed.

She was turning into a beautiful woman, and I hated the thought of those stupid fuckers at school touching her.

Just like Thane, I was protective over my baby sister.

A whole lot.

"So you'd just let her suck your dick one night if she begged you to?"

Thane laughed. "If she'd insist, fuck yeah."

I thought about it for a while, and once my brother's carefree attitude sunk in, I laughed too.

"Shit, are we really gonna fuck our baby sister?" I asked, looking at him again.

"As I said, she's a freak. She won't back down if she can reach a damn orgasm."

After grabbing a few things from the gas station, we headed home to find Azula lying on the couch with a book in hand and her legs propped up on the armrest.

"Reading for school?" I asked, knowing she wouldn't read a book if it wasn't for some school assignment.

She looked up from the page and nodded, smiling at me. "Yes, but I'm almost done. Where's Dad?"

"He's coming soon. You hungry?" I asked, walking over to the kitchen and squeezing her foot as I passed her.

"A little. What's for dinner?"

"Chicken. Wanna help me prepare?"

I usually wasn't big on cooking, but since Dad wasn't gonna make it home in time to cook and then have enough time to hang out by the bonfire, I did him the favor of preparing dinner myself.

"I'll take a shower," Thane called out from the back, but I didn't acknowledge my brother as Azula was walking over to me in that short skirt of hers.

"What do you want me to do?" she asked.

"Get the chickens out of the fridge. There should be four of them." We always had a big meal, with Reuben and Uncle Warren eating at our place most nights.

I grabbed the rest of what we needed to season the chickens, and while she was focused on placing each one on a tray, I observed her closely with every move she made.

The old sneakers she was wearing once belonged to me when I was around fourteen, and now that I had grown out of them, she wore them.

She was still growing, and soon she'd need new clothes to at least cover up her ass.

Didn't get any coverage from wearing a short skirt like that, and just like me, men would stare.

I placed the seasonings next to the tray, standing close behind her and then cupping her ass with one hand while I placed my other on the counter next to her so she couldn't move away.

"Tell me what Warren did to make you come," I growled into her ear, and as her body tensed, I squeezed her ass a little tighter.

Her breath caught in her throat, and once I was sure she wouldn't move, I placed my right hand on her hip to pull her back against me.

I continued to massage her ass, letting the skirt move up so I could touch her skin.

"Don't get all shy about it now, Azula. We all heard you moan."

She leaned her head back against my shoulder and I turned mine to look at her face.

Her eyes were closed and her lips slightly parted.

The smallest touch made her body tremble, and I liked to think that only I had this effect on her.

Clearly, I wasn't the only one though.

"Tell me," I nudged, pressing a kiss to her jaw.

"I rubbed against him," she whispered, parting her legs so my fingers had enough space to move between her folds from behind.

She was already wet, and when I pushed her panties aside to uncover her pussy, she squirmed.

"He didn't use his fingers?" I wondered, rubbing mine along her slit to wet them.

"No. I rubbed against his cock. It was hard," she explained, making my own dick jolt at her words.

Shit, I wanted the same.

Her rubbing against me, making herself come and watch her face explode in pure bliss.

"I'll let you do the same tonight if you come sleep in my bed. How does that sound, baby?"

She couldn't have nodded any quicker, fascinated by my idea.

"What about Thane?" she asked.

"Fuck him. I want you to myself tonight," I told her, but I quickly changed my mind. "Unless you want us both to touch you at the same time."

She sighed as I dipped two fingers inside her tight hole. "Yes," she cried. "I want both of you."

"Naughty girl," I muttered against her skin, sucking on it gently before letting go of her and making her turn around to look at me.

I pushed my fingers inside of her again, and with her leaned against the counter, I spread her legs apart with my knee pushed between them.

"How long have you been wishing to be fucked by us?"

A mischievous grin spread across her face, and while I kept moving my fingers in and out of her, she shrugged.

"A while now, I guess."

I moved my fingers quicker, her wetness coating me as her breathing quickened.

My dick was already getting harder, and to get at least some release, I grabbed her hand and placed it on the bulge in my pants.

She immediately started to massage it while her hips moved in small circles.

"And you're sure you can handle two dicks at once?" I teased.

"I can handle more than two," she said proudly, but I doubted she ever had more than one guy at a time.

"We'll see," I groaned, finger fucking her faster while rubbing her clit with my thumb.

"Come on my hand," I ordered.

Her head fell back again, and I took the chance to lean in and kiss her neck and the top of her tits.

She definitely needed a new bra soon too, but for now, this one would work.

"Come for me," I muttered against her skin, and only seconds later, her body tensed and stopped moving.

Her hand left my dick to grab my upper arm, steadying herself so her knees didn't give out on her.

I lifted my head again to watch her, and all the beauty on her face almost made me shoot my load in my pants without my dick being touched.

She had an insane effect on me, and I wish we'd be in bed already, fucking her.

"Oh, Wes!" she cried, her body shaking wildly.

Her pussy clenched around my fingers, and after fingering her a little while longer until she calmed down, I pulled them out and held them up to her mouth.

"Open," I ordered, and she listened like a good girl.

I pushed my fingers inside her mouth, pressing down on her tongue to get as far in as possible, letting her taste her own pussy.

"Perfect, baby," I praised, keeping my eyes on hers. "Tonight, you'll get to taste us too. Then we'll see how well you can handle two of us."

But instead of being intimidated by my words, excitement flashed in her eyes and I couldn't stop myself from chuckling.

"Let's hope you won't regret it. Haven't had pussy in too fucking long and I know I won't hold back, baby."

ten

AZULA

My heart was racing ever since we left the trailer to go to the bonfire.

Before dinner, the thing Wesson had done to me wouldn't make my legs stop shaking, and him staring at me while I was dancing only made me more nervous about what would happen tonight.

I had agreed on sleeping in his bed tonight, but there wouldn't be much of that going on.

Not with Thane already knowing what had happened in the kitchen.

He wanted in on the fun later tonight, so his eyes were set on mine as well.

Thane was sitting next to Wesson and Reuben, talking to them while all three pairs of eyes were watching me closely as I moved my body to the music blasting through the speaker.

No doubt Thane was telling Reuben about his plans.

I didn't think what they had in mind was wrong. I wanted it myself, and although they were my family, there was something more exciting about it than knowing you'd soon have sex with some guy from school.

My mind was sending me all kinds of red flags, but I quickly turned them into signs that encouraged me to go for it.

To try it just once and see how it would end.

They were my brothers, and if they thought this was wrong, they wouldn't be staring at me like that right now.

They probably wanted it more than I did.

I turned away to face Bonnie who was dancing in front of me, and although I couldn't see them anymore, I could feel their stares burning into my back.

Dad and Uncle Warren went back to the garage after dinner, saying they finally were going to get rid of that old truck.

And since they weren't around, it was the perfect opportunity for Wes, Thane, and Reuben to take me back to the trailer and fuck me.

I stopped as my mind told me I should take a few more sips of my third beer, just to numb all the negative thoughts running through my head, and once I stopped dancing to grab my beer from one of the trunks, I emptied the can.

"You got any plans tonight?" Bonnie asked, laughing at me downing the beer.

I looked at her and shrugged, unsure if I should tell her about two of the guys she had sex with before wanting to have sex with me too.

"Did your brother ever touch you when he was still around?"

She raised her brows at me at first, looking at me like I was crazy, but then she shrugged. "He kissed me when we were little while playing. And sometimes we stuck out our tongues and pressed them against each other's. We were ten or so," she said, then she laughed. "Just stupid things kids do, you know?"

I nodded.

Not sure if the things I was about to do with my brothers was just something stupid kids would do.

I turned my head to look back at Wesson who was now standing with his beer in hand, and once our eyes met, he took a sip and sat the can down before nudging Thane to get up as well.

"You don't look too well. Do you need some water?" Bonnie asked, her voice worried.

"I…yeah. I think I need to go lay down," I said, turning to look at her with an apologetic smile. "I'll see you tomorrow, okay?"

"Of course. Just come over whenever you want to. I have to help Mom clean the trailer in the morning, but I'm free after lunch."

I nodded and hugged her before walking around the fire and heading straight to the small path leading back to the street, and without having to look back, I knew Wesson and Thane were following me.

My heart was still beating fast, and once I was on the road, I turned to look at them.

They didn't say anything, but the look on their faces spoke louder than words.

They wanted me, and they knew they would get whatever they wanted.

"What if Dad finds us?" I asked, walking backward as they continued to follow me.

They were much faster than I was and they soon caught up with me, so I turned back around to fall into step with them.

"Then he can join us," Wesson said bluntly, placing his hand on my lower back.

The thought of Dad joining in on his sons fucking his daughter made my belly tingle, which should've been another red flag.

But all I was thinking of was how good my brothers could make me feel.

We reached the trailer and went inside, and after leading me into his bedroom, Wesson pulled me to him with my back against his body and his hands on my stomach.

There was no time to think about it.

This was happening.

I lifted my gaze to meet Thane's, who was standing in front of me with a grin across his face, already unbuttoning his pants.

"Have you ever kissed our baby sister, Thane? Tasted that sweet mouth of hers?" Wesson asked, moving his hands from my stomach up to my tits where he cupped them and squeezed.

"Not yet, but I've been thinking about it for a while now," Thane replied, his eyes wandering from mine down to my lips.

Wesson moved his right hand further up to cup my jaw and tilt my head back, and since he was a little more than a head taller than me, it was easy for him to lean down and kiss me upside down.

His tongue brushed over mine as I parted my lips, and once enough spit had gathered, he broke the kiss to let Thane get a taste too.

He stepped closer and placed one hand on my hip, then he cupped my pussy with the other and started rubbing it with the palm of his hand.

"Sweet Azula is already wet for us," he growled before covering my lips with his.

Thane was slightly gentler with me than Wesson, but that was because he had been holding me every night while falling asleep.

He knew I liked the way he caressed me, but I loved how they both made me feel, touching my body in different ways at the same time.

Thane's gentleness contrasted Wesson's roughness beautifully, and I leaned more into Wes as Thane deepened the kiss.

A soft moan left my chest while Wesson continued to massage my tit, tugging at my nipple through the thin fabric of my shirt and lace bra.

I've never been touched by two men at once, but I was already getting used to it.

And it definitely made me want more.

I lifted my hands to place them on Thane's shoulders, keeping him close and making sure his kiss would last a little longer than Wesson's.

He kept his hand on my jaw and moved the other under my shirt now, needing to touch my skin.

I could feel his hardness press against my lower back, and when I moved, he pushed his crotch against me more, letting out a low groan.

Thane broke the kiss after a while, and as he took off his pants and boxer briefs, Wesson lifted my shirt and pulled it over my head to then let it fall to my feet.

"Beautiful," Thane murmured, watching my tits closely as Wesson took off my bra as well.

"And she's all ours, brother. Let's see if she can take both of us at once. She sounded promising when I made her come before dinner."

Wes pushed me down to my knees and grabbed a fistful of my hair as he unbuttoned his pants with his other hand.

Thane was already rubbing his cock, and unlike Dustin the other night, his was already rock hard.

Just like Wesson's.

Having that effect on them made me feel powerful, and all the worries I had washed away in an instant.

"Go ahead," Wesson ordered, gripping my hair tighter in his fist and directing my head toward his cock.

I looked at it and licked my lips before wrapping them around his tip, already tasting the saltiness of his precum on my tongue.

"Take it all in, baby," he hissed, keeping my head in place and moving his hips to get his cock deeper into my mouth.

I looked up, trying to hold back a gag as I felt his tip hit the back of my throat, and once I got my gag reflexes under control, he started to push in and out of my mouth slowly.

I had done this a few times before but it never felt right.

Wesson knew exactly what he was doing, without making me feel uncomfortable.

Thane knelt next to me with both his hands wrapped around my throat and his face close to mine.

"Beautiful. Let him fuck your mouth," he whispered, tightening his hold around my neck.

I looked at him now, still focusing on my breathing while Wesson started to move his hips faster.

His length didn't fit all the way into my mouth, but the harder he pushed, the further in he got with each thrust.

It made me gag, struggling a little with Thane's grip closing up my airway.

"Fuuuck!" Wesson groaned, and surprisingly, he pulled his cock out of my mouth fully to let Thane kiss me.

My spit mixed with his, and he obviously didn't mind the taste of Wesson's cock on my tongue.

He pushed his deeper into my mouth, then pulled back and swallowed my spit before turning my head back to Wesson's shaft.

I took him in again while Thane stood back up, and after thrusting into my mouth a few times, Wesson growled and pulled out to let me take in my other brother's cock.

They were about the same size, though Wesson's had a slight curve to it.

They were both fairly thick, making it hard for me to take them all in.

Thane's hands gripped my hair on each side of my head, making me turn on my knees.

But unlike Wesson, Thane was a little more careful with me, and even he noticed.

"Come on, Thane. Show her how much you wanna fuck that mouth. She said she could take us both. Don't hold back."

I looked up at Thane whose facial expression quickly changed, and as his jaw clenched, his hips started to move faster and harder.

I closed my eyes and put both hands on his thighs, making sure I wouldn't choke and gag too much.

Neither of them cared though, and the faster he thrusted into me, the sooner he'd pull back out.

"That's it," I heard Wesson say, and when Thane's cock started to throb, he pulled it back out to give me and himself a little break.

"Get on the bed," Wesson said, but he didn't say it to me.

Thane got onto the mattress and leaned back against the headboard, then Wesson pulled me up and made me crawl onto the bed to kneel between Thane's legs which he had spread out to make enough space for me.

Looked like they had a threesome before, and knew exactly what position to go for.

I was on all fours, looking into Thane's eyes as he rubbed his cock and reached for my tit with his other hand.

"You okay?" he asked.

"Yes," I replied, not wanting him to worry.

This was all new to me, but up until now, no regrets were running through my mind.

I was just a little nervous still, but that's okay.

I reached for Thane's cock with my right hand and took over stroking his length, then I leaned in to continue sucking him while Wesson pulled down my skirt and panties to get rid of them.

Once I was fully naked, I heard him spit and then felt his wet fingers run through my slit where he took his time to gently rub my asshole.

"I need to stretch you before I can fuck this tight asshole," he told me, pushing one finger inside and making me arch my back.

"Don't think she's ever had dick in her ass before," Thane said, keeping his eyes on mine while I slowly moved my head up and down.

"Definitely hasn't. But I'll be her first."

eleven

WESSON

It would take a while until she could take my dick inside her asshole, and while I stretched her with my fingers, I made sure she was comfortable enough while sucking Thane's dick.

Her body language showed enough enthusiasm without her having to say a single word.

She wanted this just as much as we did, and how wrong would it be not to please her when that's all she was asking for?

Our baby sister deserved the world and we would give her whatever she wanted.

I caressed her ass with my left hand while I fingered her asshole, stretching and preparing it for my shaft.

Hearing her soft, muffled moans made my dick twitch, and whenever I looked at Thane, seeing his relaxed face tense every time she took him in deeper only added to the excitement in my chest.

I knew he was close, but I wanted him to hold it in a little while longer.

With my hand now wrapped around the base of my shaft, I brushed the tip along her wet slit and pulled my fingers out of her hole.

"Arch your back and stick that ass out more for me, baby," I demanded.

She did as I said, still focusing on Thane.

"Perfect," I whispered, observing her ass for a moment before pushing my tip against her back entrance.

"I'm gonna make you feel good, Z. Relax your body," I encouraged, noticing it tense as I slowly pushed inside of her.

It was too damn tight, but the more she relaxed, the easier it was for me to slide inside of her.

"Ah!" she cried, turning her head to look back at me.

Thane caressed the back of her head to try and calm her, and I reached over to grab her chin between my thumb and forefinger.

"Relax, or else it'll hurt. I stretched you enough, baby. Let me in."

She nodded, her breath hitching in her throat, and once she turned her head back to look at Thane, I pulled my dick out slightly to then push inside again.

This time it was easier, not feeling as much tension in her body anymore.

"That's it. Let me fuck that tight ass."

Another moan escaped her, but it was muffled again when Thane pushed her head further down to make her take in all of his length.

I placed my hands on her hips and started to move slowly, needing to adjust myself before I could fuck her harder.

Accumulating spit in my mouth, I let it drop right on top of my shaft and the edge of her hole, watching as it made my dick glisten.

Once I was pushed deep inside of her, I stopped,

looking back at Thane and giving him a quick nod. "Keep her still. I wanna fuck this ass until she can't take it anymore."

Azula's body tensed again, but only for a moment.

Thane cupped each side of her head with both hands, holding her still with his dick still inside her mouth.

His hips started to move slightly, and when I was sure I could move without her getting away, I started to thrust in and out of her fast and without mercy.

I had doubts about her being able to take how rough I could get, but only seconds later, she fully relaxed and stuck her ass more toward me.

"Fuck, yes. Keep sucking that dick, Zula. Don't stop until I shoot my load in your mouth," Thane encouraged, letting her move her head again.

I squeezed her ass tightly, then lifted my right hand and slapped it hard, making her jump and then arch her back again.

"Yeah, you like that, huh?"

I slapped her ass again on the same spot, this time even harder.

Her cries were mixed with moans, and they sounded so damn erotic that I nearly exploded inside her already.

I knew Thane was feeling the same, and from that moment on, it didn't take too long for both of us to come.

I reached around her to rub her clit, knowing she probably wouldn't be able to come by me fucking her ass, and since I now knew how sensitive her pussy was, I'd make her come fast.

"Come on, baby. Show us how much you love having both our dicks inside of you," Thane growled, his voice deep.

"Ah, fuck!" I groaned, slapping her ass with my left hand this time while continuing to rub her clit.

Her body started to tremble, and without stopping my thrusts, her tightness clenched around my length.

"That's it!" I encouraged one last time before emptying myself inside of her.

Thane had grabbed her head again, holding it still so he could unload himself in her mouth, and while he did, I tried not to lose control over her.

She was pushing back against my now slow thrusts, and the harder she moved back, the more intense the sparks inside of me got.

Sweet Azula knew how to tease me.

Thing was…the more she teased, the more I would do the same.

She hadn't come yet, although she was very close.

I moved my fingers from her clit to her wet entrance while keeping my dick inside her.

Thane had come in her mouth, and I could tell by the muffled sounds she made that her mouth was filled with his cum.

"Kiss me," he demanded, pulling her up by her hair and making me move more toward him so I wouldn't leave her.

I watched them kiss, with his cum running down his chin and dripping onto his chest.

I've seen my brother do nasty shit before, but only now I was wanting a taste myself.

I looked down and slowly pulled out of her to watch my own cum drizzle between her folds, and before it dropped onto my mattress, I wiped it off to then taste myself.

"Wes," Azula whined, sticking her ass up again. "Make me come," she begged, looking back with her lips glistening with Thane's cum.

It looked hot, and now that I had tasted myself, I wanted more.

I made her turn around and lay against Thane's upper body, and after spreading her legs far apart, I leaned in to lick along her slit.

From her asshole to her clit.

"Please," she begged again, and while Thane played with her tits, I played with her pussy.

"Keep your eyes on him," Thane demanded.

I flicked my tongue against that little nub and pushed two fingers back into her pussy, stretching her other hole and giving it the same attention.

"Oh, Wes," she cried, her hands fisting my hair now.

"Come on, baby," Thane muttered, wanting to see her body shake and tremble the way I had seen earlier this evening.

A few more strokes and her body tensed again, and with her legs trying to squeeze together, she was telling me that she was close.

I pushed her leg up with my left hand, making Thane grab it so she couldn't move, and the faster I moved my tongue, the more her body trembled.

It was a beautiful sight watching the orgasm wash over her.

"Come," Thane whispered in her ear, and sure enough, she exploded right on my tongue, letting me taste more of her sweetness as she tried to keep herself under control.

She was long gone though, falling over the edge but not coming back down anytime soon.

I grinned at Thane who had the same facial expression, and before Azula opened her eyes again, I kissed her inner thigh to help her relax.

"Beautiful. And I thought she couldn't handle us," I teased.

Her eyes were back on mine and her breathing had slowed down a little.

She didn't speak, but that wasn't necessary anyway.

"She's gonna sleep in here tonight. You can stay too," I told Thane, and he nodded.

I didn't mind sharing, as I had just shared her now, but I hoped to have her all to myself one day.

Just like he always had her to himself every other night up until now.

We took it slow and gave her the time to recover, and once she did, we all got under the covers with her lying between us.

We were all naked, and our sweaty skin rubbed against each other as we moved closer.

I placed my arm around her stomach while Thane placed his hand on her thigh, and before we closed our eyes, we both leaned in to kiss her cheek.

"It's all good, baby. There's nothing we have to worry about," I told her.

Azula didn't look worried though.

She looked tired and hazed, as if she was still swirling around in outer space somewhere after that orgasm.

"I love you," she whispered, looking at me first, then at Thane. "I love you both so much."

"We love you too, baby. Now, sleep. You need to recover," Thane replied sweetly, sounding like the usual, caring brother he was.

Azula breathed in deeply and placed each of her hands on ours, holding on tightly as she quickly drifted off into dreamland.

This certainly wasn't the last time we'd fuck her, but maybe next time, we'd have to take it a little slow at first.

Not that I was capable of that, but I could surely try.

I looked at Thane whose eyes were already on mine, and like we always did, we understood each other without saying a word.

This was new to both of us, and to Azula too, but if that's what she desired, we wouldn't take such experiences from her.

Considering all the guys running around out there wanting to sleep with Z with those larva dicks, she was better off with her brothers.

twelve

WARREN

I went straight to bed after getting rid of the truck with Viggo, and I didn't even bother going to check on the kids at the bonfire.

I came across Bonnie who was walking home from the beach, but instead of asking where the others were, I just waved and headed into my trailer.

Exhaustion came easy these days, and I wasn't getting younger either.

Still, I wouldn't trade my life with anyone else.

Not with the family I had.

I was lying awake in bed, hearing the music at the bonfire in the distance and the laughter coming from the same place.

It was almost one a.m., but as it was the weekend, people would stay out until late tonight.

Reuben wouldn't be home until the early morning, and he'd skip breakfast like his cousins often did after a long night out.

Viggo and I usually grabbed a bowl of cereal and sat outside his trailer in the camping chairs to not bother the kids sleeping inside, and we'd watch the sunrise over the trailers as our community slowly woke up.

When I heard a noise coming from outside, I wondered what Reuben was doing back home already, but after noticing the footsteps being far too light to be Reuben's, I had an idea of who was sneaking into my trailer this late at night.

Azula closed the front door quietly and then appeared in the narrow hallway leading directly into my bedroom, and after sitting up to let her know that I was awake, her body relaxed.

"Hi," she said quietly, stopping in the doorframe and leaning against it.

"No partying?" I asked, tilting my head to the side.

She shook her head and watched me closely, then looked at the empty space next to me.

The moonlight was shining into my bedroom, and I only now noticed how unsure her eyes looked.

Almost as if she was about to cry.

"Zula, what's wrong?" I asked, sitting up and holding out my hand for her to take.

She didn't hesitate and moved closer to the bed to crawl onto it before cuddling up to my side with her face buried in the crook of my neck.

I put my arms around her and held her tight, rubbing her back and trying to make her feel okay.

"Tell me. What happened?"

I gave her the time she needed to gather her thoughts, and when I knew it would take a while, I leaned back against the headboard and continued to hold her without nudging her to talk.

This was new to me.

Her needing someone to hold her because something was wrong, but I was more than happy to be the man she wanted to be held by.

I always had a special bond with her, but up until now, she never needed me the way she did tonight.

I caressed her back with one hand and cupped the back of her head with my other, pushing my fingers into her hair and massaging her scalp.

"I had sex tonight," she suddenly whispered, making me look down at her.

Not sure why she would tell me this when I knew it wasn't the first time, and before I could ask her something, she continued to talk.

"I don't know if it was okay, but it felt good. I know we're different than the people who don't live here, but I'm unsure if it was too much."

I didn't understand where she was going with this, so I waited for her to go on.

She tilted her head back to look up at me, placing her hand on my chest and tugging at my shirt while she chewed on her bottom lip.

She looked nervous now.

"I had sex with Thane and Wesson."

A knot immediately tightened in my throat, not because she had sex with her brothers, but because I had thought she'd choose me over them first.

After what we'd done in the office earlier today, I figured she wanted more.

I studied her face while she did the same with mine, trying to figure out what I was thinking.

"Are you mad at me?" she asked in a whisper.

"Of course not," I replied, cupping her cheek now.

"Do you regret it?"

She shook her head. "No. It was nice."

"Then there's nothing you have to be unsure about, Azula. Did they make you feel good?"

Now, a smile appeared on her lips. "Yes, very. They were amazing."

"Good. As long as they treat you right, you have nothing to worry about. They love you, you know?"

"I love them too. I didn't think you'd be okay with it. I mean, after what happened in the office earlier, I thought that maybe you would…" she stopped herself and dropped her gaze to my lips.

She was thinking the same.

"I know. I thought so too. But I'm happy they were good to you. You deserve to be loved," I whispered, pressing a kiss to her forehead.

She pulled at my shirt and snuggled up to me again.

As much as we both wanted each other, I had this strong urge of just holding her tonight.

As tough as she seemed sometimes, Azula needed reassurance too, and I liked to think that she could only get that from me.

She was close with everyone else, especially Viggo, but I was the only one who she really felt protected by.

"Do they know you're here with me now?" I asked.

"No, they're sleeping."

Good.

Means that she's more comfortable sleeping with me right now then with them.

"It felt strange staying in bed with them. I don't know why."

I looked down at her again and kept on brushing through her hair. "Maybe you needed a little break from them to get your thoughts under control."

Being fucked by two guys seemed exhausting, and I didn't want her to break having to handle that much at once.

She was still sixteen, and her body had yet to get used to stuff like that.

"Maybe," she whispered. "My mind was all over the place after we had sex."

"Just take it slow, okay? Don't want you to feel pressured."

That would be the worst.

Her brothers talking her into having sex with them for their own good without thinking about Azula.

She was their sister after all, and they couldn't take advantage of her.

"They were good to me," she assured, turning her head to look at me again. "I promise, Ren. They made me feel amazing."

I smiled at her and nodded. "I believe you, sweetheart. Now, get some sleep, okay? If you want, I can take you to the thrift store tomorrow and buy you new clothes like I promised."

Her smile grew and she pushed herself up on her elbow to lean over me and kiss me.

Her lips moved against mine gently, and I cupped her face in both my hands to keep her right there.

I deepened the kiss and tilted her head to the side to push my tongue deeper into her mouth, and after moving it around hers for a while, I broke the kiss to look into her eyes.

"Whatever's happening in your life right now, know that if there's anything you need to talk about, I'm right here to listen. You're starting to get to know yourself a little better by letting your brothers get that close to you, and I know they won't be the only ones doing so."

She studied me for a moment and nodded. "I'm letting you get close too."

"Yeah, you are. And I'm happy that you trust me so much. But promise me one thing, Azula," I whispered, brushing along her cheeks with my thumbs.

"Anything."

"Never close yourself off when you're feeling down. Talk, and let me in whenever you need to."

No matter how immoral it was what she had done with her brothers and myself today, and no matter what else she'd let us do, I couldn't risk her mind spiraling out of control.

She was still young, and it was important for her not to end up damaged.

"I'll be okay," she whispered, her words promising.

"You're okay now. But I can't help but think about what could be if you're not careful. Mentally, I mean."

She was trying to figure out what I meant by that, and although she wasn't naïve, she still had a long way to go until she understood how important it was to take care of her mind.

Or maybe I was just overreacting.

She knew her limits well, yet, I didn't want her to slip and fall over the edge, regretting her actions one day.

"I'll be okay," she repeated, smiling at me this time. "I love you. And I love the others just as much."

When she was being this adorable, I couldn't help but grin like a fool.

She had always said the sweetest things, but the older she got, the surer I was that she understood the words she said.

I pulled her close again, kissing her and showing her that I felt the same for her.

There weren't many things in my life I didn't love.

I had a great job, working with my brother, son, and nephews, and living a simple life here at the trailer park.

Nothing I'd ever want to change.

And Azula only added to my happiness.

***

"Quit moving around," I muttered against the back of Azula's head.

She had been restless for the past twenty minutes, and although I was holding her close in my arms, she wouldn't stop moving.

Our legs were tangled, but that didn't stop her upper body from twisting and turning.

I placed my hand on her stomach and pressed her back against my chest. "What's wrong?" I asked, wondering if she was even awake.

A sigh left her, and when her head turned to look back at me, I opened my eyes to meet hers.

"Bad dream?"

She shrugged. "Bad thoughts."

I made her turn around, and with my hand cupping her cheek, I made her look at me.

"Talk to me," I encouraged, not wanting her to drown in her own thoughts.

"I was just thinking about what Dad will think. I'm sure Thane and Wesson won't keep it to themselves for too long. They'll tell Reuben, and he never keeps his mouth shut," she whispered.

I chuckled, agreeing with her statement about my son.

Reuben was nosy.

"How do you think your father will react?"

"I don't know. I can see him getting mad at me, but also at the boys."

I brushed along her cheek with my thumb and tried to calm her. "Viggo's like me. He wants the best for you, and when he knows you wanted it, I'm sure he won't get mad. It was your choice."

She bit her bottom lip and let my words sink in for a while before a smile appeared on her lips.

"You're right. I'm overthinking again."

"Yeah, you are. But there's no need to. You know you can make your own decisions. Now, let me get another hour or two of sleep. It's early," I told her.

I didn't have to look at my phone to know that it was only around six a.m., and luckily, Azula didn't mind closing her eyes for a little while.

She leaned in closer and placed her lips on mine, kissing me softly and letting me taste her sweetness.

"Sorry I woke you," she mumbled against my lips before leaning back to look at me again.

"It's okay. Come here."

I wrapped my arms around her tightly again, holding her close against my chest and then cupping the back of her head with one hand.

It was easy to fall back asleep with Zula next to me, and I liked to think it was the same for her when she was lying here with me.

thirteen

VIGGO

I was sitting outside in my camper chair when Azula walked toward me with a wide smile on her face.

She was only wearing her oversized t-shirt she wore to sleep, and her feet were bare.

"Where have you been?" I asked, keeping my eyes on her face as she came closer.

"At Warren's. I couldn't fall asleep last night, so I went over."

She could've just come to me if falling asleep was her issue, but ever since that evening by the lake where she kissed him, I knew there was more to it than just affection.

She was into my brother a little too much for my liking, but I wasn't going to act like an asshole, telling her she can't spend time with him.

She would anyway.

"Why couldn't you sleep?" I asked, reaching out for her hand as she stopped in front of me.

I placed my cup of coffee down on the small table next to me and pulled her onto my lap.

She wrapped her arm around my neck and sat sideways to be able to look at me, and I put one arm around her back while placing my left on her thigh.

She was quiet for a while and studied her hand on her lap, then she puckered her lips and looked back into my eyes.

"I spent time with Thane and Wes, and once they fell asleep, I needed to be with Warren."

"What did you do with them?"

There was something she wasn't telling me, but it wouldn't take long for her to spit it out.

Her hand moved from my neck into my hair, wrapping her fingers around my hair and tugging on it slightly.

"They touched me," she said, her voice quieter now.

"Where?"

She looked back down to my hand before answering me.

"All over. They were good to me, Daddy," she promised.

I had no doubt about that.

Still, I wished I had known.

I had a moment of confusion when I found Wesson sleeping in one bed with Thane.

Both were naked.

I caressed her thigh and kept my eyes on her face as a frown appeared between her brows.

"They fucked you?"

"Wesson did," she replied.

We were blunt with each other, and no matter how frowned upon it was to talk about sex with your teenage daughter, I couldn't give less of a fuck.

On the contrary: I wanted to fuck her too.

"And what about Thane?"

Her eyes met mine again, and when she noticed that I wasn't mad about this situation, she smiled softly.

"I gave him a blowjob. I've done that before, you know?"

I looked at her lips now, wondering how they would feel around my dick.

Would they feel the same as Bee's lips?

I missed the feeling of her mouth wrapped around my shaft.

"They made me feel amazing. They really did," she stated, twisting my hair around her fingers.

"I believe you, baby. Just wished you would've needed me afterward instead of Uncle Warren. Why didn't you come to me?"

"Because I knew I could tell him. I wasn't sure how you'd react. I didn't want to upset you."

"How come you think you would've upset me?"

"Because you don't often speak your mind about your feelings or your thoughts. It's easy to talk to Ren. He doesn't judge. Ever."

I wasn't judgmental either, but I could see how she would think that.

I smiled at her. "I won't judge you for the things you enjoy doing, baby. You're smart, and I know you would never do anything you'd later on regret. I trust you."

Her smile widened as she listened to me speak, then she hugged me tight by pressing my head against her chest.

"I promise I will talk to you about everything from now on. I was unsure at first, but I knew you wouldn't judge."

"Never when it comes to my kids," I assured her, rubbing her back gently.

When Warren appeared in the distance, I kept my eyes on his while he observed what was going on in front of him.

He looked relaxed, and that surely had to do with Azula sleeping in his bed last night.

I'd be as relaxed too.

"Morning," I greeted as he stopped in front of us.

"Morning. Guess she told you?" he asked.

I nodded and looked up at Zula, who was still smiling like a kid who had just received a bag of candy.

"But next time she feels like she needs a break from her brothers, I told her to come to me," I teased.

We had this unofficial competition going between us ever since we were little, but with Azula being the main reason for our competition, neither of us took it too seriously.

"I think we should keep her at a distance from them for today. How about you tag along? I was gonna take Zula to the thrift store today."

Sounded like a good idea to me, so I nodded.

"Get yourself some coffee first. The boys will be sleeping for a few more hours."

Azula got up from my lap but kept her hand in my hair. "Stay. I'll get you both coffees."

She grabbed my cup from the table and then walked inside, leaving my brother and me outside.

I leaned back and stretched out my legs, making myself comfortable while he took the seat next to me.

"Didn't take her long to tell you," Warren said, squinting into the sun which was slowly rising.

"She wouldn't have kept it in for long anyway. Not surprised about what they did with her either," I stated.

"Me neither. Still, we gotta keep it all under control. Shit like this can get out of hand real fast."

I raised a brow and looked at him. "How come?"

He shrugged. "She's young. Not sure her body will be able to take that much exhaustion. She looked tired last night, and it wasn't because of the beers or her brothers fucking her."

"What's the issue then?"

"Her being overly-excited about everything that happened in the past few days. Thane and Wesson weren't the only ones touching her, but she kept her excitement inside long enough to exhaust her brain."

It made sense what he said, and there was only one solution to that problem.

When Azula came back outside and handed us both a cup of coffee, I placed my free hand on the back of her thigh and smiled up at her.

"You gonna tell us about your thoughts too the way we will? Whenever you wanna try something new, be open with us, all right?"

She smiled back and nodded, and soon enough, her eyes filled with excitement.

"I really never thought you would react this way. I'm happy you understand my needs," she told me, her voice proud but gentle.

"You're my baby. I'll grant you every wish, no matter how fucked up they are."

I pulled her down onto my lap again and wrapped my arm around her stomach while taking a sip of my coffee.

"So, thrift shopping today?" Warren asked, and Azula quickly nodded.

"I'm excited! Last time I passed the store I saw this great jean jacket hanging in the window. It's only ten bucks."

"Let's hope it's still there," Warren said.

It would be a great day without the boys around, and just like they were able to last night, I was excited to explore some more with my baby girl.

There was so much more to her than people saw, and I was glad she showed her naughty side only to the men closest in her life.

fourteen

VIGGO

Zula didn't need much in life to be happy.

She had us, but it was always heartwarming watching her eyes go wide when she saw the simplest things she liked.

This time, it was that jean jacket she had told us about this morning.

We left after getting ready while the boys were still sleeping, and once we got into my truck and drove into town, I didn't bother thinking about them for the day.

I wanted to enjoy my time with my daughter and brother, without the boys feeling the need to show off their newly found interest in her.

Because I damn well knew they'd act like possessive motherfuckers the second they woke up.

I was standing by a table with hats and beanies on it while Warren sat down in one of the two chairs in the middle of the thrift store.

He was watching Azula as she tried on the jacket, and when she turned to look at herself in the mirror, I moved closer to the chairs.

"Looks good on you," I told her, eyeing the back of the jacket covered in her long, fiery locks.

"It's the perfect size too," she announced, turning her head to look back at me with a smile.

"Does it feel good?" Warren asked.

"Yes, very. It's comfy," she stated, smiling at him now.

"Ten bucks, is it?" he then added, looking at the tag hanging from the bottom of the sleeve.

She lifted her hand and looked at it, then she nodded. "Ten. Is that too much? I can look for another jacket. I don't mind."

"Take it. Look around to see if you find anything else you like," I told her, watching her eyes widen.

"Really?" She was surprised that we were open to spend more money than we usually would, seeing as we saved every penny to get a good meal on our table every day.

This time, the boys and I made a little more money thanks to the new customers we got.

And what better way to spend the money than spoiling our little girl?

"Really. Go look around," I encouraged with a smile.

She sighed happily and walked over to me and wrapped her arms around me tightly, kissing my cheek multiple times before leaning back to look at me.

"You're the best!"

"It's his money too," I told her, nodding down at Warren so he'd get the same attention.

As competitive and sometimes jealous as we were as brothers, there were times I wanted him to feel the same I did.

Azula let go of me and leaned in to hug Warren as tightly as she hugged me, and kissed his cheek too.

"I love you guys. This is the best day ever."

If the simplest things made her so damn happy, I did a good ass job raising her.

Azula had always been selfless and put others' needs first, so why not show her that she deserved the same?

She walked over to the mirror again where a single floral dress was hung on the side of it, and she took it down to look at it closely before showing it to us and pointing at the only changing room in the store.

"I'm gonna try this one on," she told us, but instead of just nodding and waiting there, we both followed her to the large curtain which she pulled aside to reveal another big mirror and a small stool.

There were no words needed between my brother and me, and once I was inside the changing room with Azula, Warren stepped closer to pull the curtain back again.

He was standing in front of the opening so no one was able to look inside, and while Azula looked at us with wide eyes, I couldn't help but chuckle at her surprised expression.

"What are you doing?" she asked.

"Making sure that dress fits. Take off your clothes," I told her. "Can't see if it fits if you don't try it on, hm?"

She shook her head and then looked at Warren before placing the dress onto the stool and taking off the jacket.

I took it from her and hung it up on one of the hooks,

then watched her closely as she slowly got rid of her shirt.

She looked unsure, but I knew it was because there were other people in the store.

To ease her tension, I reached for her ass and cupped it with one hand, then squeezed it gently to make her look at me again.

"You're gonna have to be quiet, all right? Don't want anyone to know what's going in here, hm?"

She shook her head, and sooner than I had imagined, mischief appeared in her eyes.

Warren was still standing in the same spot, but he was now working on unbuttoning his pants.

The curtain was still covering most of him from behind, and without dropping down his pants and shorts, he pulled his dick out and rubbed on it.

"Here?" she asked, wanting to make sure.

"Here," I stated, squeezing her ass one more time before dropping to my right knee and pulling at her skirt.

She made it so damn easy for us to get to her body, and I knew she loved that.

Once her skirt was on the floor, I cupped her pussy from behind and felt her wetness on the thin fabric.

"Starting to become a usual thing, huh?" I whispered with a grin.

Azula reached back and placed one hand on my shoulder to steady herself while she let Warren grab her right hand wrap it around his dick.

"Mouth shut," Warren warned, and when she pressed her lips into a tight line to ensure no sound would come out of her mouth, I started to rub her clit with my two fingers.

We all had to be quiet, or else they'd kick us out.

Zula's clit was already throbbing by just the simple touch of my fingertips, and the faster I circled the little nub, the more her body tensed.

"Relax. He's only just started," Warren murmured.

A small sigh escaped her, and with her eyes closed, she threw her head back and gripped my shoulder tighter.

I could imagine how painful it was for Warren right now, feeling her hand squeeze his dick so damn much.

Lucky him.

I continued to rub her clit until I could smell more of her arousal, and when her legs started to shake, I pushed her panties aside to uncover her slit before sliding two fingers inside her tightness.

It was easy, and as soon as she felt them inside of her, she relaxed again.

"Oh," she cried, sticking her ass out more.

I placed my lips on her cheek and bit the soft skin gently while I kept moving my fingers in and out of her pussy, and her walls clenched around me with every thrust inside.

"Shh, Z. Keep that mouth shut," Warren hissed before covering her lips with his.

She was now leaning more into him with her back arched, and it gave me much better access to her asshole now that her legs were spread wider too.

I licked through her slit and circled the tiny hole with my tongue, making her squirm.

I could hear their kiss turn into something deeper, and if I wasn't using both my hands to please and keep her right there, I would be rubbing my dick.

It was throbbing in my pants, and it was getting tighter with each flick of my tongue.

Pulling my fingers out of her pussy again, I pushed them into my mouth before rubbing them along her slit again.

"Fucking beautiful," I whispered as I watched her folds move on their own as a reaction to my touch.

"I wish I could fuck you right now, baby. Just the thought of it turns me on so fucking much," I growled.

We all knew that wasn't possible, but I could still make her come.

"Bend down a little more, baby," Warren told her, and once she did, she was close enough to his dick to take it into her mouth.

What we were doing would not only kick us out of the store, but also have people call the damn cops on us.

If we'd get caught fucking our daughter and niece at the trailer park, no one would fucking care.

But this was thrilling, and it showed by the way Azula's body shook now that I was fingering her again.

"Fuck," Warren growled, and I wished I was in his position.

I'll get her to suck my dick eventually.

Her moans were muffled, and I looked up to see Warren look behind him to make sure no one was close, and when he turned his head back, he gave me a quick nod.

We were in the clear, so I moved my fingers faster to hopefully make her come.

It was easy with her mother, as she was so damn sensitive down there, and I was happy to find out that our daughter's body was the same.

Her legs were twitching and her body squirming more and more as I continued to drive her close to the edge, and knowing my brother, he'd try to come at the same time as her.

He kept his groans inside, not wanting to get any unnecessary attention from customers, but when Azula was close, I watched his body tense as well.

His hands were cupping her head and fisting her hair tightly, moving his hips so he could dive deeper into her mouth until his tip hit the back of her throat.

Her pussy squeezed my fingers even more now, and the faster I moved, the harder her body shook.

"Come for us, baby. Show us how much you like to be touched by your dad and uncle."

It turned me on talking about myself making my daughter come, and I knew it had the same effect on both of them.

We were all on the same page, and after a few more seconds, both of their bodies stilled and tensed.

"Oh, God!" Azula cried out as Warren pulled out of her, and I watched his cum drip down to the floor, staining the colorful carpet we were standing on.

Luckily, Azula had swallowed most of his cum, and that stain wouldn't be seen any longer after it dried.

There were spots on the carpet anyway.

I got back up from kneeling behind her, but I kept my fingers inside of her to keep on massaging her walls which had been tightening uncontrollably for the past few minutes.

I pulled her up, making her let go of Warren's dick and lean back against me with my hand wrapped around her neck.

"That's not all we can do to you. Before you let your brothers fuck you again, we'll be the ones doing so."

She looked at me through tear-filled eyes, but her smile assured me that she wasn't upset about what just happened.

It was Warren's dick in her mouth that made her eyes water.

"Yes, please," she whispered.

I tilted her head slightly to the side to kiss her, tasting my brother's cum still lingering on her tongue.

We shared the same DNA anyway.

After a long, deep kiss, I let go of her so she could finally try on that dress she picked out.

"I wanna see you in this," I told her, tapping the fabric of the dress. "You'll look beautiful in it," I added with a smile.

A wide grin spread on her lips, and when Warren was finally done buttoning his pants again, we both stepped out of the changing area to give her some space.

No one had been watching us exit and sit back down on the two chairs in the middle of the store, and I was starting to wonder if people just ignored us because they knew we weren't born and raised in this town.

We were outsiders and didn't have a glamourous life like most of the people in this town.

Yet, our lives were far more interesting than theirs.

No doubt.

fifteen

AZULA

"You okay?" Warren asked as we got back to the car.

Dad had already gotten in on the driver's side, and I stopped on the other side of the car to look up at Warren.

"Yes, I'm okay," I assured him, knowing this was about what happened in that changing area inside the store.

We didn't get caught, luckily, but it was a close call as I did see a girl my age looking at me with a strange look when we stood by the checkout.

Or maybe she was just looking at me like that because she thought I was strange.

That was an even more probable explanation, seeing as I wasn't like the girls in this town.

Warren placed his hand on my cheek and brushed along the corner of my lips with his thumb. "Thrilling, huh? What we and your brothers put you through in the past days."

I smiled and nodded, then I bit the inside of my cheek to try and not turn red.

"Will there be more?" I asked quietly.

"If that's what you want. I just want you to feel comfortable with everything you let us do to you."

"I don't think there's anything that would make me feel uncomfortable. Not when it's you guys."

I was starting to explore my sexuality, and although I've had sex before, this was different than anything I've ever experienced.

Those boys were young and just wanted to fuck a girl to please themselves, but the men in my family were adults.

They cared about me and wanted me to feel good before they reached their own orgasms.

That was the biggest difference between the boys at school and my family, and I preferred men instead of boys.

"Get in," Ren said with a nod toward the door behind me, and before I turned around to open it, I stood on my tiptoes to kiss his jawline.

I could see us lying around in his bed for hours, just talking about our feelings and thoughts, something I could never do with the others.

Still, knowing that Warren wanted me just as much as the others did made my insides tingle.

He smiled at me when I reached back to open the door, and when I got inside, he did the same.

"What have you been whispering about?" Dad asked, sounding a little jealous.

I placed my hand on his shoulder and squeezed it gently, smiling at him. "Nothing, Daddy. Just letting Warren know how much I love you guys."

"We love you too. Don't forget to show me some of that love too though."

"I won't," I promised him, letting him grab my hand and kiss the back of it before he placed both hands back on the steering wheel to start driving.

Our love was stronger than anyone ever could imagine.

And unless it involved other people, I didn't give a shit about strangers' opinions.

***

"Where have you been this morning?" Bonnie asked as she walked up to our car after Dad parked in front of our trailer.

She had nothing but a bikini on.

The sun was shining brightly and it was starting to get hot outside, and I already knew where she was headed.

"Shopping with Dad and Warren. Wanna see what I got?" I asked, smiling brightly at her.

"Hell, yeah!"

I reached into the backseat to grab the bag from the thrift store and pulled out the jean jacket first, letting her look at it and even try it on.

"That's the one we saw last time, right? God, I wished I had ten bucks to spare and get it myself."

"You can wear it sometimes," I told her, seeing as we shared almost everything.

I had a pair of her old heels laying around in my bedroom which I had once worn out to a house party of one of our schoolmates.

We had been sharing things ever since we were little, and I one time gave her the same body spray I always used because she liked it so much.

That's what best friends were for, right?

"I also got this dress." I pulled out the floral dress which I had tried on after Warren and Dad finally left me alone in the changing room, and I fell in love immediately after seeing myself wearing it.

It was a light blue fabric with small flowers covering it.

It hugged my waist perfectly and flowed gently from my hips down to the middle of my thighs.

"Oh, my God! This is gorgeous!"

"Right? And it was only eight dollars. I wonder who owned that dress before."

"Maybe a woman in her early forties. Looks like a dress she'd buy to get over her husband who cheated on her, and with that dress she wanted to show off that she was still young and beautiful," Bonnie said.

"People are still young at forty, Bonnie," Dad told her with a chuckle.

"But at fifty, not anymore," she shot back, mocking him.

Dad shook his head and muttered something under his breath while Warren grinned, slapping his brother's back.

"Bonnie's right. Look at all that white hair peeking through. Doesn't matter if our hair is blond. White still shows, big brother."

Dad laughed. "I'm old when I say I am. I still feel good at fifty-three."

"As you should," I told him, looking back at the dress. "I'm gonna wear this tonight."

"Wanna come down to the beach for a swim? I can't stand this heat," Bonnie sighed.

"Let me go put on my bikini." I grabbed the jacket again and put it back into the plastic bag with my dress, then I headed inside to walk straight into my bedroom to get my bikini.

It was already past lunchtime, but Thane and Wesson were still sleeping.

Or at least they were still in bed and not ready to get up.

I didn't think last night would've been so exhausting for them, but even I was able to wake up early enough this morning.

I changed into my bikini and then walked into the bathroom to get a towel, and when I passed Wesson's bedroom, I saw them both lying there, naked, but with their eyes open.

The TV was also on, which I only now realized.

"Morning," I greeted, stopping by the door and trying not to stare at their boners.

They didn't bother pulling the covers over their bodies, and when they looked at me, they both grinned.

"Where have you been this morning?" Wesson asked, placing his right hand on his shaft.

"Thrift shopping with Dad and Warren. They said they're gonna prepare some lunch and bring it down to the beach, so if you wanna eat, you better get up. It's almost one," I told them.

As much as I tried not to look, I couldn't help but let my eyes wander down their bodies.

Thane's left leg was wrapped around the covers, but other than that, there was nothing keeping my eyes from seeing his beautiful body.

Wesson had a tan line across his lower abdomen, and I knew his skin would only get tanner now that summer was coming closer.

Just like Thane, I didn't tan at all.

I would only get burned, and I only now remembered to put sunscreen on before heading down to the beach.

"We're getting up soon," Wesson replied, moving his gaze down to my body.

"Did you put sunscreen on?" he then asked, always making sure I was safe.

"I will take it with me to the beach," I told him with a smile, then I looked back at Thane who was now observing his brother's hand massaging his cock.

He watched Wesson the same way I did, and I was starting to wonder if Thane wished to have been in my place last night.

When Thane's eyes met mine, he shot me a crooked grin and held out his hand.

I stepped into the room and around the bed to get to him, and once I reached him, I placed my hand in his and leaned in to kiss his cheek.

"Something on your mind?" I asked.

He looked a little lost in his thoughts today, but he shook his head. "Just not fully awake yet. I'll meet you down at the beach."

"Okay. I'm sure Reuben will come too if he knows Bonnie's down there as well."

"Don't think Bonnie will be the reason for him to come down there," Wesson said, smirking with a knowing look on his face.

Thane nudged Wesson's side with his elbow. "Shut it," he muttered, then he looked back at me. "We'll be there in a few," he promised me, then he pulled me back down to kiss my lips softly.

I kissed him back immediately and placed my hand on his chest to not fall onto him, because once I did, I wouldn't get back up.

The narrow space between my brothers looked cozy, and although I had escaped from that exact spot last night, I wanted to crawl back into bed with them.

"I want a kiss too," Wesson said, and once I broke the kiss, I laughed softly.

They were both needy, but I wouldn't hold back from giving them what they wanted.

I sat down on the bed next to Thane and leaned over him to get closer to Wesson, and once he placed his hand at the back of my head, I kissed him too.

I could feel Thane's eyes on us while he caressed my back, sending shivers down my spine with his gentle touch.

"Staying in bed all day long sounds much better than the beach," Thane said quietly, making me smile into the kiss.

Wesson's tongue brushed along my bottom lip, but he broke the kiss just seconds after to respond to Thane.

"Can't keep her in here all the damn time. And I think our baby sis has something to tell us." Wesson looked at me with a knowing look. "Think we aren't the only ones who wanna keep her to ourselves."

I watched him closely as I sat back up, and when my eyes met Thane's again, I bit my bottom lip.

"Tell us," Wesson urged. "What else did you do this morning at that thrift store?"

How on earth did he know there was more to it than just shopping?

Although he expected an answer, there was no reason for me to give him one.

He knew Dad and Warren touched me.

"Guess Reuben's the only one left. Don't think he'll want to miss out on the fun," Wes said in a husky voice.

I had never thought about Reuben being into me, or ever wanting to get closer to me.

I did have a lot of fun with him growing up, playing house and sharing all kinds of stories.

Reuben had been like a best friend, but the older we got, the more he distanced himself from me and started to hang out more with Bonnie or other girls.

"You'd let him fuck you, right?" Wesson asked.

"Yes."

I didn't have to think twice about it.

He smirked and cupped my jaw to squeeze my cheeks, then he let go of me again to run his hand through his hair.

"Sharing you is easy, Azula."

That statement didn't need any explanation or more words added to it.

"I'll meet you at the beach," I said after we were all quiet, then I got back up and left the bedroom.

It was easy for them to share me, and even easier for me to let them do so.

sixteen

THANE

"Reuben will kill us when he finds out about us fucking Azula," Wesson muttered after Azula left the room.

"Think he's just gonna be upset. He's been into her ever since he was little. Remember that time he told us he would one day marry her? Guess that idea isn't as strange and disgusting as it was when we were younger."

Wesson chuckled and shook his head. "Back then I didn't think we would turn into sick bastards like we are now. She's got five of us wanting her now."

Zula was a lucky girl having all these men wanting her, and although I hadn't been inside her yet, it didn't bother me sharing her.

Just like Wesson said, sharing her was easy, especially when the other guys were people I loved.

I had my gaze back on the TV, but from the corner of my eye I could see him still stroking his cock like he had been doing ever since Azula first appeared.

My dick was hard too, and I wished someone would be touching it again like Zula did last night.

During the blowjob she gave me, I often looked at Wesson, but that only made it harder to keep from coming.

I had always admired Wesson.

He was slightly taller, tanned, and his face wasn't covered in freckles like mine in the summer.

Not that they bothered me, but it was clear that most girls preferred him over me especially when we were still in high school.

When he wrapped his hand fully around his shaft, I couldn't stop myself from looking at it and watching him rub along his hardness slowly.

There was already a drop of precum on his tip, and if I hadn't held back when I had the chance to fuck that guy from school before, I would've known how cum tasted.

Well, I did get a taste last night when Azula kissed me after swallowing my cum, but that didn't really count in my eyes.

Wesson's dick was long and wide, maybe even slightly bigger than mine, and when he fucked Azula's ass last night, I wished it was me he was thrusting into.

My dick twitched when Wesson squeezed his tip gently, but instead of touching my own to ease the tension, I gripped the side of the mattress to stop myself.

"The hell are you staring at?"

My heart started pounding in my chest at his harsh tone of voice, but when I looked into his eyes, there was amusement in it.

"Nothing," I replied quickly.

We talked about a lot of things, but our sexuality had never been something we discussed.

It was clear to me from a young age on that I was attracted to a certain type of man, and Wesson was one of those types.

Maybe it was because he was my big brother, and I had always seen him as a role model.

"You wanna suck it?" he asked, making my eyes widen and look at him again.

"Huh?"

He chuckled. "You heard me right. Do you wanna suck my dick?"

As shocked as I was, I couldn't turn down that request.

It would be my first time, but if I was being honest, I wanted this more than fucking Azula.

"But you're not into men," I stated, frowning at him.

"Who said that?"

Touché.

I shrugged. "I guess I never thought of you being into men."

"Didn't think that about you either up until I noticed you staring at me from time to time. And the way you watched me while I fucked our sister told me that you'd rather be in her place than your own."

He couldn't be more right, and having him acknowledge that made my heart beat even faster.

"So? Gonna suck me dry or not?"

At this point, there was nothing that could surprise any of us.

Our family was already deep into this twisted shit, so why not go even further down the rabbit hole?

I watched him for a moment before sitting up, and while he did the same, I moved between his legs.

Wesson wasn't nervous, whereas I was almost exploding.

My mind was racing.

Wesson's hand ran through my hair and he gripped it tightly at the back of my head to guide me closer to his hardness leaned against his stomach, and once I wrapped my hand around its base, I lowered my head to put my lips around his tip.

There had never been any practicing for sucking dick in my life, but having Wesson be my first made things a little less awkward and much easier.

He wouldn't judge me, and also…how hard would it be to suck a dick?

I took him in deeper, and for a short second, I wondered how Azula did it.

Granted, she had some practice before.

"Fuck…" Wesson growled as I took him in deeper, and when the taste of his precum hit my tongue, I immediately wanted more.

Shit…how was I only now exploring the male body?

I reached between my legs to stroke my own dick while I continued to suck his, and my balls immediately tightened at my touch.

"That's it," he groaned, pushing my head down more and making his tip touch the back of my throat.

Yeah, this was something I had to practice.

Maybe I could get some tips from Azula, I thought, making myself laugh internally.

And I had always thought as the older brother I would teach her stuff.

I knew how hard it was to keep yourself from coming after waking up with a boner, and I also knew that Wesson wouldn't be able to keep it in for much longer.

His dick was already throbbing, and only seconds later, he held my head still and bucked his hips to take control over me.

"God!" he groaned, throwing his head back and pushing my head down again, making it hard for me to breathe.

His cum flowed down my throat immediately, and to stop me from choking on it, he let me move back up and have the rest of his cum accumulate in my mouth.

I looked up at him and watched a smirk appear on his lips, and once I swallowed his cum, I chuckled.

"What's so damn funny?"

"Nothing. Just never thought I'd let my little brother suck my dick one day."

He covered my face with his hand and pushed me aside jokingly, and when I rolled onto my side to lie next to him again, I grinned up at him.

"You liked it," I stated.

"Whatever," he muttered with the same smirk plastered on his face.

I wasn't ashamed, but I could see him not wanting to repeat this or do more in front of the others.

I also wasn't going to push him to be open about this, but I sure as hell wouldn't deny it if the others found out about it one day.

"I think you liked it so much that you'll one day fuck me in the ass the way you did with Zula."

He watched me for a moment, then he shrugged and ran one hand over his face.

"We'll see," was the only thing he said.

That was good enough for me.

***

Wearing only my swim shorts, I headed over to Reuben's while Wesson followed Dad and Warren to the beach.

Warren told me that Reuben was probably still in bed, but when I arrived by the trailer, he was sitting on the front steps of the trailer, smoking a cigarette.

"Zula was here this morning," he said after acknowledging me.

"I know. Did you talk to her?"

I sat down next to him and grabbed the cigarette he handed me.

Taking a long drag, I looked straight ahead into the distance.

"No. I heard her talk to Dad though. Something about me finding out about you and Wesson. Thought Dad was the only guy she had a thing for."

I raised a brow, handed him the cigarette again and looked at him.

"Don't look at me like that. This home has thin walls. Even heard them kiss. How come I don't know about this secret of hers?" he asked.

He sounded hurt but annoyed at the same time.

Reuben had always had a crush on Zula, but as her cousin, he could never get too close to her.

Unless we let him in on what we've been doing with her.

"Z's starting to explore a little, and she decided to use us as her little guinea pigs."

He let my words sink in, then he laughed. "Shit, really? Means I'm not the only one who's ever fantasized about her?"

I chuckled. "No, and let me tell you…she's pretty open too. Baby sis is freakier than I thought."

"So you fucked her?"

"No, but Wesson did."

"What about my father?"

I shrugged. "She never mentioned him fucking her."

His facial expression relaxed a little when I told him that. "Shit," he repeated under his breath, then he let out another harsh laugh. "Where's she now?"

"At the beach with Bonnie and the others. I'm headed there too. You coming?"

I knew his response already, and while I got back up, he took the last drag of his cigarette, then put it out by throwing it to the ground and stepping on it.

"You think she'll ever let me get closer?" he asked, sounding insecure.

"Would it be fair letting us all get close but not you?" I asked back with a raised eyebrow.

"Guess not. She's always made sure that everyone's happy."

That was true.

She'd always make sure everyone got the same treatment, no matter what it was about.

"And you deserve to be happy too. Now, go change. I'll wait right here."

He looked up and squinted into the sun, and after taking a while to think about my words, he finally got up and headed inside.

There was no problem with Azula letting him touch her too, but he had to be careful not to catch feelings for her or shit could get complicated.

If that wasn't already the case.

seventeen

REUBEN

As much as I wanted to get close to her, something inside of me stopped me whenever I saw her.

What Thane told me about the things she let the others do to her made me jealous at first, but for some reason, she made me insanely nervous whenever she stood in front of me.

That's why I hadn't talked to her all day, even though she was right there.

She was heading into the water for the third time this afternoon, and the urge to follow her was getting stronger.

The more she was exposed to the sun, the more freckles appeared all over her body, and although I liked the ones covering her nose and cheeks the best, the freckles right underneath her ass at the back of her thighs were starting to become my favorite ones.

"She's getting prettier each day, hm?" Viggo murmured next to me.

We were both sitting in camping chairs, holding a beer while letting the sun hit our skin.

I looked over at him after tearing my eyes off Azula's backside, then I sighed. "Am I literally the only one who hasn't gotten close to her yet?"

Viggo chuckled and shrugged. "Looks like it. Didn't think you'd be into her though. Thought you had a thing going on with Bonnie."

It stunned me how casual he was talking about being attracted to his daughter, but only for a little while.

"Bonnie smells exactly like Z. Why the fuck do they have to have the same body spray anyway?"

"That the only reason why you fuck Bonnie? Because she smells like Zula?"

There was amusement in his voice.

"Bonnie's also as close as I can get to Z. They're best friends."

I didn't have to state the obvious.

Not to her father.

"Don't you think Bonnie would get jealous if you'd start fucking her best friend?"

"I don't care. If you can fuck your daughter, I wanna fuck my cousin. Looks like we're all sick bastards here anyway."

Viggo didn't respond to that.

He knew I was right, but there was nothing normal about us anyway.

When I was little, I had always known Azula would one day be the girl I'd marry, and for a while I had thought that would actually happen.

Now, knowing she let four other men touch her, I was starting to lose that hope.

Still, she would surely let a fifth show her how loved she was.

"Maybe you should talk less and follow her onto that floating dock. Bonnie's already coming back out."

I looked back to the water to see Bonnie walk toward us, then she grabbed her towel and sighed, looking at me with an apologetic look.

"I was hoping to spend some time with you today, but I forgot that Mom needs help with something. See you tonight?"

I watched her before moving my gaze to Azula who was pulling herself onto the floating dock further out on the lake, and before I'd get lost in my thoughts because of her, I looked back at Bonnie.

"Uh, sure. Tonight."

She left with her towel wrapped around her body, and I quickly got up to head into the water.

Z was all alone, and seeing as her brothers and Dad were busy kicking around the soccer ball, I took the chance to get to her before anyone got the idea to join her out there.

"Don't go too hard," Viggo advised, sounding amused again.

"I definitely won't fuck her on that dock."

"Good. It's my turn to fuck her anyway."

Not sure he could decide who got lucky with her next, but for now, I just wanted to be alone with her.

Even though their eyes would be on us.

I put my beer down and walked closer to the water, and once I was inside, I started swimming toward the floating dock to get to her.

Azula saw me get into the water, and while leaning back on her elbows, she could watch me swim toward her.

As I got there, I placed both hands on top of the dock and pushed myself up and out of the water.

"I was hoping someone would come join me," she said with a smile.

"Someone, or me specifically?"

She shrugged. "Someone. You've been a little distant lately."

That was true, but I had my reasons.

Her not being attracted to me was one of them.

"Mind if I join you though?" I asked, hoping this conversation would ease the tension between us a little.

"Of course not," she replied, smiling brightly. "Bonnie has been talking a lot about you lately. She has a huge crush on you."

Ah, fuck.

Good way of starting a conversation with a girl you secretly like more than the girl you're hooking up with.

"She's nice."

"*Nice*? Just nice? Seems a whole lot more than just nice to me if you spend so much time with her."

"It's easy to pass the time with Bonnie," I explained.

"So you're only hanging out with her to pass the time? There are other things you can do, you know?"

Of course, but unless those things included her, I didn't wanna do them.

I sat down next to her and ran a hand through my wet hair. "I heard you and Dad last night."

Keeping it a secret wouldn't last long anyway, and if I ever wanted in on the fun, I'd better tell her now.

"You did?"

She didn't sound as surprised as I hoped she would, but on the other hand, this would make it much easier to talk about.

"Yeah. You know those things you let your brothers do to you are wrong, right?"

117

She didn't reply at first, and after a while of staring into each other's eyes, she raised a brow. "But you wish to do the same things to me as they do."

Wasn't denying that.

"You'd let me?"

Her skeptical look eased, and by pulling her knees to her chest, she placed her head on them sideways to keep looking at me.

"Remember when we were little and we used to play husband and wife?" she asked.

"Of course, I remember. Those are my favorite childhood memories."

"You once said that a husband always kissed his wife, but you only ever kissed my cheek because you already knew that kissing my lips wouldn't be right."

I didn't know where she was going with this, but it did seem a little controversial, knowing about the things she did with her brothers.

And uncle and dad.

"We were kids, Z," was my only explanation.

"I know. But I never had that thought in my mind that kissing you would be wrong. How is something wrong if it feels right?"

"It's wrong to others."

"And you think we should care what others think?" she asked.

Although she was only sixteen, sweet Azula was very wise.

I smiled at her and studied her face closely. "No, I think we shouldn't give a shit about what other people think."

"Then why do you keep your distance from me when you clearly want to get closer?"

Damn.

"Probably because I'm an idiot."

She laughed softly and shook her head, then she reached out her hand and placed it at the back of my head while still keeping her head on her knees.

"You're not an idiot. But you would be one if you'd continue to sleep with Bonnie just to feel as if you're close to me."

She was right, or course.

I was using Bonnie but didn't even get what I actually wanted.

My eyes dropped to her lips, and by leaning in closer, I brushed my lips against hers before kissing her gently.

The nervousness in my chest exploded and turned into excitement which soon moved all the way down to my lower abdomen.

Although she wasn't the first girl I'd ever kissed, it sure felt like it.

Azula was special, and knowing she wasn't pushing me away made me feel proud and happy.

Drops of water mixed with our kiss as I parted my lips, and when our tongues touched, I didn't want this to end.

So much about her was addicting, but I wouldn't be the only one to get a taste of her in the future.

Everyone else already had gotten this close, and I was taking in this moment before I'd have to share her.

I deepened the kiss by tilting my head more to the side, placing my hand on her knee to then gently push her back until she was lying on her back.

I held myself over her with my left hand next to her head, and to feel more of her, I pushed my knee between her legs to tangle them with mine.

Her hand moved into my hair while she placed the other on my chest, sliding it downward to feel my muscles move underneath her touch.

Azula took it slow to discover every inch of my body, and I wanted to do the same with hers, but not here on a damn floating dock.

If Dad got to be alone with her, then I wanted the same but without all of the other guys watching.

I cupped her cheek with one hand and brushed my tongue along hers one last time before breaking the kiss and looking at her.

"Why did you stop?" she whispered, her voice sounding slightly desperate.

I smiled down at her and touched the tip of my nose to hers. "Just taking in this moment."

She was so fucking beautiful.

I wanted to kiss every single spot on her skin and show her how loved she was, but she'd get enough love from the others as well, and I didn't wanna come off as annoying.

Or maybe you should just stop thinking too much and do what you think is right.

Placing my lips on hers again, I could feel her smile into the kiss as she pulled me closer with both her arms wrapped around my neck now.

I didn't care who she let touch her body before, because all I cared about was how she made me feel.

And, hell…kissing her was the best feeling I've ever felt.

eighteen

REUBEN

My lips still tingle from that kiss with Azula a few days ago, and seeing her walk up to my trailer made my heartbeat pick up speed again.

We had a lot of work to get done at the garage, not leaving much time for us to spend time with Azula.

Today, Dad and Viggo sent us home early while they finished up working on a car, and I had just gotten out of the shower when I saw Azula.

I went to the front door with only a towel wrapped around my hips and my hair still dripping, then I opened it before she reached the front steps.

"Hi," she greeted, making that insane feeling inside of me grow.

"Hey. What are you doing here?" I replied with a grin.

"Came to see you. It's been a few days." Her smile was heartwarming, and I couldn't stop looking at her face while she stood there with her arms loosely crossed in front of her.

"Warren's not home yet either, huh?" she asked.

I shook my head and leaned against the doorframe, then I crossed my own arms over my chest. "Your brothers didn't tell you Dad and Viggo are staying a little longer tonight?"

"No. Wesson went straight into the shower and Thane dropped into the bed. They looked exhausted."

I was tired too, but having her here right now kept me awake.

"Wanna come in?" I asked.

She was wearing her new dress which fit her perfectly, and her feet were bare as usual during the warm days of the year.

"You want me to?" she asked back, making me grin and chuckle.

"I don't think I would've asked you otherwise. Come on in."

I stepped aside and let her enter, and once she was inside, I closed the door behind me and then wrapped my arms around her stomach.

Leaning in, I kissed her cheek and walked toward the narrow hallway to get to my bedroom.

It's been a while since I last had her in here.

"Are you coming to the bonfire later?" she asked, leaning back against me as we stopped in front of my bed.

I placed another kiss to her cheek, then trailed kisses all the way down to her shoulder. "How about we go out tonight? I can take you to grab burgers and fries, and then we can watch the sunset somewhere."

She was quiet for a moment, then she turned around

in my arms to face me and place her hands on my chest.

"Like…out on a date?"

"If you want it to be one, why not?"

She looked unsure, but then she smiled and nodded. "That sounds perfect. I haven't had a burger in months."

"Perfect. Let me get dressed and then we'll leave." I leaned in to kiss her lips, letting her grip my hair tightly with both hands and pull me even closer to her body.

Catching feelings for her wouldn't be a good thing, but as long as I got to be with her, I didn't care.

Now that I had opened up to her about that long-lasting crush I had on her, I couldn't just take all the things I said when we were little back.

I placed both hands on her ass and squeezed gently as she deepened the kiss, but as quick as our kiss turned passionate, she broke it again.

"Get dressed."

I grinned and pressed one more kiss to her lips before turning and grabbing clothes out of the closet.

"How was school today?"

"It was okay. We watched some movie about a guy swallowing a tapeworm to show what that does to a human body. It was weird."

I laughed. "He swallowed a tapeworm on purpose? Did he end up getting rid of that thing?"

"He was able to get rid of some. They explained how that tapeworm got longer every day and it probably split a few times. So he's still got some of it inside of him I guess."

I scrunched up my nose and looked back at her. "Thanks for telling me about all that stuff. I'm even hungrier now that I listened to your tapeworm story."

She laughed at me and shrugged before leaning back against the headboard.

"You asked how school went."

True, but I didn't expect her to tell me about damn tapeworms.

I put on a pair of shorts and a shirt, and since it was warm outside anyway, I didn't bother drying my hair.

"All right. Ready to go?"

I observed her as she took in a deep breath, silently telling me that she was too comfortable to get back up, but then she reached out her hands and I grabbed them both to pull her back up.

"Don't tell me you're tired from sitting in school all day," I teased.

"Hey, school's tiring. But no, I'm energetic enough to have dinner with you." She smiled up at me by tilting her head back, and I wrapped my arms around her lower back to hold her close.

"Good. Don't think we'll get another great opportunity to spend time on our own."

"Me neither," she replied, licking her lips. "And I hope Wes and Thane won't see us leave. They'd get jealous for sure."

I agreed, and to not spend any more time hoping we wouldn't get caught, I grabbed her hand and pulled her outside to my old car.

It was still in perfect condition, but it was almost twenty years old.

I just knew how to keep it alive for long enough without having to get a new one.

I opened the car door for her, and once she was inside, I walked around the front to get in myself.

"Hey, can we go for tacos instead?" she asked,

looking at me with question in her big, beautiful eyes.

"We can just get both. Burgers and tacos," I suggested.

"You sure? Do you have enough money for that?"

I chuckled and started the car. "Did you really just ask me that? You do know that we're not as broke as people think we are."

"Then why do we live in the trailer park?" she shot back with a raised brow.

"Because this is where we were born and raised. You don't leave your home unless there's a good enough reason to do so."

My answer made her think, and although I didn't have as much money as I wished I had, I owned enough to take sweet Z out on our first ever date.

I needed this, knowing that soon I won't have her all to myself anymore.

***

Watching Azula eat four tacos, a burger, fries, and ice cream in less than thirty minutes was astonishing.

She's always been a big eater, but tonight, she even ate more than I did.

Maybe it was because I was nervous, being alone with her for once.

"Full?" I asked with a smirk as she leaned back against the car seat, throwing her head back and closing her eyes.

"Yes, very. I think the ice cream was too much," she replied with a chuckle.

"I'm glad you ate. Viggo won't have to worry about feeding you for the next week or so," I joked.

She laughed at my words and opened her eyes again to look at me. "I'm gonna be hungry again first thing tomorrow morning. Aren't you going to finish that?"

I looked at my second burger which I had only eaten half of, then I shook my head. "Guess not. I had a sandwich before coming home from work."

"That's a bad excuse," she shot back, grinning at me.

I reached over and squeezed her side gently, making her jump and laugh. "It's not an excuse. Besides, those burgers were huge."

I grabbed the waste from her lap and piled everything into the big bag we got with our food inside, and after opening the car door, I got out and walked to the next bin.

The sun had already set while we were eating, and now that the stars and moon were shining brightly in the sky, I wanted to enjoy that sight with Zula.

"Get out of the car," I told her before I closed the door to then get in front of the car.

I had parked it in a parking lot further up the hill overlooking the town, and in the distance, we were still able to see the lake and trailer park.

When she got out, I didn't intend on pulling her to me and kissing her, but I did, surprising the both of us.

With my lips pressed against hers, I held her close to me with my hands on her waist.

She wrapped her arms around my neck and tilted her head slightly to the side to deepen the kiss.

If her brothers didn't exist, and her dad and mine wouldn't be into her, we could've been an actual couple.

Dating, spending time together daily, and everything couples usually did.

But that would never happen.

Not with her wanting four other guys.

I didn't have a problem with that, but if I was in control in all of this, I would just keep her to myself.

Her hands moved into my hair and gripped it tightly, pulling at the ends while her body pressed against mine.

She tasted of fast food, which didn't bother me one bit.

While she continued to pull at my hair, I moved my hands down to her ass, squeezing it gently as I leaned back against the hood of my car.

She stood between my legs as I stretched them out, and by pulling her as close as possible, I showed her how much I adored her without having to say a word.

Our kiss turned passionate, and I moved my tongue with hers gently, slowly tasting every inch of her mouth while her perfect scent moved up my nose.

Bonnie wouldn't have kissed me right after eating burgers and tacos.

She wouldn't have let me near unless she'd brushed her teeth.

Azula was different.

Cared less about what others would think, and didn't care about unnecessary and little things.

Just as I thought our kiss would last forever, a car parked right next to mine, and since I had expected this to happen for a short moment throughout our date, I wasn't surprised as I opened my eyes to look to my right.

nineteen

AZULA

"What are they doing here?" I whispered as I saw Thane and Wesson get out of the car.

Thane had a smug grin on his face while Wesson's frown was the exact opposite of Thane's expression.

"Did you really think you'd get away with this?" Wesson asked, his brows raised now.

His words were directed at Reuben, and I hated the annoyance mixed with sadness in his eyes.

He was so happy and excited to spend time with me alone, and although I would never choose any of them over the other, I was having a lot of fun with him alone too.

"I didn't think shit," Reuben murmured, turning his head to look at me again with an apologetic smile. "Sorry," he then whispered.

I cupped his face with both hands and smiled back. "Don't be. I had a lot of fun tonight."

I leaned in to kiss his lips gently before looking back at my brothers who were both leaning against the side of their car with their arms crossed over their chests.

"Mind a little company?" Wesson asked, his voice mocking the both of us.

"Why are you here?"

Wesson shrugged. "Woke up from a nap and couldn't find either of you. Thought that was strange and so we came looking for you."

"And how did you know we were up here?" Reuben asked with a raised brow.

"Got her phone's location. You know I always wanna keep my baby sister safe."

Wesson was starting to get on my nerves, but as annoying as he was, I couldn't help myself from feeling protected by my older brother.

"Reuben and I just wanted to spend some time together since you two were tired. He took me out for dinner," I told them.

They didn't reply.

They had just ruined a beautiful moment between Reuben and me.

We were all quiet for a while, but Wesson broke the silence with his growly voice.

"Come here," he demanded, keeping his arms crossed over his chest and his eyes dark.

I looked at Reuben to see if he'd have an issue with that, but he didn't move a muscle or react at all.

I stepped away from him and walked over to Wesson, hoping he would soon drop his bossy attitude.

It wasn't necessary.

His jaw clenched, then he reached for my hand and pulled me closer with his eyes staring into mine.

Before he could say a word, I spoke first. "Are you jealous?"

His brow shot up, then he let out a harsh laugh. "Jealous of Reuben spending time with you alone? No. We share you, and you damn well know it," he said with an amused undertone. "If I wanna spend time with you on my own, then I will. But I'd much rather share you."

"Why?"

Thane laughed next to us. "Don't you like it better having more than one guy touch you? You profit from it the most."

I looked at him for a moment, but what Wesson said next surprised me and made me look back at him.

"You'll profit from it too."

I wasn't sure how to interpret that, but I'd soon find out.

Wesson lifted his hand and gripped my jaw gently, tilting my head back while keeping his eyes on mine.

"Gonna do as I say?" he asked, his voice all collected and calm.

"You know she does," Thane replied.

"Go stand in front of Reuben again," he ordered.

I didn't hesitate, quickly turning and walking back to Reuben who pulled me to him with a sweet smile.

Words weren't needed, and no matter what Wesson had in mind, I knew I'd be safe with the three of them.

Wesson walked over to us and stopped behind me, cupping the back of my head with his large hand.

"Pull down your pants," he told Reuben, and for a short moment, I wasn't sure he would do what Wes said.

When I smiled at him and nodded, Reuben unbuttoned his pants and pushed them down along with his boxer briefs, revealing a hardening cock.

I had an idea of what Wesson had in mind, and when he pushed my head down to get closer to Reuben's cock, I immediately wrapped my hand around his base to then take him into my mouth.

"Ah, fuck..." Reuben muttered, cupping my head with both hands.

To our luck, this place wasn't visited much by others, so I knew we wouldn't get caught up here.

Even if...I wouldn't care much.

I couldn't see what was going on behind me, but it took a while until two hands pulled down my skirt and panties.

It was Thane.

His hands weren't as rough as Wesson's.

"Your turn to fuck her, little brother," Wesson then said.

I continued to move my head up and down, taking Reuben's shaft in deeper with each movement.

"Beautiful, baby," Reuben whispered, caressing my scalp with his fingers buried in my hair.

I had heard Bonnie give him head in the bathroom at the garage last time, but it had sounded like he had taken control over her.

With me, he was being gentle.

I hoped that changed though.

I liked it rough, and although I hated being bossed around, it was different during sex.

When Thane's tip brushed through my slit, I widened my stance so he had better access, without having to tease me too much, he could easily slide inside of me, stretching me the same way Wesson did.

I moaned, arching my back a little more to stick my ass up toward him.

"Fucking tight. Shit…how did you hold back that long when you fucked her?" Thane asked, making Wesson chuckle and Reuben tense.

I hoped he wasn't too upset about what was happening right now, but he definitely wouldn't have let me suck him if he wasn't okay with it.

"Self-control," Wes replied, and I heard him open his pants as well.

What was he up to?

They'd have to take turns with me, but instead of moving closer to me, I heard Thane grunt.

And only then I realized what was going on.

Oh…

THANE

Wesson was stroking his dick while his other hand moved over my ass, his wet fingers leaving a trail all over my skin.

I didn't expect him to go as far as to fuck me, and I had imagined that blowjob I gave him was the last time a guy let me touch him.

I was so fucking wrong.

My heartbeat picked up speed again and the nervousness I felt that day reappeared deep in my chest.

It felt strange at first, having his fingers move between my ass cheeks.

My balls were already tight from thrusting in and out of Z, but his touch made everything even more intense.

It wouldn't be easy for him to fuck me, not unless he'd stretch me the way he did with Azula.

And that's exactly where he was going with this.

The tips of his two fingers rubbed around my tight asshole, and I tried not to tense too much and make it even harder for him.

I continued to move my hips and fuck Azula's wet pussy while doing my best to avoid eye contact with Reuben, unsure of how he would react to what Wesson was doing to me.

But when he groaned, thanks to Z working her magic with that perfect mouth of hers, I couldn't stop myself from looking directly into his eyes.

We were the same height, and having Azula bent over allowed us to see each other.

He looked surprised but not disgusted or weirded out, which made me relax and enjoy my brother's touch.

We were all sick, and there was little that could shock us.

Reuben grabbed a fistful of Azula's hair, and although he looked down at her, I kept my eyes on him.

I needed to look at someone while Wesson slowly moved his fingers inside of me, and Reuben was handsome anyway, making it easy to enjoy everything that was happening.

"So damn tight," Wesson hissed, pushing his two fingers deeper inside.

With my eyes glued on Reuben, I started to move my hips faster, fucking Azula faster and harder and pushing deeper each time.

Her muffled sounds got louder when she lifted her head, but Reuben was quick to push her back down.

I was holding on to Azula's hips with both hands, but Wesson reached for my left hand and placed it on his dick, letting me stroke it.

The whole situation was starting to get overwhelming, but I didn't wanna miss a thing.

I focused on Azula while I watched Reuben's emotions on his face change.

He looked hot as sweat dripped down the side of his face, and I wanted to lean forward and lick it all off to taste the saltiness of it.

I wondered what his cum tasted like.

Would it be like Wesson's?

"Make them come, Azula," Wesson ordered, and as if those words were directed to Reuben and me, we both started to move our hips faster.

Her gags got louder with each thrust of his hips, and with me pushing into her from behind, her body started to tense more and more, making me question whether or not she was enjoying this.

I felt Wesson's finger stretch me more as he added a third inside of me, and the faster I moved, the quicker my orgasm started to creep up on me.

I was still rubbing his dick, but I couldn't focus as much as I liked to.

"Stop," I heard Azula cry, but as selfish as we were, we wouldn't stop.

Her body switched from tense to limp in a matter of seconds, and when she tensed again, I slowed down for her to adjust.

"Please," she begged, but at that point I had no idea what she was begging for.

Maybe for us to stop?

An orgasm?

"Argh!" Reuben groaned as every single muscle on his body tensed, and I soon followed behind with my own orgasm hitting me.

"Come," Wesson murmured close to my ear, then he pressed a kiss underneath it, making me shiver.

I threw my head back and closed my eyes and my balls tightened, and after the first drop of cum shot into her, I stopped moving and pressed myself against her.

"FUUUCK!"

Reuben and I were the only ones enjoying this moment, because the second I looked back down at Azula, there was puke all over the hood of Reuben's car.

"Shit...Z, you okay?" he asked frantically, pulling her long hair back to see her face.

She had missed him by only a few inches, but I didn't think he would've cared if she had thrown up on him.

"What the hell happened?" Wesson asked.

He had pulled his fingers out and was now acting like the usual protective older brother.

I was stunned by what just happened and needed a second to come back down to earth.

"Baby, are you okay?" Wes asked, brushing back her hair and pulling her up against his body. "Hey, what happened?"

Azula was paler than usual, if that was even possible, but she wasn't well at all.

"I think it's the food. She had a whole lot," Reuben told us, guilt washing over his face.

"Shit," Wesson murmured. "Let's get her home. Think we took it a little too far tonight."

Well, at least he realized that.

Azula was still young, and her body wasn't used to what we had just done to her.

But as much as I hated seeing her all sick and tired, I couldn't help but think about the next time we'd do something like this.

It was exciting, and my mind was getting more twisted by the minute.

twenty

WESSON

She had her eyes closed during the ride back home, and Thane shot me worried looks whenever I looked at them through the rearview mirror.

It wasn't really my fault what had happened to Azula, and her throwing up definitely had something to do with all the food Reuben claimed she had eaten before we arrived on top of that hill.

Sure, I was the one initiating things, but Azula was old enough to communicate to us how she was feeling.

"What happened back there?" Thane asked her quietly, brushing her hair back and caressing the side of her face.

She didn't reply right away, but after a few seconds, I could hear her murmur something.

"I'm sorry. We should've stopped when you told us to. I guess we both weren't thinking straight in that moment," Thane told her with an apologetic tone in his voice.

He was talking about himself and Reuben, because all I was doing was fingering Thane's asshole.

Seeing it this way, I didn't have anything to do with Azula throwing up as I wasn't touching her, but I knew she felt pressured by just my presence.

I had no right to be angry at her or the boys.

"I'll make you a tea when we get home and you'll feel better soon, all right? Maybe this whole fucking more than one guy shit is too much for you," I said to her.

"No." Her reply came much faster than expected. "It was because of the food, I swear. I had too much."

I watched her sit up in the back, and while Thane was still worried, I couldn't stop myself from laughing.

"The food just added to the mess, Z. The boys were too much to handle, and because they didn't listen when you told them to stop, you got overwhelmed."

She furrowed her brows, trying to figure out if what I was saying made sense.

"Let's not tell Dad about this, okay?" she then said.

"That you threw up or the other thing?" I asked.

She rolled her eyes at me and leaned back against Thane, then she turned her head to look outside to see Reuben driving close behind us.

"I was having a really good time with him, you know? We were just talking."

"We know, but Reuben's had a crush on you for years, and if he can't put those feelings aside, this won't end well," I told her.

Reuben was already in too deep, and although I didn't have an issue with him falling in love with Azula, I knew it would only cause jealousy on his part.

It would happen someday.

There was no doubt.

Azula didn't reply to me, and for the rest of the drive, we were all quiet.

As we arrived at the trailer park, Reuben drove directly to his own trailer to park the car.

He'd have to clean up the puke on his hood.

When I stopped the car, the door to our trailer opened, revealing Dad standing there with a frown between his brows.

"Where the hell have you been?" he asked even before we got out of the car.

I looked back at Azula with a raised brow, silently telling her to keep what happened to herself.

We got out and she quickly walked to the front door, wanting to hide from all of us.

"What happened?" Dad growled, grabbing her wrist and stopping her from walking past him.

She looked up and smiled, but she couldn't hide her sadness and unsureness in her eyes.

"Nothing. I'm just tired," she lied, making Dad look at me and Thane.

"What happened?" he repeated, not letting go of Zula.

"Nothing, Dad. We just went out to eat dinner," Thane told him. Well, that was only half a lie, but Dad didn't believe him either.

"Someone better tell me what the fuck happened and why Azula smells like a damn dog has thrown up all over her."

Well, shit.

"It wasn't a dog," I said, no longer able to keep this from him.

He'd squeeze it out of us eventually.

"Reuben took her out to dinner and Thane and I found them later on. We had a little fun with her but she couldn't take it and threw up on Reuben's car. Nothing to worry about."

Dad's facial expression relaxed a little, then he looked back at Azula and sighed. "You okay?"

"Yes, I'm fine," she replied, sounding slightly annoyed now. "I just wanna go to sleep."

I leaned against my car with my arms crossed over my chest while Thane just stood there, watching Azula.

"Go to my room. Think you've had enough of your brothers for tonight," Dad said.

Without looking at us, Azula headed inside, and after Dad closed the door, he looked ready to throw fists.

"The hell is wrong with you? You fucked her until she threw up?"

"It wasn't like that, Dad," Thane said with a sigh and a shake of his head.

"Then what was it like? Because it looks like you just used her for your own advantage."

I shook my head at him and laughed. "It's not like she said no. It was too much for her in that moment, but we didn't use her. We would never and you damn well know it. Makes you look like you're just fucking jealous that you didn't get to fuck her yet."

It was a low blow, but Dad didn't take it too personal.

He knew I was right.

He looked at me for a while, then at Thane before he muttered something under his breath. "Next time, make sure she's okay. Not just in the beginning. She shouldn't come to the point of throwing up."

That's settled then.

He turned back around to get inside, leaving us standing there.

"She'll be fine," I told Thane who looked even more worried now. "She'll learn to understand her body better."

"She's not gonna let us touch her again."

"If that's what you think, then you don't know our sister well. She'll think about what happened, get over it, and act like nothing's ever happened. She's figuring shit out just like you are."

He raised a brow at me but sighed soon after, not wanting to argue with me.

He knew I was right, and that there would be days where he'd try and figure his own things out too.

Thane liked men and women, but up until the day he sucked my dick, he didn't accept that fact about himself.

I reached into my pocket and pulled out a pack of cigarettes, then I lit one as Reuben was walking toward us.

"Where's Z?" he asked.

"Went to sleep. Did you clean your car?"

"Yeah, don't think Azula knows how to chew her food. There were pieces of zucchini and unchewed beans all over my hood."

I chuckled. "She got that from us. Wouldn't be surprised if I ever threw up a whole steak."

"Did Viggo say anything?"

I nodded, but didn't feel like telling him about the conversation we had with Dad, so I kept it short and simple. "Dad knows what happened."

Reuben nodded and leaned against the car next to me, then he looked up at Thane and studied him closely.

"Since when are you into guys?"

I smirked.

I loved how uncomfortable Thane got when he was confronted with things that applied to him but he wasn't sure how to handle them himself.

Thane shrugged. "Guess for a while now."

"And Wes was your first?"

"He never fucked me," Thane quickly replied, almost as if he was defending himself.

"But you want him to."

This time, Thane didn't reply.

"Come on, man. It's not like I'm gonna judge you for it. If that's what you're into, why not be proud of it? Means we get more of Zula," Reuben said with a grin, making me chuckle again.

"Just because I like dicks doesn't mean I won't fuck Azula again."

Good point.

We were all quiet after Thane's statement, and I continued to smoke my cigarette while we listened to Dad's muffled voice inside talking to Azula.

He wasn't mad at her for what happened, and although he didn't look like he was mad at us for what we had put her through, I was a hundred percent sure he wasn't going to let us near her tomorrow.

He'd cuddle her tonight, make her feel comfortable and loved.

Suddenly, a second voice appeared, which couldn't have been Azula's as it was way too low.

"Warren's in there too?" I asked surprised, looking at Reuben again.

"Seems like it. He wasn't home when I got there."

"Looks like we're taking turns," I said.

"Let the old men have their fun too. They know they can't compete with us when it comes to sex," Thane added with a grin.

"Wouldn't be so sure about that, brother. You'll probably change your mind if Dad or Warren ever fucked you."

Just the thought of me talking about shit like that made everything feel unreal.

No brother would ever fuck his sister and then talk about his damn father fucking her too.

It was abnormal, but then, we weren't born in a normal world after all.

twenty-one

AZULA

As unwell as I felt the moment before throwing up and during the drive back home, I knew my limits could be pushed even further.

I wanted to experience more moments like these, feeling helpless but loved at the same time.

It wasn't usual to like having boundaries being pushed, but I've always known there's something wrong with me, and my own mentality didn't shock me much.

When I went inside the trailer, Warren was sitting on the couch, drinking a beer.

After hearing what we had talked about outside, he didn't look at me like he was sorry for me.

He looked intrigued, but also slightly unsure about what he had heard.

I smiled at him when Dad closed the door behind me, and without saying a word, I walked into the back to change into my pajamas.

Warren followed me and stopped by the door to watch me change, and when he just kept quiet, I decided to be the one to talk first.

"How was your day?" I asked.

"Long. Exhausting. Looks like you had fun tonight." His voice was quieter than usual, almost as if he didn't want the others to know that he was inside with me.

"I did. Reuben took me to have dinner and Thane and Wesson then joined us. We were up hill overlooking town. You know, on the other side," I explained.

"I know. And you should know that you have a voice to tell them when things are too much for you."

I rolled my eyes at his words. "I know, Ren. But there was no reason for them to stop. I didn't want them to."

"Doesn't look like that to me. You're paler than usual. No clue how that's even possible. Did they tell you not to tell the truth about what really happened?"

Just because I didn't have a certain reaction to what went down, didn't mean I was being silenced by my brothers.

"They didn't say anything. I'm fine. I had fun. I threw up and now I wanna go to sleep. Is it so hard to believe that I'm not upset about what happened?"

He studied me for a while, then he smiled. "You'd tell me if you ever feel pressured, right? You won't just keep it inside."

"Of course I would tell you, Warren. I tell you everything."

He nodded and then smiled, letting that frown disappear again. "Go brush your teeth," he told me, then he walked back down the hall as Dad came back inside.

I heard them talk, and when I entered the bathroom, I saw the boys still standing outside, smoking cigarettes and talking.

Reuben was there too, and I couldn't help but smile at him.

It wasn't just him who had to be careful not to fall in love, because after our date, I sure felt different than when I was with the others.

I changed into my pajamas and brushed my teeth, then I headed into Dad's bedroom like he had requested to.

I didn't feel the need to sleep on my own tonight, and since the boys had their turn already today, I wanted to spend some time with Dad and Ren.

I didn't have to ask him if he would stay, because when I entered the bedroom, he followed close behind, already taking off his shirt.

"Dad coming too?" I asked.

"He's just gonna clean up the dishes. Had to eat dinner by ourselves tonight."

I got under the covers and moved to the middle of the bed so both of them had enough space. "And that's a bad thing?"

"No, of course not. I enjoy spending some time alone with my brother sometimes. Just wished you would've told us where you went so we didn't have to worry."

"But you knew I wasn't in danger."

"Yeah. Still."

He climbed in next to me and I immediately cuddled up to his side, letting him pull me into his arms and hold me tight.

"I'd still appreciate you telling us where you are," he whispered, kissing the side of my head gently and rubbing my back.

"I promise I'll let you know in the future."

I placed my hand on his chest and pushed my leg between his, wanting to get even closer.

I'd have to give Dad some attention too as soon as he came to bed, but for now, I wanted to enjoy this moment with Warren.

He was still the only man who was able to make me feel calm without having to say or do much, and he knew that he had this effect on me.

I could tell by the way his body tensed but not in a bad way.

He was protective over me, and without having to say a word, I felt that protection from afar.

I turned my head to nestle my face into the crook of his neck and then I placed a kiss to his skin, moving my fingers from his chest to the side of his face.

"I love that all of you are so different. Every single one of you makes me feel special," I whispered.

He let out a soft chuckle and cupped the back of my head. "Wouldn't expect anything else from the others and myself. You've always been our baby. You deserve all the love in the world, Z."

"You guys deserve love too," I replied, tilting my head back to look at him.

"We do. But you give that to us already. You know how damn lucky we are to have someone like you?"

I smiled at him and felt my cheeks warm. "You've felt this kind of love before though, right?"

"Yeah, I have. But this is still different."

"You loved Shayleen, right?" I asked, knowing bringing up his ex-wife wasn't gonna cause issues.

"Sure did. For a long time. She was a good mother to Reuben, and a great aunt to you guys. Until she decided cocaine and vodka were more important to her than her family."

"And you think it's necessary to talk about your ex right now? It's late." Dad's voice made me turn my head and look at him.

He never liked to talk about Shayleen or Mom for that matter.

"We were just talking," Warren said calmly.

"Don't you miss them, Dad?" I asked, meaning Mom and Shayleen.

He shrugged. "I think about them sometimes, but then I wonder what life would be like to still have them around. Can't imagine them still being here."

Dad wasn't heartless.

He just accepted people leaving his life and never returning.

It was easy for him to forget.

"Let's not talk about this anymore. I see it's going nowhere anyway," Warren whispered to me.

Dad got into bed next to me in only his boxer briefs, and to give them both the same attention, I turned onto my back and let them get closer with their hands wrapped around my body.

Dad kissed my temple, and I smiled as Warren stretched out his arm over my head to play with my hair.

"You comfortable like this?" he asked, looking at me.

"Very."

Their warmth was soothing, and I quickly forgot about my stomachache.

"It sounded like fucking torture that you threw up because of them fucking you, but how much did you eat, baby?" Dad asked, making me laugh.

"Four tacos, a burger, fries, and ice cream," I told him.

"Damn," Warren laughed, looking over at Dad with a grin. "We raised her right."

"Sure did. Shit…not surprised it all came back out of you."

I pressed my lips into a tight line to hold back laughter. "It was delicious," I assured them, then I let them cuddle even closer with Dad burying his face into my hair and Warren placing kisses on my cheek.

"But they treated you right, huh?" Warren asked.

"Of course they did. You know they would never treat me without respect."

And I was lucky that was the case, because any other girl would love to be in my position, being loved by not just one, but five men at once.

twenty-two

AZULA

I preferred to sleep with my brothers and Reuben than with Dad and Warren, because Dad turned away from me in the middle of the night and Warren wouldn't stop waking up and telling me to stop kicking off the covers.

It got too warm between the two of them, so I woke up early, headed into the kitchen and made myself a cup of coffee before I went to take a shower.

At only six-thirty, I went outside and walked over to Bonnie's trailer, knowing she would be up this early due to her intense morning routine.

Not surprised her mother screamed at her multiple times a week for letting the shower run for too long in the morning.

The lights were on in her trailer, and I knocked at the door, waiting for her to open.

When she did, she frowned at me. "You're up early. What are you doing here already?"

"I couldn't sleep. Wanna go grab a muffin or something before school? We could eat it at the park in town. I took ten dollars out of Dad's pocket."

"Bad girl. Give me a minute."

She turned around and headed back into her bathroom, and to not stand outside, I went inside and closed the door behind me.

School wouldn't start until eight, so we had enough time to enjoy the sunrise and quietness before the town woke up.

"Who is it?" Wanda called out from her bedroom.

"Zula," Bonnie replied.

"It's not even seven. What the hell are you up for already?" That question was directed at me, and when she appeared in the narrow hallway, I smiled at Bonnie's mother.

"Couldn't sleep so I came to pick her up. How are you doing, Wanda?"

She studied me for a moment and shrugged, grabbing the cigarettes from the table in the middle of the living room. "Could be doing better. Still looking for a job and not finding one."

"Sorry to hear. Maybe I can ask Dad if he needs someone to take care of all the paperwork at the garage. Warren does it at the moment, but I'm sure he'd rather be working on cars than papers."

Wanda smiled and waved a hand at me. "Don't think those guys want a woman working for them. But, thank you, Azula. I wished my daughter would be this kind and attentive."

"I am kind and attentive. You just don't appreciate me."

They fought a lot, but as soon as their fights started,

they finished again seconds after.

"I'm sure you'll find a job soon, Wanda. You're a great woman and you did your last job very well at that daycare."

"Yeah, I did. Wished those other women working there wouldn't have told my boss those stupid lies."

I didn't care much about her problems and issues she had at work, but it wasn't right what she was fired for.

"I've been telling you to apply to that other daycare. But you won't listen," Bonnie muttered.

Wanda didn't reply. Instead, she grabbed a glass of water and a cigarette, then she headed outside to sit in one of the chairs in front of the trailer.

I looked at Bonnie and puckered my lips, hoping to change the subject. "Let's go," she said, grabbing her backpack and walking past me.

I reached for her wrist before she could go outside, and she looked at me with a frown, wondering what I was doing.

"Don't be so hard on your momma, okay? She's trying."

She studied me for a moment, then she sighed and looked away. "I know. I'm trying."

I believed her, but I knew their relationship wouldn't change as quickly.

"Have a good day, Wanda," I said to her as we headed outside, and she smiled at me without saying a word.

"Sometimes I feel like she'd rather have you as her daughter than me," Bonnie murmured.

"Of course. I'm better than you," I replied with a smirk.

After grabbing some baked goods from the bakery,

we sat down on a park bench while the sun slowly started to rise.

I bit into my chocolate croissant while squinting into the sun, enjoying its warmth on my skin.

Luckily, I didn't need to put on sunscreen in the morning as the sun wasn't as hot as it would be in the afternoon.

"Where were you last night, by the way? I came by but no one was around."

"Uh, I was out with the guys. We had burgers and tacos," I replied.

"Reuben too?"

"Yeah."

"Sounds like you had a lot of fun."

I wasn't sure if telling her about what really happened last night was a good idea, knowing how much she liked Reuben.

"Your silence tells me that there's something you're hiding from me. Spit it out, Z. Not gonna sit here and try to figure it all out myself."

I laughed and then sighed, knowing she wouldn't stop bugging me about this.

I looked at her and took another bite of the croissant, and after swallowing, I sighed again.

"Remember that time we talked about you being into your brother? Or that you definitely would sleep with him if he was still around?"

"I remember, and I haven't changed my mind about that either."

"So you know that incest isn't right but you would totally let your brother fuck you?"

Bonnie nodded. "We're all just people, Z. Who the

fuck cares who we have sex with? I'm sure you would let your brothers do the same to you."

I was silent after her statement because it was the damn truth, and because she'd soon figure out what happened last night herself.

Just as I expected, she kept her eyes on me and studied me carefully while her thoughts ran wild.

I continued to stare at my half-eaten croissant and waited for her to put all the puzzle pieces into place.

Once she did, she punched my arm. "Who did you have sex with, you slut?"

I laughed at her surprised tone of voice, then I looked at her with a grin.

"Guess."

"Well, shit...Wesson, maybe? He seems liked he'd just pull you behind a tree and fuck you mercilessly."

To be fair, I only had actual sex with some of them, but I wouldn't keep that from her after this conversation.

"I would let him fuck me too if he were my brother. Was it Wes?" she guessed again, and I nodded slowly.

Another punch to my arm, and I laughed. "But then there was also Thane."

"You're fucking kidding me. Wait...and Reuben? Z, don't tell me you let him fuck you too. I'm gonna be so mad if you did."

Her crush on him suddenly didn't seem as serious as before, seeing that excited grin plastered on her face.

"Maybe. And maybe Dad and Warren are in on it too."

"Shut up!" she squealed, holding her hand over her mouth now. "No fucking way. Azula, are you serious?"

I nodded and watched her face go from surprised to

confused, then back to surprised. "Shit…I knew your family was one of a kind, but I'd never imagine you letting all that happen. And you're feeling okay? I mean, mentally?"

I've never been normal, so this shouldn't have come as a surprise to any of us, and even after what happened last night, I knew I wanted more.

More of their touch, more of their kisses, more of them.

"I know you like Reuben, and I would understand if you were mad at me now," I told her, but instead of being angry at me for sleeping with a guy she was into, she laughed.

"Are you kidding me? I wish I could watch you do all that crazy shit. I didn't think I'd ever say this out loud to anyone, but the only porn I watch is incest porn. Literally. It turns me on."

I knew about her porn addiction.

She even once showed me her collection of vibrators she accumulated, which essentially were just small, battery powered massagers used mostly for other parts of the body.

She used them to get off most nights.

"So you would actually just sit there and watch them fuck me? Wouldn't you want in on the fun?"

"No. I don't think your dad or uncle would want me to be part of it. I'm speechless, honestly," she said with a chuckle.

I laughed and looked back at my breakfast in my hand and thought about her words.

If she'd really be into watching, why would I not invite her the next time I'd have some fun with the guys?

Looking back at her, I watched her for a while

before suggesting something I never thought I would.

"I could invite you to dinner tonight and then try and seduce them. Then you could watch."

It sounded like a scene straight out of a porn, but if that's what excited us, why not live it out?

Bonnie didn't hesitate to take me up on that offer, and I already started to plan how to seduce the guys tonight at dinner.

It was exciting, but I knew they would appreciate a little attention from my side instead of them having to initiate things all the time.

twenty-three

AZULA

Thinking about the guys and planning what I had in mind all day long made school pass in no time, and now that I was home, waiting for everyone else to arrive, I was slowly starting to get nervous.

I didn't know what plans they had for tonight, if we'd eat at home or at the beach, but either way, I was hoping to not mess up.

Bonnie was excited, and she had already texted me multiple times, but other than telling her about them not being home yet, there wasn't much for me to tell her.

In the meantime, I decided to do my homework and finish reading the book we'd discuss next week, and soon after I was done with it, I heard cars pull up to the trailer.

I got up from the couch and walked over to the door to open it, revealing all five men getting out of the car with their usual oil stains all over their clothes and skin.

"Hi!" I greeted, happy to see them all again.

"Where did you run off to this morning?" Dad asked as he approached me, and when he stopped in front of me, I smiled up at him.

"I woke up early and thought I'd go grab something to eat with Bonnie. I took ten bucks out of your pocket," I confessed, but I knew he wouldn't be mad at me for that.

"And how was school?" he asked, passing me with his hand on my waist.

"Good. I did my homework and all already. What's for dinner?"

I was overly excited all of a sudden, and they noticed.

There was a smirk on Thane's face, and Warren looked at me as if I was on some drugs.

"You okay, Z?" Thane asked.

"I'm fine."

"We can tell. Feeling much better today," Wesson stated, his brows furrowed and his lips curled up into a grin.

"Much better. But I'm hungry, and I want to know what you're gonna cook tonight."

Dad chuckled behind me and I turned around to look at him standing in the kitchen already. "I was thinking of heading down to the beach and getting a fire started. We got some meat in the fridge. And we also need to get rid of all this oil so a late-night swim would be great."

Perfect.

If we spent the evening at the beach, I knew my plan would definitely work out.

"Awesome! Are we going right now?" I asked.

"Sure. Help the boys put all the food in the cooler. I'll take care of the drinks with Warren."

I nodded and already walked over to the fridge to get everything out that we needed, and with Reuben and my brothers helping me, we were ready to head down to the beach quickly.

"Tell me," Reuben said as he stepped closer to me, and I looked up at him with question in my eyes.

"Tell you what?"

"Tell me why the hell you're so happy tonight. I honestly thought you'd need more time to get over last night."

I smiled, shaking my head at him. "I don't. I'm just happy to see you all again. And I'm excited to spend time with you. I've always been like this."

My words made Wesson laugh out loud, and Thane soon followed. "That's a load of bullshit, Z. What's going on?"

Okay, maybe this wouldn't go as I had hoped it would, but I didn't want to disappoint Bonnie who was still very much excited about tonight.

Reuben wrapped his arm around my shoulders and pulled me closer while Thane stepped to the other side of me with his arms crossed and his eyes on me.

"Come on, Zula. What's going on?" he asked.

Dad and Warren were listening to our conversation while they put all the cans of beer they could find into the second cooler, and since I wouldn't get out of this trailer without spilling what I was keeping secret from them, I sighed heavily and decided to just tell them about my plan.

There were two ways they could take this.

They'd either be into the idea, or they'd look at me like I was crazy.

Well, it was only the part about Bonnie watching us

that could've come off strange, but seeing as they had already done things to me no other parent or brother would do, I had a little bit of hope left that they would be okay with it.

"Well...I was talking to Bonnie this morning," I started, looking over at Dad and Warren who now turned around to look at me.

They were all standing around the kitchen with their eyes on me, almost making me feel uncomfortable.

How did I get so damn lucky?

They were all handsome, but definitely intense.

I could handle them though, despite what had happened last night.

"I tell her everything, and I think you guys know that. But we were talking about...porn and sex. And while we talked, I told her about *this*."

That was the only way to describe what we had.

Hell, if there even was a way to describe it.

"She knows?" Warren asked, concern washing over his face.

"She won't tell anyone," I assured him. "She once told me that her brother kissed her when they were little. I think she's the last person who'd judge us. In fact," I said, stopping right there to watch them all carefully before I continued. "When I told her, she said she'd love to watch."

They were all quiet, taking in my words.

The moment I told them didn't feel real, and I felt as if I was in some sort of movie.

To be fair, since this was about sex, I wouldn't be surprised if someone brought out a camera and filmed it all to then put online.

Shit, Z...you're sick.

But the thought of it excited me more than I was expecting, and when they all started to smirk and chuckle, I knew they were in on this too.

"Well, fuck. Our baby really wants us all to fuck her while another one watches," Dad said.

"You sure about that?" Reuben whispered next to me, and I nodded before looking up at him.

"I'm sure. Last night I realized that no matter how sick I felt, I wanted to feel more. I wanted to be pushed more because I hadn't reached my limit. I know I'm young and I don't know much, but I know my body and needs. I wanted more and I know you can give me more."

They kept looking at me, and when I moved my gaze to Warren, I smiled at him because he was the only one still unsure about this.

I stepped closer to him and reached for his hands, squeezing them gently. "I want this. You know I wouldn't ask you to do this when I wasn't a hundred percent sure, right?"

He studied my face for a while, then he looked at Dad and the others before his eyes met mine again.

"I know you wouldn't."

"Okay, then there's nothing you have to be worried about. I promise," I said quietly.

Their trust was important to me, but I understood that it wasn't easy for him to accept my decision.

He'd get over it though.

He had to, unless he wanted to be the only one excluded from the fun we'd have tonight at the beach.

twenty-four

VIGGO

I should've said no.

She was too damn excited for my liking, and knowing us men, this wouldn't end up with us cuddling her and treating her like a princess.

We were animals, and while we had fun taking turns, tonight Azula might realize that letting us fuck her all at once wasn't such a good idea after all.

I was selfish though, and backing out now would only make me feel like a coward.

It was her wish to have sex with all of us while her best friend watched, and I wasn't going to upset her by telling her no.

She was old enough to make decisions about things like this.

We arrived at the beach and set up everything for the fire, and while the boys started the fire, I helped Warren with the food.

"You're not sure about this, huh?" he asked, keeping his voice low.

"I don't think she's sure about it. She'll have to figure it all out herself. If this is what she's into, then I won't keep her needs and wishes from her."

My way of parenting had always been different.

I let my kids learn by doing instead of lecturing them on every little thing that came their way.

They quickly learned not to mess with teens when they were still kids, and that throwing stones at cars would only get them in trouble.

And the worst part of it all was Azula doing everything the boys did.

She followed in their footsteps, but when she noticed them getting shouted at by the neighbors for breaking a window, she knew to never throw stones again.

She was smart enough in that way, but I was starting to doubt her decision she made today.

"You can still put a stop to it all," Warren said.

I knew that.

But even after all the things that ran through my mind just then, I was sick enough to want to see how far we'd really go with her.

See if she could really push those limits like she said she could.

"You're not backing out now, are you?" I asked him, knowing my brother often changed his mind in a matter of minutes.

He shrugged. "I'll be there mostly for moral support. She needs me there, but I won't add to the damn group sex."

That made me laugh.

He wouldn't be able to just stand there and watch.

"You both will be part of this. She wants us all, and you can't fucking deny that you want her too," Wesson muttered as he stepped closer to us.

He'd be the one without mercy.

As much as I loved my sons, they surprised me in negative ways at times.

Not because of their actions, but because of their words.

Wesson had always been careless, especially when it came to others' feelings.

Other than his sister, he didn't care about the women he used to fuck, and it was surprising when he started to spend less time outside and more time at home without the company of another girl.

Almost as if he turned off his addiction for sex and wanted to enjoy some time without fucking.

"Just gotta make sure she can handle it all. Don't want her breaking down like last night," Warren said.

"She didn't break down. She felt sick because she had just eaten a lot," Wesson clarified, but the way of them fucking her definitely had something to do with it.

Not just the food.

When I saw someone approach us, I looked over to the trees to see Azula walking over to us with Bonnie following her.

While Bonnie looked excited, Azula looked nervous.

Clearly one of them was going to have more fun tonight than the other.

"There they are," Wesson announced with a smug grin on his face, and when they stopped in front of the fire, Azula nervously played with her hands.

"Bonnie asked if the beach is a safe place to do what we have planned," Azula said, looking at me as if I had the answer to everything.

"We're the only ones out here right now, and if people come by, they'll leave again when they hear what's going on," I told her.

"They don't give a shit anyway," Wesson added, making Azula relax a little.

"And you're sure you just wanna watch and not join in?" Wesson then asked Bonnie.

She blushed, and then quickly shook her head. "I like to watch."

Reuben and Thane joined us around the fire now, and for a short second, it felt awkward standing there without anyone saying a word.

We all knew what was going to happen.

"Always knew we lived in a fucked-up place," Thane said, watching Bonnie closely.

"That's not a bad thing," I told him. "Let's eat."

"Don't eat too much," I heard Reuben say to Azula in a worried voice, and I couldn't stop myself from grinning.

"Let the girl eat what she wants," I told him, then I looked at Azula who was still picking at the skin around her fingernails.

"I had a sandwich after school. I'm not that hungry," she assured us all.

She didn't intend on throwing up again.

We all sat around the fire and put the steaks and sausages on the grill, and so we wouldn't eat just meat, I added a few bell peppers and potatoes on it wrapped in some foil.

There wasn't much talking going on, and we all got lost in our own thoughts as we awaited what would happen later.

It was strange at first, but the longer we were silent, the more normal it all seemed.

We were all like-minded people, and although I never expected Bonnie to be a dirty one, I liked knowing she would be right there to hold her once the fucking was over.

Lucky them for being such good friends who told each other everything.

And Bonnie wasn't even mad about Reuben being into Azula.

Good for her.

***

We were all still dirty and stained with oil from work, so after eating, we all got rid of our pants and shirts to then bathe in the lake and clean ourselves a little.

We'd all be taking a shower at home later on of course, but this was enough for now.

While the boys swam over to the floating dock, Warren and I stayed close to shore where Azula and Bonnie stood with their feet in the shallow water.

They were talking silently, but their eyes were on us the whole time, letting us know that they were talking about us.

"She's scared," Warren said, running his hand through his wet hair.

"She's not scared. She's nervous. She'd be long gone if she was scared."

He knew that was the truth, but he was trying to get Azula out of this situation.

"We're gonna break her," he muttered, making me laugh.

"She wants us to break her. She's exploring herself. Quit being such a pussy."

I didn't get a response after that.

Instead, Warren got out of the water and headed straight to Azula.

Looked like he was going to comfort her before we jumped her all at once.

I'd let him have that moment.

Only for a little while.

twenty-five

AZULA

As Warren walked up to me, I looked over at Bonnie who was watching him closely, and when he reached me and placed his hands on my cheeks, she stepped away to give us some space.

I guess we were starting already.

My heart was beating fast, but with Warren's lips on mine, I calmed down quickly.

His wet hair was dripping all over me, and I placed my hands on his chest to steady myself.

Tilting my head back, he deepened the kiss and moved his tongue along my bottom lip before dipping it into my mouth and tasting every inch of it.

Having him around helped calm my nerves a lot, but as hard as I tried to stay cool, deep down I couldn't stop shaking.

From the moment that Warren kissed me, I pushed all the worry aside and focused on him.

I forgot about Bonnie watching, or the possible neighbors walking by and catching us.

Warren's left hand moved from my cheek down to my hip, pulling me against his body and holding me close.

"You sure?" he muttered against my lips, and I didn't hesitate to nod.

I heard someone walk toward us as the water splashed, and I knew it was Dad when his hands grabbed my waist.

His hands were rougher than Warren's, but I liked the contrast of both pairs on me.

Dad didn't say a word, but his actions were enough to make my body tingle.

My knees were starting to give in, and I leaned back against him while pulling Warren with me to keep him right there.

Both their bodies were pressed against me from the front and back, and while Warren continued to kiss me, I felt Dad's hands move lower and finally cup my ass.

I was still wearing what I had on at school, and with a skirt on, it was easy for him to pull it up and get rid of my panties.

He let them drop to my feet, and when I stepped out of them, he moved his fingers through my slit from the back to feel my wetness.

My pussy clenched as he moved through my folds, then his fingertips reached my clit where they circled it gently.

I moaned, leaning my head back against Dad's shoulder and breaking Warren's kiss.

When I looked at him, his eyes were on me and studied me carefully, making sure I was okay and comfortable.

He had nothing to be worried about.

In the end, this was my plan.

I wanted this, and even with Bonnie watching us from afar, there was no way I would stop this now.

"Beautiful," Warren muttered under his breath, placing both his hands on my tits now.

He started to massage them carefully, pinching my nipples through the thin fabric of my shirt.

I smiled at him, assuring him that everything was okay, and when he gained the confidence to open up, he pushed my shirt up to expose my breasts.

Leaning in, he pulled one nipple into his mouth and continued to play with the other while Dad worked his magic on my clit.

It was throbbing, just like Dad's dick in his shorts.

I could feel it against my lower back, and to tease him, I pushed back against him, making him groan.

"So damn wet already. Wanna let me get another taste of that sweet pussy, baby?" he asked, whispering into my ear.

"No," Warren said after letting go of my nipple, surprising Dad and me. "It's my turn."

He lifted me up and I wrapped my legs around his hips to let him carry me over to the fire where all the chairs and towels were, and he let me down onto one of the camping chairs, then he knelt in front of me, pushing my legs apart.

Thanks to Dad already taking off my panties, Warren had easy access to my clit which he immediately pleasured.

I pushed my hands into his hair and held his head close as his tongue licked through my folds and over my clit, circling it before sucking on it gently.

I arched my back and threw my head back again, but this time Dad's shoulder wasn't there to lean against.

Instead, he was standing next to me with his hand cupping the back of my head and grabbing a fistful of my hair to turn my head to the side.

He had already taken off his shorts, and his cock was already rock-hard, ready for me to take it in.

I lifted my right hand and wrapped it around his base, then I started to stroke along his length before taking him into my mouth.

No one needed to tell me what to do.

I knew what they'd like, and with the other guys slowly approaching us, I got excited knowing I was all theirs tonight.

And they were all mine.

"Fuck," Dad growled as I swirled my tongue around his tip, and when I took him back in, he pushed my head down until I could feel his tip against the back of my throat.

Dad was definitely one of the more dominant out of the five of them, right next to Wesson and even Reuben.

Thane and Warren were definitely the more careful ones, and with Thane I understood because he was still figuring some things out.

He liked men, and maybe he even liked them more than women, but I wasn't mad about that.

If he liked the attention of Wesson more than mine, I would let him enjoy that.

Warren flicked his tongue faster, making me buck my hips uncontrollably until he gripped both my thighs to keep them still.

It was hard to focus on just one thing, which is why Dad took control over me.

He kept moving my head to meet his thrusts, and just as I tasted his precum on my tongue, he pulled away to bend down and kiss me.

It was a gentle kiss, but his dominance shined through as he wrapped his hand around my throat and squeezed tightly.

I held my breath and tensed my body, trying to hold back the orgasm already creeping up on me.

It was either me being insanely sensitive, or them knowing exactly what to do to make me come.

Either way, I didn't want this to stop.

Dad stood back up and pushed his cock back into my mouth as I heard Wesson say something in the distance, and when they reached us, Dad pulled out again.

"Let us have some fun too, old man," he said to Dad, making him chuckle and step aside.

I looked at my brothers and Reuben standing there in their shorts, water dripping down their bodies.

Even in the moonlight they looked incredible, and I would be okay just sitting there and looking at them all night long while Warren continued down there.

"Who do you want next, Z?" Wesson asked.

I didn't care, so I kept quiet.

"Not gonna choose?" Thane asked with a chuckle, his hand already stroking his cock through his shorts.

I looked at his hand for a moment, then my gaze moved to Reuben who was watching his Dad between my legs.

I smiled, knowing that he wanted a taste too, so I gently pushed against Warren's head to make him stop and get up, then I reached for Reuben, wanting him to kneel in front of me.

"Shit," he muttered as he moved closer with his hand in mine, and once his unsureness faded, his lips pressed kisses from the inside of my thigh to my folds.

Warren stayed close to me by kneeling next to me, with his arm around my shoulders and his face close to the side of mine.

"On your knees," I heard Wesson say, and since it couldn't have been me he was talking to, I looked at Thane who obeyed our older brother.

When Wesson stood in front of him, I moved my gaze to Dad to see his reaction.

There was none.

Did he know about it already?

Wesson pushed down his shorts, then let Thane start sucking his cock.

Something about seeing them do this warmed my chest, and the fact that neither Dad or Warren said something against it made me even happier.

But then again, there was nothing that could ever surprise any of us anymore.

"Guess it's still my turn," Dad said as he stepped a little closer again, and with my hand on his cock, I took him back into my mouth.

Warren leaned in to pull my nipple into his mouth, and with Reuben's tongue moving fast, I was soon back to where I was before.

The orgasm creeped up on me again, making me want to squeeze my legs together.

Reuben stopped me from doing so by holding on tight to my knees and pushing them apart.

I still had my skirt scrunched up around my waist and my shirt pushed up over my breasts, but I wanted both things off as they were bothering me.

I'd have to wait though, and to make my orgasm come faster, I rocked my hips against his tongue until an overwhelming feeling washed over me.

I cried out as Dad pulled out, and my body shook as the orgasm sent me over the edge and quickly threw me back down to earth.

"Tastes like heaven," Reuben said, caressing my thighs now to help me calm down.

I smiled at his words and managed to open my eyes before looking past him and seeing Bonnie sitting on the other side of the fire.

Her jean shorts were down to her ankles, and her hand was pushed into her panties as she played with herself.

She was really into this, but I didn't think she'd be masturbating while watching.

It didn't bother me, and I thought the guys enjoyed having someone watching them fuck me.

It was a win for all of us, and since we weren't pushing anyone to join us, we weren't doing anything wrong.

twenty – six

WESSON

As much as I liked having Azula suck my dick, I was starting to enjoy Thane's mouth around it a little more.

Maybe it was because of his effortless tries to get me deep inside his throat, and sucking me off better than any girl ever has.

I had seen Bonnie masturbating on a chair on the other side of the fire, and although she said she liked to watch, I wouldn't have anything against her joining us.

Two girls were better than one, but since we wanted to spoil Azula, it was okay for Bonnie to just sit there and watch.

Turned me on just knowing she was there staring.

I looked back down to Thane pulling me in deeper, making my tip press against the back of his throat with each thrust.

When I heard Azula moan, I looked up to see Dad already pushing inside her, with Azula now kneeling on the chair backward and facing Reuben who was standing behind it.

I enjoyed watching them take control over the situation while Z just let them do what they wanted.

She wasn't scared of them hurting her, and her confidence only grew with all the praises Dad said to her.

His words didn't only turn her on though, and I found myself listening to Dad's words while Thane continued to suck me dry.

It wouldn't take too long for him to make me come, just like the last time, but I wanted to keep it in to enjoy coming inside of Azula.

I wanted all of us to come inside of her, and I knew that without saying it, the others would catch on and follow my plan.

Thane placed his hands on my hips as I started to thrust my hips faster, and by pressing his head against me, I stopped him from moving back.

I wanted him to hold his breath and beg for me to let him breathe, and when he tapped my hips, he was doing just that.

Letting go of his hair, he leaned back and breathed in deeply while looking up at me, and I grinned at him, liking his facial expression when he was all worked up.

"Come on, brother…I know you can take more than that," I said, brushing his hair off his forehead.

He looked at me for a while, then I pulled him closer again.

I moved my gaze to Zula again, and she looked pretty comfortable while Reuben fucked her mouth and Dad her pussy.

There was one more hole of hers we could fill, and Warren was the only one left out of the fun.

As if he could hear my thoughts, he made the two others stop so he could sit down on the chair and pull her on top of him, and now that he was inside her pussy, Dad carefully pushed inside her asshole, stretching her and making her arch her back.

Reuben's dick was back in her mouth, and muffled sounds came out of her.

Thane was now the only one not being touched, but I would soon change that.

He was supposed to have some fun too.

THANE

As much as I liked what I was doing to Wesson, I felt like we weren't part of what the others were doing to Azula.

When Wesson pulled his dick out of my mouth again, I turned to look at Azula who looked like she was struggling a little bit with both Dad and Warren inside of her.

She was trying to relax though, and the more they pushed into her, the more she got used to them.

I got up to stand next to Reuben and Wes stepped closer to him as well, looking down at Azula while rubbing ourselves.

It would be my turn soon, and I would let Dad and Warren enjoy their moment as they started to move faster.

It didn't take too long for them to start groaning and growling, telling Azula that they were close.

Z didn't complain, and she kept her eyes on Reuben while he held her head still, slowly thrusting in and out of her mouth.

Just watching all this go down was enough for me to make myself come, and when I looked over at Bonnie still sitting there with her hand in her panties, I understood her liking of watching a little better.

It was erotic and hot, and us all being related only added to the fantasy.

Well, wasn't a fantasy anymore.

This was real, and as disturbing as it may be, none of us would regret this in the morning.

"Fuuuck!" Dad groaned, and from the veins on his arms and neck popping out, I could tell he was close.

He moved his hips faster, thrusting into her mercilessly until he stopped deep inside of her to empty himself, and imagining the tightness both Warren and Azula were feeling, I knew Warren would follow close behind.

Reuben stepped away from Azula to let her catch her breath by closing her eyes and collapsing on top of Warren, and while he held her tightly against his body, he groaned as his load filled her.

Two down, three to go.

twenty-seven

AZULA

I was already exhausted.

Feeling them both stretch me was a strange feeling, and even when I got used to it, I couldn't adjust properly.

But that didn't push my limits yet, and I knew that I still had some strength in me to let the other three fuck me too.

I also felt an orgasm slowly coming over me, but it wasn't enough to push me over the edge yet.

I needed more.

"You okay, baby?" Warren asked, breathing heavily after he had just shot his load inside of me.

I felt his and Dad's cum come out of me and run down my inner thighs, but that didn't bother me much.

"I'm okay," I assured him, smiling gently and then looking back at Dad as he pulled out of me.

He brushed his hand over the back of my head, showing me some affection before Warren made me stand up so he could get up himself.

There was no time for me to recover, and Wesson already nodded at Reuben to sit down where his Dad was sitting so we could be in the same position as before.

Reuben sat down and pulled me on top of him, cupping my jaw with one hand and kissing me while he rubbed his tip along my folds.

With all the cum dripping out of me, it was easy for him to push inside me, and it was the same for Thane who moved behind me to be in the same position Dad just was.

"Now you'll see what it's like to fuck a tight asshole," I heard Wesson mutter, directing his words at Thane.

His words always made me shiver, no matter if he was talking to me or not, and I knew they had the same effect on Thane.

I broke Reuben's kiss to look back, and when I saw Wesson standing behind Thane, I knew exactly what his plan was.

Thane didn't try to push his cock inside of me right away. Instead, he used his fingers to stretch me a little, making sure he wouldn't hurt me.

He wouldn't, but I loved how careful he was.

When he started to finger me, I turned back to look at Reuben who was already buried deep inside of me, and by Thane's sighs, I knew Wesson was using his own fingers to stretch him.

During all of this, I felt Bonnie's eyes on us the whole time, and I wondered what it would be like to just sit there and watch and not get in on the fun.

Although I would let her, I wanted to have these guys all to myself.

I wanted them to exhaust me the way they did last night, and I wanted to feel numb again, forgetting about everything in the world.

And to my luck, it didn't take too long for Reuben, Thane, and Wesson to put me in exactly that situation.

Reuben started to thrust his hips while Thane carefully pushed inside of me, and with Wesson doing the same to him, they soon found a steady rhythm.

I closed my eyes and enjoyed the way they made me feel, but after a little while, I had to open my eyes again to see what Dad and Warren were up to.

They were both standing on either side of me, rubbing their cocks slowly.

They weren't as hard as they were before, and at first, I didn't know what they were up to.

I focused on the boys again, figuring out that whenever I clenched my pussy together, Thane and Reuben groaned loudly.

They liked it, and I continued to tease them.

"Look at you, getting fucked by all of us, baby," Dad muttered, his voice low.

He sounded proud, and when I looked up at him, I smiled. "I love you," I told him, but my words were meant for all of them.

At times, they were the only things keeping me alive.

I wasn't depressed or anything, but without them, I didn't think life would be half as good.

Without them I'd be lost.

Dad caressed the back of my head, and I was starting to feel that orgasm creep up on me again.

"Perfect, baby. Let them make you come."

"Oh, yes!" I cried as both Reuben and Thane moved their hips faster.

I could hear Wesson groan behind me, making Thane's body tense as he was feeling just as much as I was.

Guess we were the lucky ones in this situation.

"Don't stop," I begged, arching my back a little more and looking back at Reuben who was watching me closely.

One of his hands was covering my tit while Warren played with the other, giving my body as much attention as possible.

I enjoyed being loved by all of them at once, and no matter how intense this would end up being, I knew it wouldn't be the last time.

"FUUUCK!" Wesson groaned, letting us all know that he was so damn close.

And just as expected, Reuben and Thane both came inside of me simultaneously, making my body tense and grip Reuben's shoulders tightly.

It was easier for them to come, whereas I was trying to hold on to my orgasm, not wanting it to fade away right before falling over the edge.

"Come on, Z," Reuben whispered, moving his hand between us now to rub my clit.

"Keep moving," he then told Thane, and while he did, Reuben's fingers circled my most sensitive spot until I got sent straight into space with shivers and sparks running through my body.

For a moment it didn't feel as if what we had done was as exhausting as it felt in the beginning, but as I slowly came back down, I felt my body numb.

Just like I wanted.

I felt weak and tired, although it wasn't me doing all the work.

I could hear my breath hitch as my body trembled, and only when my back hit the now cold sand, I opened my eyes again.

They were all standing around me, naked, and observing me like a statue at a museum.

No one said a word, but I could tell they all knew what was going to happen next.

Their cum was still inside of me, slowly oozing out and tickling my skin.

I took them in one by one, and while Reuben looked at me with hearts in his eyes, Dad and Wesson were ready for round two.

I would be up for it, but I wasn't sure how long I could keep my eyes open.

My body felt limp, weak, and my brain was slowly shutting off.

I didn't even have the strength to check on Bonnie, but I didn't have to, as shortly after having that thought I could hear her moan.

"Took her long enough," Wesson said, making the others chuckle.

Their voices sounded faded, and I couldn't keep my eyes open any longer.

As much excitement as there still was inside of me, I didn't even bother checking if the warm, almost hot, liquid hitting my body was what I thought it was.

I was already gone, feeling like I was dreaming as they peed all over me.

I wasn't grossed out, and for some reason, what they were doing made me feel like they were marking me once more to show me that I was theirs.

My skin burned, but in the best way possible, and as I slowly drifted off, I dreamt of everything that had just happened and experienced their love and affection all over again.

I was theirs, and I didn't care what they did to show me.

REUBEN

Humiliated would be the word to describe the situation Azula was in right now, and we put her there.

We should've felt bad, hated ourselves for doing this to our little girl, but all those bad thoughts washed away quickly when I reminded myself that Azula wanted this.

She didn't complain, didn't stop us.

"What now?" I asked, keeping my eyes on Zula as she lay there, sleeping in the sand.

"Now we get a taste," Viggo said, still rubbing his dick gently while observing his daughter.

There was no regret in his eyes, but then, I didn't expect anything from him.

"Taste?" I asked.

Wesson nodded and turned around to look over at Bonnie who was still sitting on that chair, watching all of us.

"Come here," he ordered, and after thinking about it for a little while, Bonnie got up and walked around the fire to get to us.

Wesson grabbed her by the neck and pushed her to her knees next to Azula, and by leaning down to get closer to her, he whispered into her ear. "You're a dirty little thing, aren't you? I want you to lick this up," he demanded, pointing at the small pool of piss on Azula's belly button.

Bonnie looked at Wesson as if she had seen a ghost, but she should've known that she wouldn't get away with just watching.

"Come on. Isn't this the shit you watch every night? It's just piss," he said, his voice deep.

Bonnie looked back at Azula, still unsure but not ready to back away.

We were all watching her, and when Viggo moved, I looked at him as he got down on his knees on the other side of Azula, pulling apart her legs.

"Go on," he encouraged Bonnie, then she finally leaned in and licked our combined juices off her best friend's stomach.

"That's it. Swallow it all," Wesson growled, keeping his hand on her neck.

To my surprise, Viggo moved closer and leaned in himself, licking through Azula's slit where all of our cum was still lingering.

I never would've thought he'd do something like this, and he also surprised his sons and brother.

Guess Uncle Viggo had his own little secrets too.

Was just as dirty as all of us.

I looked over at Thane who couldn't tear his eyes off Azula, but there was no regret on his face.

"Perfect. Now you were part of this too. Not just from afar," Wesson praised Bonnie, and when she got back up, Viggo was done tasting his daughter as well.

"Let her sleep," Viggo told us, and without saying another word, he turned around, grabbed his clothes and one of the coolers and headed up the beach to get to the road.

I was unsure about what to do, but when Wesson and Thane followed their Dad back to their trailer, and Bonnie also disappeared, I looked at Dad.

"We can't leave her here," I told him.

"We won't."

I knew deep down Dad wasn't okay with this.

As much as he added to Azula's body breaking down tonight, I knew he would soon feel sorry for her.

He couldn't just push it aside like his brother did, and since I was his son, I'd soon feel the same way.

I watched Dad pick up all our clothes, and before picking Azula up, I wrapped her into one of the towels so her body was covered.

"We'll take her home," Dad said as he turned back to me, and after brushing back Azula's hair gently, he sighed and looked at me.

"Your mother would've killed us."

She definitely would've, but she wasn't here. "Do you regret it?"

He was quiet for a while, then he shrugged and looked back at Azula. "She wanted this. If she wakes up regretting tonight, I'll regret it too."

I understood what he was saying, and no more words were needed.

We walked back to our trailer where sweet Z would be safe and warm, and hoping she would wake up the next morning with no worries and regrets on her mind.

Until then, I would hold her close, and Dad would too.

twenty-eight

AZULA

My body ached when I woke up.

I wasn't sure if it was a good or bad aching, but when I felt arms tightly wrapped around my body, I relaxed and eased into them a little more.

Without having to open my eyes, I knew I was in Warren's bed.

His bed wasn't as hard as Dad's or mine, and I could tell Warren and I weren't alone in his bed either.

Reuben was right in front of me, his hand cupping my face gently.

I remembered last night and as tired as I was, it didn't feel like I slept enough to regain strength.

It was mostly my mind that needed it, not my body, but since it was my idea for the events that happened last night, I shouldn't complain.

Warren's arms tightened as I tried to stretch, and when I opened my eyes, I looked directly at Reuben's handsome face.

He looked calm and relaxed, just how he should be feeling.

Lifting my left hand, I placed it on his covering my cheek and brushed my thumb along the back of his hand gently.

Although a voice inside my head was telling me not to feel bad about what I made them do to me, I couldn't help but feel slightly uncomfortable with myself.

Sure, we all consented to it, and I even hatched that plan and not them, but I still had a feeling of remorse inside my chest.

I knew what Reuben felt for me, and even if it was only a crush he had on me, it still felt wrong to have made him share me with the others.

With my eyes still on his, I watched as his slowly opened, looking straight into mine.

I smiled at him, hoping the regret I was feeling wouldn't reflect in his eyes.

"Hey," I whispered, keeping my hand on his as he took me in carefully.

He was trying to figure out if I was okay, but he didn't have to worry about that.

I was fine, just a little exhausted.

"Hey," he whispered back. "How are you feeling?"

"I'm okay. How are you?" I asked.

His eyes were narrow and looked tired. "Okay," he replied quietly, then he let his eyes wander down to my upper body which they must've covered with one of their shirts before putting me to bed.

"You passed out last night. I don't know why we let it go so far, but I was worried," he told me, keeping his voice low to not wake up Warren.

"I don't want you to worry. I'm okay, Reuben," I promised, placing my hand on his cheek now.

"You didn't look okay to me last night. You were…gone. And we just kept going. We should've stopped before you passed out."

"No. Reuben, I wanted it. I wanted you guys to push my limits as much as possible and I wanted to do the same with myself. I don't want you to feel guilty."

A frown appeared between his brows now, trying to understand what I was saying.

Maybe the things I wanted couldn't be understood by others, and that's okay.

Everyone had something only they comprehended, and for me it was feeling that extreme sense of lightness in my head and body while others used my body for pleasure.

I was young, and most girls my age wouldn't even go as far as to experience something so intense, but that exact feeling was something I craved.

The feeling of being loved, yet used.

The feeling of being in control, yet losing it.

It was what my body craved.

What my mind craved, and although I was just at the beginning of getting used to it being what I wanted, I knew last night wasn't the last time they brought me to the point of consumption.

"You don't remember what we did to you when you were passed out," Reuben stated. "It felt wrong. You weren't even aware of what we were doing."

"I don't care."

"Why not?"

His question almost made me laugh.

God, he was so damn sweet.

"Because I don't. Don't you have something you know is not normal but you just can't stop doing or thinking about? A sort of obsession. Something others wouldn't understand but even if they knew you wouldn't care."

He studied me closely, thinking about my words until a gentle smile appeared on his lips. "There's one thing I know no one would understand."

"Tell me about it," I whispered, caressing his cheek.

"No. You'll think I'm weird."

"I already think that," I teased. "Come on, Reuben. You know I would never judge you for anything."

He sighed and shook his head, but then he ran his fingers down my neck and over my shoulder.

"I'm obsessed with your scent. Peaches and honey. That's what you smell like. You didn't smell like that last night though. Dad and I cleaned you up before putting you to bed," he explained.

I felt cherished knowing he liked my scent, but his other words made me wonder what they really did last night.

"What did I smell of yesterday?" I asked.

He scowled, looking back into my eyes. "Of piss and cum. It was all over you. If Dad and I wouldn't have taken you back home, you'd still be lying there on the beach."

I didn't have to ask any more about the piss and cum.

It was clear to me what happened.

Leaning closer to him, I pressed a kiss between his brows to stop him from frowning, then I placed a kiss to his lips, silently thanking him for what he had done for me.

"I don't want you to worry about me," I whispered against his lips.

"You can't tell me not to, Z. Let me worry."

I looked back into his eyes, seeing how serious he was. "Okay. I'll let you. Only if you let me be myself."

He wasn't too happy about that, but he couldn't change the way I wanted to be handled by them.

I needed their touch.

Their way of loving me.

It slowly started to feel as if without it, I couldn't survive.

"Fine," he mumbled.

"Stop fighting," Warren hissed from behind me in his sleepy voice. "We're all different."

He didn't have to say much to get the message through, and I agreed with him.

Not everyone will agree with you in life, but as long as those people respected you, there was no reason to fight or even try to find an even ground.

***

"Full?" Warren asked as I got up from the table.

We ate breakfast together, just us three, and before heading to school, I wanted to go see Bonnie.

"Yeah. Do you want more coffee?" I asked him as I got up to walk over to the sink to place my plate in it.

"No, thank you. It's still early, Zula. Why are you in such a hurry?"

"I'm not in a hurry," I told him, not fully believing myself. "I wanna go pick up Bonnie."

He studied me and Reuben lifted his gaze to look at me as well. They both looked worried, but their frowns quickly vanished.

"Don't you at least wanna take some coffee with you?" Warren asked.

I shook my head.

I had already put on my clothes they brought back here last night, and although I wore them all day yesterday, I didn't mind.

Skipping school was my plan for the day anyway.

"I'll see you tonight," I told them, walking back over to the table and leaning in to kiss Warren's cheek first, then I moved to Reuben and kissed his lips gently, knowing that a kiss on the cheek wouldn't be enough for him.

"Sure you're okay? You're acting a little strange," he whispered.

I smiled at him. "I'm okay, I promise. I'll see you tonight at dinner."

I pressed another kiss to his lips, then I headed outside and walked straight to Bonnie's trailer.

Wanda was sitting outside, enjoying the early morning sun rays hitting her face and drinking her coffee peacefully.

"Hi, Wanda. Is Bonnie up?" I asked.

"She's in the bathroom. Been there for the past hour. At least she didn't shower for that long this morning."

I laughed softly and passed her to get inside, and when I walked down the hallway to get to the bathroom, Bonnie peeked her head out before I reached it.

"Hey," I greeted, but there was silence on her side. "Are you okay?"

No answer, though she chuckled and shook her head.

Then, finally, she spoke. "Are *you* okay? Those guys broke you last night. If I had known it would be that erotic, I don't think I would've watched."

I frowned. "But you did."

"Fuck, of course I did. But seeing your body go limp and you not responding to any of them was scary to look at. Did you faint?"

Puckering my lips, I leaned against the doorframe and looked at my hands. "I passed out from exhaustion, I guess."

"Mental or physical exhaustion?"

I shrugged. "Both, I guess."

"Shit. You don't remember much, do you?"

I shook my head this time, looking back up at her. "Will you tell me what they did to me? We can skip school and hang out at the park."

She looked at me like I was crazy, but then her face eased and she sighed. "I'm scared to, but I will. You wanted it, right? No reason for you to regret any of it."

No, there was no reason to.

And no matter what she would tell me, I knew I would let them do it all over again.

twenty-nine

AZULA

Bonnie had told me every little detail, and since she sat there masturbating while the guys fucked me, she remembered every single moment of that night.

As harsh as her description was, it didn't stop me from letting them do it all over again.

And even now, lying here surrounded by the five of them for the fourth time in the past two weeks, I knew I would let them have their fun with me again.

Dad's loud grunts in contrast to Warren's gentle touch made me feel lightheaded, and while Dad was the only one left to come, I couldn't do much else than lay there on the grass in our backyard, fisting it tightly on either side of me.

My eyes were closed, but I could feel the other three standing there, watching as Dad fucked me mercilessly.

My stomach was flat on the ground, but with my head on Warren's thigh, my back was slightly arched.

He had sat down in front of me with his legs spread apart, rubbing his cock while I leaned the side of my head against him.

He had pulled out a few minutes ago and was now only caressing my cheek, knowing I would soon fall back into that intense state of unconsciousness.

There was cum on my back and ass, and Dad was rubbing it into my skin while he continued to thrust inside of my pussy, growling and hissing curses.

Bonnie wasn't here tonight, but from what she had told me, I knew once Dad was done one of them would turn me onto my back and taste the mess they left behind between my legs.

I've never been awake during that part of our time together, but tonight, I wanted to watch.

I was trying the best I could to stay awake, and although my eyes wouldn't open, I knew I would be able to hold on to my consciousness a little while longer.

"Argh!" Dad groaned, slapping my ass hard before gripping it tightly with both hands and burying himself deep inside of me as he came.

Out of the five of them, Warren was the one who never made me feel pain, just pleasure, which in Dad's case was the exact opposite.

Thanks to him, my skin burned for hours after they fucked me, and he left marks and bruises all over my body.

Reuben was gentle with me too, though he had his moments of possession overcoming him, whispering to me how much he loved me and wished to have me to himself.

Thane was gentle too, but he added a few spanks and slaps when it was his turn.

Much like Wesson, though his were almost as painful as Dad's.

Safe to say that they were the most aggressive ones, whereas the other three cared if I was hurting or not.

Still, I didn't want them to change the way they treated me.

Or as Bonnie would say, used me.

They used me for their pleasure, but whatever they felt, I felt too.

It wasn't one-sided, but if for some reason that would one day be the case, I'd make them stop.

I was enjoying it, loving every second of their touch, and each time it happened it felt different.

A new experience every single time, and the more we did it, the more I wanted.

It was becoming an addiction, and in that moment, I didn't realize how much it would break me soon.

"Turn her around," Wesson said, and I snapped out of my deep thoughts and finally managed to open my eyes.

It was dark out, but from the sun shining all day long, it was still warm out.

I couldn't see clearly because of the tears stinging my eyes, and when one tear rolled down the side of my face onto Warren's thigh, I breathed in deeply to assure myself that I was still alive.

I felt pure bliss each time before losing consciousness, but I could truly live it out now that I was awake and aware of what they were doing.

"She okay?" I heard Reuben ask.

"She's fine," Dad muttered, pulling out of me and helping Warren turn me onto my back.

"Baby," Ren whispered, making me look up at him.

"Feeling okay?"

I managed a nod, then I moved my gaze to Reuben who was looking like he had just witnessed someone being murdered.

If this was what he always looked like after they were done with me, I'd have to talk to him to not make him worry so much.

Even if I told him I would let him worry, I didn't like seeing him in this much agony.

I was okay, and I would recover again.

Like I always did.

"Whose turn is it?" Wesson asked, sounding amused.

They took turns?

"She does look delicious tonight," Dad added in the same tone of voice.

"So?" Wesson looked at the other three, and when no one answered, I opened my mouth to talk.

"Warren," I whispered in a croaky voice, feeling him tense immediately.

"You heard her," Dad said, raising a brow at him.

Looking back up at Warren, I tried my best to smile at him. "Please," I begged, wanting to feel his tongue on me.

He brushed back my hair and studied me for a while before finally moving.

He positioned himself between my thighs, pushing them apart before leaning in to kiss my stomach.

I lifted my right hand and pushed it into his hair, and when his head moved further down, I kept him there as his tongue came out to lick through my folds.

There was cum inside of me.

Dad's, Thane's, and Warren's.

It seemed that none of them cared much about a possible pregnancy, but since it hadn't happened yet, none of us were worried.

Why would it happen?

It would be wrong to have kids with someone related to you anyway, right?

God, that would make the town talk.

Warren flicked his tongue against my clit in fast movements, making me move my hips in circles and moaning softly with every spark lighting up inside of me.

I closed my eyes again, enjoying their eyes on me.

It wouldn't take long for him to make me come, and while I was getting closer, I could hear him suck all the cum out of my pussy slowly.

He was enjoying this too, just like the others had all those times before.

Only difference was, I was awake and I would push myself to stay awake the next time too to experience this again.

It felt like heaven.

"Oh, Ren!" I cried, pulling at his hair as the orgasm came over me.

He grunted, sucking at the little nub until it started throbbing against his tongue.

"Look at her," Dad whispered, admiration filling his voice. "She's a damn goddess."

His words made me feel proud of myself, and no matter how careless he sometimes seemed, I knew he loved me more than anything on this planet.

I wanted to stay awake and know what would happen next, now that I had experienced something new, but my eyes and mind slowly shut, letting my dreams take control over my body as I slowly drifted off.

***

I woke up in Dad's arms.

I was clean and dressed, but I didn't feel as good on the inside.

My stomach was twisting and turning, making it hard to breathe, and when I opened my eyes and sat up, my head ached.

It was still dark out and I didn't feel as if I had slept many hours before waking up again, and while I tried to figure out why I was feeling this way, Dad's arms loosened around my body.

"Why aren't you sleeping, baby?" he asked in a deep, raspy voice.

"I don't feel good," I told him, placing my hand on my stomach and turning to look at him.

"Is it your stomach again? Did you eat too much last night?"

Could be, so I shrugged.

"Need to go to the bathroom?" he asked, sitting up and brushing my hair away from my face.

I nodded this time, pushing the covers off my legs and getting out of bed to head straight to the bathroom.

Dad followed me and stopped behind me as I knelt in front of the toilet, but while I was hovering over it, nothing came out of me.

I could smell the unsettling smell of puke in my mouth, but my stomach wouldn't empty itself.

"Told you not to eat so damn much, Zula."

Ever since this all started, I ate more than usual.

Before, I would eat not even half of what the guys would eat, but for some reason, all the excitement surrounding me made me eat more.

I should've been taking it slow though, seeing as my body wasn't taking it well.

"Let me go make you a tea. Maybe that will help your stomach."

I gave him a nod and stayed right there in case my body decided to change its mind.

It didn't take long for him to come back with a cup of tea in his hand, and when he stood in the doorway, I sighed and looked up at him with a crooked smile.

"Sorry I woke you," I whispered.

"Don't worry about that. Come back to bed and drink some tea."

When I got up, he handed me the cup and let me pass him, and while I got back into bed, I heard him pull the bucket we usually used to put water and soap in to clean from under the sink.

It was also the bucket we used to throw up in whenever we were sick.

Dad came back into the bedroom and placed the bucket next to my side of the bed, then he walked around it to get on his side and under the covers.

"If it doesn't get better by tomorrow morning, I want you to go to the doctor."

We didn't have medicine around the house other than cough syrup Thane once got when his throat was sore, and although the pain was bearable right now, I'd take something for an upset stomach to not deal with it all day long.

"Okay," I replied, taking a sip of the tea and leaning back against the headboard.

Dad placed his hand on my thigh and caressed it while he watched me drink, and thanks to the tea warming me from the inside, I soon put the cup away and fell asleep feeling a little better already.

thirty

REUBEN

Azula was paler than usual, and that usual smile she wore on her lips in the morning wasn't there to light up her face.

When I walked into Viggo's trailer, my cousins were all sitting around the table, already eating breakfast while my uncle made more coffee.

No one was talking, and seeing them like this looked as if nothing happened last night.

It was another rough time with all of us men using Azula's body for pleasure, but that had become normal.

"You okay?" I asked her as I sat down next to her, placing my hand on her thigh and squeezing it gently to get her attention.

She turned her head and nodded, then she put her hand on her stomach. "I've not been feeling well."

"Did you throw up?" I wondered, but she shook her head.

"No. But it feels like I have to."

"She's going to see a doctor before school," Viggo announced.

I kept my eyes on Azula and smiled at her, thinking going to the doc was a good idea. "Is Bonnie going with you?" I asked.

"No."

"Do you want me to come with you?"

She shrugged, but since her brothers and father weren't set on taking her to the doctor's office, I figured I would.

I looked over at Dad who sat down across from us. "Mind if I take the car? You can drive with them," I suggested.

Dad nodded and eyed Azula before taking a bite of his bread. "Make sure that doc gives you the real stuff. Heard a lot of them are starting to turn to that herbal medicine shit."

"Those aren't bad," Thane said.

"Didn't say it's bad. Just saying that if she's in pain and needs something for a stomachache, she should take something that kicks in immediately."

Not that Dad had any experiences with herbal medicine, but the way he put it, I believed him.

"When's the appointment?" I asked Zula, caressing her thigh gently.

"In twenty minutes. I just need to pack my backpack before we leave."

I nodded and started eating too, and when we were done, with Azula not having eaten too much, she went into the back to get her school stuff.

"When did the pain start?" Dad asked Viggo.

"In the middle of the night. Made her tea but she didn't get much sleep."

"We're exhausting her body," Wesson chimed, not sounding worried about his sister at all.

"She'd tell us to stop if it was because of us fucking her. She's got an upset stomach. That's all," Viggo replied.

"Probably just some girl problems. She's always had pain during her period," Thane explained.

"Is she on her period right now?" I asked, raising a brow at him.

"How would I know?"

"Z, are you on your period?" Wesson then asked her as she came back from her room.

She looked at her oldest brother with a confused look on her face, trying to figure out why he would ask her that.

"Uh, no, why?"

"Maybe that's why you're feeling sick."

She shook her head and looked at me. "We can go."

"All right. Let's go."

I placed a hand on her lower back to guide her to the door, and before exiting, I looked back at the guys to let them know that I would be at the garage after dropping off Azula at school.

Of course, only if she felt like going.

No need for her to sit there when she could be in bed recovering.

We walked down the street to get to my car, and when we arrived, I opened the door for her so she could get in.

"Do you think you've got a fever?" I asked as she put her seatbelt on.

"No, other than feeling sick, I'm okay."

I studied her for a moment before closing the door and walking around the car to get inside myself, and while I put on my seatbelt, Azula sighed heavily.

"You don't think this is because of all the sex I'm having, right? I mean, I've heard stories of people getting injured during sex."

I chuckled. "I don't think those injuries affect your organs. I'm sure it's just something you ate that makes you feel sick. You'll be okay, Z."

She relaxed as I drove out of the trailer park and into town, but every once in a while, Azula tightened her arms around herself and let out a small cry.

"Is it getting worse?" I asked concerned, reaching over to caress her thigh again.

"A little."

"If you need to throw up, let me know and I'll stop on the side of the road."

I hoped that wouldn't be the case as we were driving down the main street, but to our luck, the doctor's office wasn't too far away.

I parked my car and got out immediately, jogging around the car to get to her side and open the door.

"All right, let's go inside."

As we entered the office, not many people were there.

Luckily, Azula had called early in the morning and got an appointment immediately, and we didn't even have to wait in the waiting area as the nurse behind the counter told us to go directly into one of the check-up rooms.

I knocked, and when a deep voice from inside called out for us to come in, we did just that.

"Morning," the doctor said, not looking too happy to be up this early. Guess not everyone was in a good mood doing their job.

"Morning," both Azula and I replied, then we sat down on the chairs in front of his large desk.

"What can I do for you?" he asked, looking at the papers in front of him.

When he read the name, he looked at Zula, knowing I wasn't the one who needed to be checked out.

"My stomach's been aching all night long," she replied, keeping her answer short and simple.

"Have you thrown up?" he asked, typing something into his computer.

"Uh, no, but I feel like I have to. I had to a few weeks ago, but that was because I ate too much and—" she stopped herself before spilling too much, and after pressing her lips into a tight line, she continued to speak. "I didn't eat that much last night so I don't think it's because of what I ate."

The doctor kept typing, then he got up and nodded toward the bed. "Take off your shirt and lay down, please."

She did, and he then started to feel around her belly. "Have you eaten anything this morning?"

"Yes. A slice of bread with honey."

"Did you drink something?"

"Yes, water."

He was quiet again, reaching for his stethoscope, he listened to her stomach.

"I don't hear anything abnormal. Are you having issues going to the bathroom?"

"No."

The doc looked clueless, but then, it was hard even for him to figure out what was wrong when someone just had a stomachache.

"I can give you something for the sickness and pain. Think it's just an upset stomach you have there," he told her.

"Okay, that's good," she replied. At least he'd give her something to make her feel better.

There were too many doctors telling their patients they didn't need anything to heal.

Azula got back up from the bed and sat back down next to me while the doc typed more into his computer, then he handed her a note with two different medications written on it, telling us to get those things at the front desk.

"And if it doesn't get better, just come back here. But I'm positive it will go away in no time," he said to her, making her smile hopefully.

"Thank you."

Back in the car, Azula studied the medication she had already taken, and I was feeling confident that she'd be up on her feet with no pain in no time.

"Feel like going to school?" I asked.

"I'd rather stay home today. Can you drive me back?"

"Of course. Want me to stay home with you? I can take care of you," I suggested.

She laughed softly, looking at me with glowing eyes. She was tired from not sleeping much, yet she was beautiful.

"I'm not sure Dad will let you stay home just because I'm sick."

I shrugged. "I don't care. Spending time with you sounds way better than working on cars all day. I could use some time to myself too, you know?"

She smiled and then looked back at the medication. "I'll be okay, Reuben. I think I'll be sleeping anyway."

I had to respect her decision, and although I would've loved to stay home and cuddle her, letting her be was what I needed to do.

thirty-one

AZULA

Once Reuben had dropped me off at home, my plan to sleep all day and ignore the pain didn't work out the way I wanted it to.

I couldn't close my eyes, and it seemed as if that medication had only made my pain worsen.

It was unbearable, but it immediately stopped after I finally managed to throw up.

I had to force it, which wasn't fun, but I was relieved afterward and felt a whole lot better.

It was the middle of the afternoon when Bonnie knocked on my door, and when I opened, she asked if I wanted to go for a walk.

Some fresh air would make me feel good, so I changed back into the clothes I wore this morning and headed outside.

"From the symptoms you've been having, I don't think you have the stomach flu," she said.

"What do you mean?"

"Last time I felt sick like that, I had to get an abortion a few days later."

I raised a brow at her. "I'm not pregnant. I had my period." Although it wasn't like my usual periods.

The blood was much darker, and there were only a few spots on my pads.

"I'm just saying. Wouldn't hurt to get a pregnancy test. None of the guys ever wore a condom, so maybe it would be safer if you'd get tested. Just in case."

I didn't like the idea of that, although it wasn't out of this world to ensure that there wasn't a baby inside of me.

"Right now?" I asked with a sigh.

"We got time. And if you take one, I'll take one too."

"Why?" I asked, laughing.

"Because while you got five dicks, I had one reoccurring one. Watching all that fuckery got me needy."

"And who's the lucky guy?"

"Dustin."

"Huh?"

"I felt bad for him after Wesson stopped him from fucking you, so I started talking to him and made him feel a little better about himself. It's fun with him."

I couldn't help but chuckle. "And you haven't been using a condom?"

"Not always. So, we're both gonna take a pregnancy test and find out if either of us is pregnant. Will be fun," she told me.

Not sure what's fun about that other than finding out that you weren't pregnant.

That'd be very fun.

***

"These two minutes feel like two hours," I murmured.

We were both standing in the small bathroom of her trailer, just staring at the two tests sitting face down on the counter.

We decided not to look at them, but we both knew which one was whose.

"Ten more seconds," she said. She wasn't as nervous as I was, and I was trying to keep my cool while the time just didn't go by.

"What if we're both pregnant?" she asked, grinning at me.

"God, I don't even wanna think about that. We'd be the town's teen moms."

"You'd keep the baby?" she asked surprised.

There was no doubt that I was scared of being pregnant, but getting an abortion sounded wrong, especially when the possible father was a man I adored endlessly.

I knew it was immoral being impregnated by any of the five men, considering our relationships, but if I were pregnant, that baby would be a result of love.

"Probably."

We didn't need to discuss the issues it would cause if I were pregnant by any of them, so we pushed that conversation aside and looked back at the tests.

"Can we look?" I asked, already reaching for mine.

"You go first," she said, and I couldn't pick up the pregnancy test fast enough.

One line.

It's one line, I thought, staring at it without taking my eyes off it.

"What does it say?" Bonnie asked, leaning over to try and get a glimpse of it.

"I'm not pregnant," I told her, but it was then that I realized I had just been blocking out the second, very faint line.

It couldn't be.

It must've been a mistake.

"Zula…" Bonnie said, laughing softly. "That's two lines."

"No, it's not. It's one. The other one is faint."

"It's still a line, Azula. Congrats, girl. You're gonna be a momma!"

Her words echoed in my head, making my body shake and mind feel dizzy.

Shit.

"Well, I'm not pregnant. Had luck this time," I heard her say, obviously sounding happy about it.

I kept staring at the pregnancy test and the lines slowly started to blur as tears stung my eyes.

"Hey…" Bonnie sighed, rubbing my back as she stepped closer to me. "It's gonna be okay. You can still decide if you wanna keep it or not," she told me.

I knew that, but I was also sure of my decision I had made only minutes before.

I wasn't going to get an abortion, no matter whose baby this was.

"How am I gonna tell them?" I asked, trying to keep from crying. I wasn't sad or upset, just a little surprised.

But then, it would've happened someday if I let them fuck me without a condom.

"Doesn't matter how. Just matters that you *will* tell them. They have a right to know."

My heart was racing and my legs felt weak, and when I finally managed to look at her, the tears rolled down my cheeks. "I'm only sixteen," I whispered.

"So? My mom had me at fifteen and I turned out great, didn't I?" she said with a grin. "It'll be okay, Z. If you wanna keep it, I'm here to support you, and if you don't wanna be a momma this soon, that'll be okay too. Know that. You have the right to make that decision on your own."

If I didn't have her as a friend, I'd be lost.

Her kindness and support were what I needed.

I leaned against her and closed my eyes, still holding the test tightly in my hands.

Words didn't come out of me in that moment, so I let her hold me while I let my mind wander all over the place, making up scenarios about how each of the guys would react to the news.

Telling them would be hard, but if I took it slow, and after being sure about my choice, I knew they wouldn't judge me.

"If you want, you can tell my mom about it. She'll understand and be supportive. You know she loves you like a daughter," Bonnie said.

I had no doubt that Wanda would be supportive, but I had to process this first.

We stood in the bathroom for a while, then we went into Bonnie's room to lay on her bed.

"We worry too much," she whispered.

We were facing each other and holding our hands clasped together between us.

"There's so much going on around us, yet we think everything revolves around us. I can tell you're worried about what people will think, but they can go fuck themselves because it's not their shit to care about."

There weren't many times when Bonnie said something I agreed with, but this time I did.

It was hard to ignore those kinds of people, which made it hard for me to just push them aside and focus on what really mattered.

What went on in my life was for me to handle, and any opinion coming from people who didn't even know me was unnecessary.

"I'm not going to tell you what to do with this baby, and I won't try to change your mind on whatever decision you make. I'll be right here by your side."

I smiled at her and locked the words she said into my heart, not wanting to forget them.

"If your test would've been positive too, I'd say the same to you," I told her wholeheartedly, making a laugh bubble up inside of me at the thought of us both being pregnant at the same time.

"Really? Even when knowing that Dustin would've been the father?" she asked with her brows raised and a smirk on her lips.

I scrunched up my nose and thought about it for a while before laughing. "Okay, no. Maybe not with Dustin being the dad. You can do better than him," I told her.

"That's what I thought." She pulled my hand closer to her and kissed the back of it, then she smiled at me. "We'll keep it to ourselves for a little while, and when you're ready to tell the others, I'll be there with you for moral support."

I could use a lot of that.

"Thank you, Bonnie. I don't know what I would do without you."

"You'd probably be lost without me. I watched you have sex with your freaking family, Z. I'll probably be there for any other major events in your life."

True, but I wasn't sure there'd ever be a bigger event than me having sex with my dad, brothers, uncle, and cousin.

thirty-two

AZULA

Spending time with Bonnie was just what I needed.

I went back home a few times to get whatever I needed for school, but other than those times, I didn't see the guys much.

I told them I needed a little break from them, and luckily, they allowed it.

Not that they could ever hold me hostage and keep me from hanging out with my best friend.

Besides, they needed a break from me too.

I kept the baby to myself.

I wasn't ready to tell them yet, but the urge to tell Wanda was getting bigger.

She knew what it was like to be pregnant as a teenager, and as a woman, she'd be more helpful than any of the guys.

Bonnie had told me that telling her mother would help me out, and I had no doubt that Wanda would be just as supportive as Bonnie.

As we got back from school, Wanda was sitting in her usual spot, smoking a cigarette and drinking what I guessed was wine out of a mug.

She wasn't so slick about her drinking, but at least she had it under control.

"How was school?" she asked as we stopped in front of her.

"It was okay," Bonnie replied with a shrug, then she looked at me with an encouraging smile. "Azula's got something to tell you."

Already?

Shit...okay.

"What is it, darling?" she asked, looking at me and squinting because of the sun shining bright behind me.

"Uh, well," I started, unsure of how to put it. As much as I trusted Wanda, I didn't know how she'd react when she'd find out that I got pregnant after sleeping with my family.

She wouldn't judge, that was for sure, but it was still an awkward thing to tell someone.

Maybe keeping that fact to myself for now would be best.

"I'm pregnant," I told her without skipping a beat, but Wanda didn't seem surprised at all.

"I know."

"You do?" I was confused. How did she know?

"Who do you think cleans this damn trailer? I found two tests in the bathroom bin and figured Bonnie would've told me immediately. And since I'm not having sex, that leaves you to be the one with a baby."

Touché.

I didn't say anything and waited for her to resolve all my problems. Because that's what mothers did, right?

"Took you long enough to tell me. Do you know who the lucky guy is?" she asked.

"No."

"She doesn't because there's been five guys," Bonnie blurred out, making me nudge her side with my elbow.

"What? It's the truth. You have no idea who the daddy is."

"Five possible daddies? Do I at least know one of them?" Wanda asked.

I nodded but didn't go further into that matter.

I wasn't ready to tell her, and luckily, she respected it.

"All right. Next step would be to get you an appointment to get that baby checked out. Any idea of how far along you are already?"

I had no clue, seeing as there was some spotting a few weeks ago which I had mistaken as my period.

It wasn't regular either, so I never actually noticed when I was missing it.

Should've kept track.

"I don't know," I told her, placing my hand on my belly. "I don't feel pregnant."

Wanda laughed softly and took the last drag of her cigarette before putting it out in the ashtray. "I'll call my midwife and she'll help us out a little. It's been a while since I last heard from her."

I smiled at Wanda, feeling happy that she knew exactly what to do.

If I were to go through this on my own, I would be googling every single thing to figure out what to do.

"Thank you, Wanda. I don't know what I'd do without you," I said to her with a smile.

She got up from the chair and waved a hand at me, then she placed it on my shoulder and squeezed gently. "You'll be okay. And from our talk just now I'm guessing you're sure about keeping the baby, hm?"

I nodded.

I had thought about it and for some strange reason, it felt as if this baby was already part of me.

I couldn't even call it a baby yet, but I was already incredibly happy that it was growing inside of me.

"That's good. Just remember that you'll have to tell the daddy."

"But how if I don't know who it is?" I asked.

"There's blood tests you can take pre-birth, unless you wanna wait nine months. That's up to you, but maybe it's best if you let those guys know. So they're prepared, you know?"

That wouldn't be a big issue.

Just had to figure out how to tell them.

***

Wanda made an appointment for next week and said that she'd come with me for support.

There was no reason for me to be scared, but I had bad thoughts running through my mind when I thought of the possible issues this pregnancy could bring.

I knew that having a child with one of your family members was a big risk, but what if that child was loved so much already?

I sat down next to Bonnie on the couch while Wanda was cooking dinner, and when I turned to look at my best friend, she smiled at me. "You okay?"

Nodding, I leaned back and pulled my legs against me and hugged them tightly. "I think I'll tell Warren first. I'm sure he won't get mad," I whispered.

"You think any of them would get mad? I mean, wouldn't they be excited?"

"Maybe, but I have a feeling that Wesson won't take the news well."

I kept my voice low, but I could tell that Wanda was listening carefully.

"Why would he be mad about getting a niece or nephew?" she asked, making me turn my head to look at her.

I kept quiet for a few seconds, then I looked back at Bonnie who nodded at me, silently telling me to let Wanda in on my secret.

Sighing, I turned back around and bit my bottom lip before speaking. "Because it could be his."

Wanda stopped stirring whatever was in the pot, eyeing me closely before smiling. "He'll have to accept it. You made your choice, and once we're sure that baby has a heartbeat, there's no more going back. Who are the other guys?"

"You can't judge her for this, Mom," Bonnie warned, but Wanda raised a brow at her, looking slightly annoyed.

"Why the hell would I judge her? We live in a fucked up world with fucked up people. We can do whatever the fuck we desire. You think I've never done anything like that before?"

This was getting interesting…

Bonnie and I were all ears, waiting for Wanda to spill her secrets. "Shortly after you were born, I had an affair with my cousin. We did it all over this trailer, and since your father wasn't up for the job, my cousin helped me raise you and your brother. Then he ran away. Left me here with a four and three-year-old."

See?

I wasn't the only one who went against this country's laws.

She didn't get caught, so why would I?

"Did you love him?" I asked.

"Of course, I loved him. He was a good man. And something tells me that either of those five guys are men you adore. The way your eyes are glowing is enough proof."

I did love them.

So much so that I sometimes wondered how I was able to feel so much love inside of me.

"I do," I replied quietly.

Wanda nodded. "Then there's no reason for me to ask who those other four men are. And believe me when I say that you are loved by all five of them."

I knew that, but hearing it from someone made my heart warm.

"You're a lucky girl, Azula. Live your life and fuck what others think."

I could do that, but it would be hard with a growing belly.

I'd have to quit high school, which for some reason didn't seem too bad.

There had never been a goal I wanted to reach in my life. Never wanted to go to college, but rather imagined myself working for Dad at the garage.

And just because I didn't have a clue what my life would end up being, didn't mean I had no control over my life.

thirty-three

AZULA

Spending some time apart from the guys was nice, but I was starting to miss them a lot.

Other than that, I was having lots of fun with Bonnie and even Wanda, talking about this and that and hanging out at one of the diners in town or their trailer.

Being around women was nice for once, but tonight, I had to go back home and sleep in my own bed again.

She didn't tell me, but I could tell Bonnie was getting tired of me.

I was walking back to my trailer, passing Warren's but not looking at it so I wouldn't feel guilty.

Whenever I went back home to grab a few things, they all looked at me like I had just ripped their hearts out and abandoned them.

Though, they knew not to push me and just let me live.

After those nights, I needed a break from them.

When I got home, the front door was open and I could see Wesson sitting on the couch.

He had nothing but boxer briefs on as it was getting warmer each day.

"Hi," I said as I stepped inside, and when he looked up, a smile appeared on his face.

"Hey, baby. Had enough of Bonnie?" he asked, noticing my backpack which was filled with all the clothes I wore the past few days.

"More like she's had enough of me," I replied with a tight smile. "Where's everyone else?"

"Dad's still at the garage with Warren and Thane went to grab a few things at the store. Reuben's with him."

I nodded and put my backpack down, then I sat next to him and let out a heavy sigh. "Do you know what's for dinner? I'm starving."

"We'll probably have steak. We got some discounted yesterday. Actually, there were many great things that happened lately," he said, making me raise a brow at him.

"Oh, yeah? Like what?"

He pulled the corners of his mouth down, then shrugged and turned to look at me. "Like…all of us guys playing games and watching sports. You know, just us doing things you wouldn't be into."

I laughed softly. "I bet you still missed me."

"'Course I did. You just went silent and didn't talk to us for days. Tell me nothing's wrong and I won't worry."

"You never worry," I said, pulling my legs up against my chest.

"Believe it or not, sis, but I did worry. It's not usual for you to ignore us like that, and even you need a break from Bonnie at times. So, tell me. What's wrong?"

I couldn't lie to him, but telling the truth wasn't my plan either.

I kept quiet and stared at the TV in front of us, letting him watch me closely as I didn't speak.

"You know you can tell me anything, right? I'm your brother, Z. Just because we don't have *that* kind of bond, doesn't mean you can't trust me with your secrets."

"It's not that I don't trust you, Wes," I sighed, turning to look at him now. "It's just that…"

I stopped, studying his face as he tried to figure out what was going on.

"Is this about what we did to you? You would've told us if we took it too far, right?"

"Of course, Wes. That's not it," I said quietly.

"But there is something, and keeping it hidden from me and the others won't help solve whatever the problem is."

Being pregnant wasn't a problem, but telling them and hoping they would all react positively was stressful to think about.

"I'll tell you when I'm ready."

He kept his eyes on me and nodded, thankfully accepting my decision and not pushing me to talk the way he would've done if he wouldn't have noticed how serious I was.

"You're spending the night here though, right?"

"Yes," I replied, smiling at him now.

"Good. Sleeping with just Thane in bed is getting boring."

"You two sleep in one bed?" I asked surprised, though I was happy to hear that.

"Ever since you started spending the night with Bonnie, yeah."

"And have you two…"

Wesson chuckled and looked back at the TV screen. "It's strange, huh? I never would've thought I'd ever be into that kinda stuff."

It made me happy knowing that they were exploring new things, whatever those things were.

"I still prefer pussy over dicks, Z," he then said, sounding a bit more serious now.

Puckering my lips, I stopped myself from grinning. "You don't have to justify yourself, Wesson. I'm happy you and Thane have something in common."

I moved closer to him and let him pull me against his side, and once I was cuddled up to him, I wrapped my arm around his waist and closed my eyes.

"Did Dad say anything while I was gone?"

"Not really. Guess we all needed a little break. I'm glad you're okay," he told me.

His fingers rubbed along my shoulder, making my body relax from all the tension that had built inside of me.

"I feel great," I assured him, but as truthful as my words were, they didn't feel that way to me.

I still had a huge lump in my throat, knowing that I'd have to tell them about me being pregnant.

"That's good. And if there's ever a day you don't feel as great as you do now, I want you to tell me. Or tell any of the others. But don't keep it to yourself because you know we'll always help you."

His words made me smile like a fool. "You've never said anything like this before, Wes. What happened?"

He chuckled and shrugged, pressing a kiss to my forehead. "Guess I'm starting to realize that talking to each other is important. I've been quiet too damn often and just watched from afar although I was sitting right there. I'm not saying I'll stop being that grumpy and protective older brother, but I'll try to talk to you and the others more."

Imagining Wesson starting a conversation was strange, but definitely not unthinkable.

He just had to get over himself and ignore his pride.

"I love you," I whispered, nestling my face into the crook of his neck and placing a kiss to his warm skin.

"Love you too, Z. Always."

***

At dinner, Dad talked about work while Warren kept staring at me, wanting to talk to me alone but having to hold back as I didn't feel like answering all his questions.

I could tell he was worried, and for some reason, not even Reuben was as worried as his dad.

Thane was holding my hand under the table, caressing my skin while we both continued to eat and listen to Dad.

I tried to ignore Warren's stares, but once dinner was over, I'd have to talk to him and let him know that everything was okay.

"Want some more salad?" Reuben asked, holding the bowl out to me.

"Oh, no, thank you. But I'll have another slice of bread," I said, pointing to the plate with the bread they had put onto the grill next to the meat to get it crispy.

"What did you do while you were gone?" Dad asked, his eyes on me now.

"Not much. Went on walks into the city and had dinner at the diner a few times. Wanda also showed me how to make sour dough bread. I can try and make some if you'd like."

He gave me a quick nod but wasn't interested much in the bread. "You're sleeping here tonight. You've been away for too many days now," he said.

Why was he like this all of a sudden?

And even if I were to go back to Bonnie's place, why would he have to tell me where I can and can't sleep?

"That's my intention anyway," I told him, trying not to sound too sassy.

"And next time you wanna stay away for that long, you better tell me."

Jesus...

"Since when do you care how long I'm gone for?"

Dad shot me an angry glare. His mood changed in a matter of seconds, but that hadn't happened in a while now.

"Don't talk back to me like that, Azula," he warned.

"Relax," Warren muttered. "She was in the neighborhood and she showed up a few times. No reason for you to go all bossy on her."

"She's still my daughter. Least she can do is tell me what she's up to."

Instead of ending this conversation normally, Dad got up and grabbed his beer, then he headed outside without saying another word.

I frowned at my plate and pulled my hand from Thane's, fisting it tightly to keep my anger inside.

Not telling him where I was had never been an issue, and all of a sudden, he was acting like the strictest Dad on this planet?

Something wasn't adding up.

"He's had a rough day," Thane explained, but that wasn't an excuse to act like this.

"He'll calm down again," Wesson assured me. "Eat up."

It took me a moment to push Dad's behavior aside and finish my food, and although I was still mad, I already planned on going to find Dad and talk to him.

I couldn't go to sleep like this.

Not without knowing what had gotten into him just then.

thirty-four

VIGGO

I've never been mad at my daughter.

There were never moments in which I had the urge to ground her, but right now, that's all I wanted to do.

To tell her that she had to stay in her room and not come out until I got over myself.

She was a teenager, and when her brothers were her age, I let them stay away from home even longer than she had, so why the fuck was I so damn upset?

I had to leave the dinner table to keep my nerves under control, and so the beach was where I went to calm down.

It didn't take Azula long to find me though, and when her hand touched my shoulder, I looked up at her and sighed.

"Can I sit?" she asked sweetly.

I nodded, taking another sip of my beer and looking back at the lake.

The water was calm, and because it was so warm today, I had imagined others hanging out here.

There was no one around, leaving Azula and me surrounded by quietness.

She didn't speak right away, having to think about how to put her words and start this conversation because she knew that I wouldn't.

I was stubborn.

"I didn't mean to upset you," she said quietly, making me shiver as we both knew that she wasn't at fault. Yet, I didn't stop her from feeling guilty.

"I thought it was okay for me to spend some time away from home. I had a lot of fun with Bonnie and Wanda," she explained.

She clasped her hands tightly in front of her, playing with her fingers nervously.

I hated seeing her like this, but I wasn't one to get over myself that fast.

"I don't understand why you got mad just then, but I'm sorry and I don't want you to be angry with me. I'm sorry I was away for so long."

Shit.

Her voice was shaky, sounding like she was about to cry.

And all that because I couldn't act normal at dinner.

I put my bottle down and turned in my chair to look at her, and when our eyes met, I could see all the unshed tears in hers.

I was a fucking asshole, letting my daughter feel like this when it was me who was the one causing all the hurt.

Reaching out to her, I pulled her closer and wrapped my arms around her shoulders, letting her bury her face into my chest. "I'm not mad that you stayed away from us for so long, baby," I whispered, placing a kiss to her head.

"What's the reason then?" she asked, looking up at me with confusion in her eyes.

I was making this whole situation worse by not speaking my mind, but that's exactly what I should've been doing.

Time to tell the truth.

"When you finally came back home, I had hoped for you to fall into my arms. To show me how much you missed being away from me. Guess my hopes were too high. You didn't seem happy to be back home," I told her, caressing the back of her head.

Her brows furrowed and she tilted her head to the side. "That's why you were mad?"

Yeah, now that I said it, I sounded like a fucking idiot.

"Dad…you know I love you. Just because I didn't react the way you hoped I would, doesn't mean I wasn't happy to be back home. I had fun with Bonnie, but I missed you and the others a whole lot every night."

"Then why didn't you come back? What was the reason for you leaving without telling us?"

Sure, she hadn't gone far, but an explanation as to why she wanted to take time apart from us would've been nice.

She shrugged and looked at her hands in my lap, tugging at my shorts. "I'm scared to tell you."

That surprised me.

Azula wasn't one to shy away from things, seeing as she let us do all those things to her.

We used her, made her feel things she never had, and introduced her to her new self.

She had changed in a matter of weeks, grown mentally and explored herself in ways not many sixteen-year-olds would.

"Why would you be scared?" I asked, eyeing her beautiful face.

She didn't look at me, but I could tell she wanted to let me in on her little secret.

"Did we take it too far? You would've told us if we did," I stated, answering my own question.

"Yeah, I would've. That's not it," she whispered, finally lifting her gaze to meet my own.

Her bottom lip was trembling and she tried to hide it by chewing on it.

"Hey," I sighed, cupping her face with both my hands now. "Did something happen at Bonnie's?"

What else could be the reason for Azula being upset and sad?

She's always been a happy girl, and the only times she cried were when she wasn't feeling well as a baby.

Or when she fell and hurt herself while playing outside.

Other than those times, my little girl was tough.

"No," she croaked out, trying her best not to cry. "Promise me you won't get angry. I don't want you to."

I chuckled softly. "I might be a grumpy old man, baby, but I'll be right here by your side to help you out no matter what. You can count on that."

My words made her smile, but the unsureness still lingered in her eyes.

"Promise?"

"I promise, Z. Don't ever doubt me, all right?"

She took a deep breath and closed her eyes, and as she took the time to get her thoughts in order, she finally told me what the big issue was.

"I'm pregnant."

At first, her words didn't make any sense.

She was so damn young, but I was forgetting an important part of what we had been doing.

No condoms, no protection whatsoever, and I was shocked to hear that my little girl was now pregnant?

Guess I'll never receive an award for best dad in the world.

"Okay," I said quietly, keeping my eyes on her as she studied me carefully.

She looked afraid, scared that I would start shouting. I wouldn't.

"Is it?"

"Of course, it is, baby. Shit...we all should've known it would happen someday," I told her, looking down at her stomach now. "Is this why you stayed away from us?"

"Yes, and I know I should've told you earlier but...I didn't know how."

I shook my head at her and sighed. "I understand, Zula. This is wonderful," I said, smiling at her. "When did you find out?"

"Bonnie made me take a pregnancy test the day I wasn't feeling well. She said she had felt the same when she got pregnant."

I had heard about Bonnie getting an abortion a while ago, which was probably the best idea for a young girl.

But in Azula's case, I knew that she wouldn't give this baby up, no matter her age.

Hell, I didn't want her to get an abortion, but there was one thing sending out alarms in my head.

"You don't know who the dad is," I stated, not needing an answer from her.

Azula kept quiet and rubbed her flat stomach with both her hands, almost as if she was protecting that little being inside of her.

"The others don't know, right?"

"No. Bonnie and Wanda do. They're taking me to see a midwife soon. It'll be my first appointment and Wanda said the midwife will run a few tests."

I had no clue how to go on about a pregnancy, even though I had three kids. It wasn't much in my interest to know what went on during the pregnancies, but I was more into the babies being born and finally being able to hold them.

I was the proudest father ever when each of my kids were born, but knowing that my baby was having one of her own excited me more.

I reached for Azula's hand and pulled it up to my mouth to kiss the back of it while keeping my eyes on hers, and when she smiled, her body eased a little.

"I'm happy for you, baby. We'll have things to figure out, but I promise you that I'll be there for you no matter what."

"Thank you, Dad."

She got up from her chair to sit down on my lap, and once she wrapped her arms around my neck, I hugged her close to me and kissed her neck gently. "My baby's gonna be a momma," I whispered.

It sounded strange, but I had no doubt she'd be a better momma than Bee was.

Wanda would be a big help too, and I was glad she's around.

"Dad?"

"Yes, baby?"

"Can we keep it to ourselves until after my first appointment? I'm not ready to tell the others."

I had no issue with that, so I nodded and held her tight to show her just how much I supported her.

It would be a wild and bumpy ride, considering it was one of us five men who impregnated her.

But whoever the father was, that baby would be loved endlessly.

thirty-five

AZULA

On the day of my first ever midwife appointment, my heart had been racing ever since I woke up in the morning.

After telling Dad about me being pregnant, I felt a little more at ease and knew that if Dad was okay with it, the others would be too.

I was nervous to say the least, but with Bonnie and Wanda by my side, I managed to get through the appointment.

The midwife, whose name was Mona, was around Dad's age and an incredibly kind woman.

She asked me a lot of questions, wanted to know where I lived, if I've had any pregnancies before, if I used drugs or drank alcohol, and other personal things.

The only question I couldn't answer was who the father was.

I wasn't sure if telling her that I had no idea was better than just telling the truth.

Well, in a way I really didn't know who it was, but at least I could narrow it down to five men.

As she noticed my uneasiness, Wanda stepped in and explained my situation, and while I was embarrassed by the truth, Mona smiled at me with the most sympathetic smile ever.

"Dear, I don't think I have to tell you about the possible complication there may be if you carry out this pregnancy, hm?"

"No, I know. But I want this baby," I told her.

"And that's okay. I'm not going to talk you out of it. Just want to make sure you're aware."

I was very aware, especially after googling all night.

Having this baby was a risk, but I was in pain just thinking about getting rid of it.

It was my baby, and I wanted to hold it in my arms.

"Am I selfish?" I asked, looking at Mona and then at Wanda.

"Selfish? Darling, it's your body, your baby. If you had decided on an abortion, we'd still be here supporting you. This is your decision to make, and whoever tried to change your mind about it can go suck it."

"What she said," Bonnie agreed with her mother, and I smiled at them with my hands back on my stomach.

I felt ready to become a first-time momma, and the more I thought about it, the less I cared who the dad was.

All five of them would love this little human being, and that's something I could count on.

"Can you imagine us going clothes shopping for the baby? Gosh, I'm so excited! I should've kept mine when I had the chance to," Bonnie sighed.

Wanda slapped her shoulder, shaking her head at her daughter. "You need to get your life together first. No grandkids for me anytime soon."

I laughed and looked down at my stomach, gently rubbing it with both my hands. "I can't wait to hear your little heartbeat," I whispered.

Mona had told me that it was hard to find the heartbeat this early on, and since I was almost six weeks pregnant, I'd have to wait another ten weeks.

She also told me that the sickness I had been feeling in the past few weeks weren't usual that early on in the pregnancy, and that the actual morning sickness would start soon.

I was prepared for that though.

"I'll send in the tests and when I get them back, I'll call you so we can look at the results. You're still going to school, right?" Mona asked.

"Yes," I replied, but that would soon change.

I didn't want to be the pregnant girl in high school, and since I didn't have a plan of graduating anyway, I was hoping to just drop out.

Sure, dropping out might be even more frowned upon than being pregnant at sixteen, but like Wanda said, *others can go suck it*.

If I was happy and content with my life, no one's judgment mattered.

***

Back home, Dad was already home while the others were probably still at the garage.

It was Friday, so people from the trailer park would hang out by the beach tonight, and I was excited because I knew we'd be going to have some fun.

Even without alcohol, I'd have a great time.

"Hey, baby," Dad greeted as I entered the trailer, and

I immediately walked over to him to hug him. "How did it go?"

"It went well. The midwife's name is Mona and she's really nice."

"Did she ask who the father is?"

Didn't think he'd ask about that. "Yes, but she knows that I have no clue."

Dad nodded and kissed my forehead before turning back to the fridge he was standing in front of. "I told the boys to go grab a few things at the store and then we'll meet them at the beach. Do you need to change?"

"Uh, no. I'll wear this," I said, rubbing my hands down my oversized t-shirt which was covering most of my shorts.

Although I wasn't showing yet, and wouldn't be for a while, I didn't wanna wear skirts.

"All right. Then go grab the coolers. They're next to the couch," he told me.

After doing what he asked me to, I placed them next to him as he turned back around to face me.

With a smile on his lips, he put his hands on my hips and pulled me closer to him, making me stand between his legs as he leaned back against the counter.

"You look happy."

I smiled up at him and placed both hands on his chest, holding myself up and leaning into him more.

"I'm happy," I told him. "I'm a little scared of what will be, but I'm happy."

"That's good. I might not have acted the way I should've last night when you told me, but I hope you know that I'm happy too."

Dad didn't often show emotions, but today I could tell that his words were truthful. His eyes were bright and his smile genuine.

Something I hadn't seen in a while.

He focused on work a lot and didn't care much about what went on around him, but having him this excited made joy bubble up inside of me.

Moving my hands to his face, I cupped both his cheeks and stood on my tiptoes to kiss his lips.

It felt natural, and our lips immediately started to move against each other slowly, melting into one another and feeling all the love between us.

He moved his right hand down to my ass, cupping it gently and moving his other hand up to cup the back of my head.

He was being careful, almost as if I was made out of glass, and his touch felt nothing like those nights he showed me just how rough he could be.

Although I was pregnant, I didn't want to stop having sex.

In fact, I was already feeling my hormones going wild.

I parted my lips and pushed my tongue between his mouth, and by tilting his head to one side, he let me in and let his tongue move against mine.

For not having many women in his life, and especially for his age, he kissed as good as the others.

Going to the beach didn't sound as appealing anymore, but just as our kiss turned into something more, Dad leaned back and pressed one last kiss to my nose before looking at me.

"We should head down," he said, brushing back my hair and tugging it behind my ear.

"Don't we have a few more minutes?" I asked with a pout. I was starting to like this side of him.

All caring and sweet.

He chuckled. "Maybe tonight. Last night you slept in Wesson's bed. I want you in mine tonight."

I was okay with that, and so I stepped away to help him put the drinks and food into the coolers to then take down to the beach where we'd meet the others.

***

"Are you going to tell them tonight?" Bonnie asked as she sat down next to me.

I was watching Thane and Reuben talk to one of the neighborhood girls who was around their age, but other than talking, there wouldn't be more to their little interaction.

Thane had been looking at me every two minutes while Reuben kept his eyes on me, staring straight past Brenna.

"I don't know what it is, but I have a feeling that they somehow know something's up," I told her, taking a sip of my coke.

"How would they know? You only told Viggo, and I don't think he would spill the beans without your consent."

"No, he wouldn't. But they're acting weird. Especially Reuben."

"Reuben's in love with you. He probably hopes to spend the night with you alone after being away for so long."

As inviting as that sounded, I had already promised Dad to sleep in his bed tonight.

I smiled at Reuben, silently calling him over to me.

When he approached me, I turned to Bonnie. "I'll tell them tomorrow, I think. I don't wanna ruin their evening. Besides...Wesson's in a mood."

She laughed softly and looked back at Wesson who was standing next to a big rock, kicking sand against it.

I'd have to go talk to him later.

"Hey, Z," Reuben said as he stopped in front of me.

I looked up and put my cup into the cup holder of the chair and got up, then I wrapped my arms around his shoulders and hugged him. "Something wrong?" I asked quietly, rubbing his back to calm him.

"No, just happy to see you. It was a long day," he said, his voice low.

"Tired?"

"A little. Why aren't you drinking?" he then asked, looking down at my cup. "Still feeling sick?"

"No, I just didn't feel like drinking tonight," I explained.

"And do you feel like dancing? I know Thane's already waiting on you to get him away from Brenna. She can't shut up about her new job as a bartender at that sports bar in town."

I laughed and looked at Thane who was downing his beer while Brenna continued to talk to him.

I felt bad for him, and although I wanted to go talk to Wesson first, I figured he could wait for a little while.

"Let's put him out of his misery," I said, grabbing Reuben's hand and pulling him past the fire and toward Thane.

It was hard giving all of them the same attention, but they were patient with me, and once I had danced with Thane and Reuben, I'd go talk to Wesson, and then I'd go find Warren as he didn't show up at the beach.

thirty-six

VIGGO

Azula being pregnant meant a lot of things.

It meant dropping out of school and having her whole life turned upside down because of the baby.

It also meant working even harder and earning more money to give that baby everything it will need.

Our trailer wasn't big enough to house one more human being, but with a few changes, I'd make it work.

Azula was happy, even happier than she had been in the past weeks, and going against her and making her get rid of that baby would be wrong.

She'd turn seventeen a few months after the baby's born. That is, if my calculations were correct.

At seventeen, her mother was already working and had a home of her own here at the trailer park, and although I had offered to help Bee out with financing her life, she always declined to show off how strong she was.

That strength one day vanished when she found out she was pregnant with Wesson.

For some reason, taking care of kids wasn't what she wanted to spend her life doing, but that didn't stop us from conceiving.

I loved my kids, all three of them, and since Bee would've talked Azula into an abortion, I wanted her to have this kid even more.

I was determined to have my kid's lives be perfect, something I could've only wished for my own life.

"Sometimes I wonder which one of us makes her the happiest," Warren said as he sat down next to me.

I tore my gaze off Azula who was dancing with Thane and Reuben to look at my brother who had spent a little longer at the garage today to get all the paperwork done.

"We all make her happy."

There was no need to add more to it.

Azula didn't have a favorite either, and although she wasn't the same around all of us, she loved us all the same.

"Gonna take her to bed tonight?" he then asked, taking a sip of his beer.

I nodded.

"Mind if I join?"

His request made me chuckle for whatever reason. "Do whatever you want, brother. She likes more than one man by her side."

We continued to watch our kids dance as Wesson finally joined the crowd.

He had been standing further away, kicking sand and downing beers like it was nothing, and when he came to a stop next to me, I looked up and raised a brow.

"You okay?"

"Yeah, why?"

"Because you look like there's something on your mind," I told him, studying his face carefully.

"We all have shit on our minds, Dad."

Right, but my oldest son usually wouldn't make it this noticeable. "What is it?" I nudged.

Wesson sighed and shook his head at me before running his hand through his hair. "I don't know. I feel like there's something wrong. I feel like shit, but at the same time, I've never felt better."

"Definitely something wrong," Warren said with a laugh. "You've never been this sentimental."

Wesson muttered something in response, then he sighed again. "It's probably nothing. Guess I'm still recovering from Azula being away for so long and now acting like nothing ever happened."

Wesson sensed that there was something going on with her, but I wouldn't be the one to break the news to him.

Azula had to do that herself, and giving her the time she needed to let the others know was the least I could do.

"She's happy. Get over yourself and go have some fun with the others. She's been watching you ever since she noticed you standing there like an idiot."

He didn't need any more motivation to put down his beer and head over to Azula and the guys and join them dancing.

Azula smiled brightly as she saw Wesson, which made me smile too.

"As lucky as we are to have her, she's even luckier to have all of us," Warren said, sounding insightful.

"Yeah, she's pretty damn lucky," I said, letting my eyes wander down her moving body.

There'd soon be changes to it, with her belly growing, and I couldn't wait to see her that way.

Bee had looked incredible while pregnant, and I knew that Azula would too.

***

"Tired?" I asked as Azula plopped down onto my lap.

"Very. They didn't wanna stop dancing," she breathed, wrapping her arm around my shoulders and leaning into me.

"They're gonna stay out here for a while. Ready to go to bed?" I asked, placing my hand on her lap and caressing her skin.

She nodded and then smiled at Warren who had gotten rid of all the beer cans we emptied, and when he reached for her hand, she slid hers into his and let him pull her off my lap again.

"You look beautiful," he told her, placing his hands on her cheeks and tilting her head back to make her look at him.

"I do?"

As if she didn't know.

She was rare.

She was someone people looked at for minutes to try and figure out if she was pretty or not.

She was, of course, but her beauty needed to be appreciated, and luckily, we did just that.

"Most beautiful girl on earth," he complimented, making Azula blush.

"Quit making her uncomfortable," I said with a chuckle as I got up from my chair.

"I'm just telling the truth."

I watched as he leaned in to kiss her lips, making her melt into him and hold on to his shirt tightly.

People around us were minding their own business, but I'd be more comfortable if they didn't make out right here.

"Let's go home," I said, placing my hand on her waist to make her break the kiss.

When she did, Warren smirked and shot me an amused look.

"You've had too many," I murmured, taking Azula's hand as she let go of his shirt, then I pulled her away from the fire to head home.

"You leaving?" Reuben called out, and I let Warren answer his son while I continued to walk with Azula.

"How are you feeling?" I asked.

"Good. I don't think I'll be dancing like this in a few months," she stated.

"Probably not. But you've been dancing enough in the past," I said.

She slid her fingers through mine, holding on tightly as we walked along the street to get back to our trailer. "I think I wanna tell Warren."

That wasn't a surprise.

She trusted Warren more than me, at least that's how it felt, and I knew that they often had secret conversations when no one else was around.

They had their own special little bond, but having her tell me about her pregnancy first still made me feel proud.

"Tonight?"

"I think so. I almost told the boys, but I don't think they'll react the way you did. Especially Wesson."

"I don't think you have to worry about them. They're not stupid, and they know that fucking without protection can lead to pregnancies. If they had something against becoming a dad, they wouldn't have fucked you without a condom."

She let my words sink in, then she smiled and nodded. "I'll tell Warren first, then the others. I think they need to be sober when I tell them anyway."

I laughed. "Yeah, that's probably best."

We got back to the trailer and headed inside with Warren close behind. Walking straight into my bedroom, Azula took off her clothes and got into bed.

Warren had disappeared into the bathroom, and once he was out again, we switched places and I went to get rid of the beer and cigarette smells.

I heard them talk, but I didn't give them enough time to themselves before I went back out and into the bedroom.

Though, it had seemed that Azula already told him about her little secret.

"You knew?" Warren asked, standing there beside the bed with his hand on his hips.

I looked at Azula, then back at him and nodded. "She told me last night."

"Shit," he murmured, looking back at Zula with worry in his eyes. "Is that why you stayed away from us?"

"Yeah. I didn't mean to upset you."

"I'm not upset, Z. God, you're really pregnant," he said, needing to say it again to believe it. "And you've already decided that you wanna keep it? You know being a mother can be hard. And what about school? You're in the middle of your sophomore year."

"I know, but I've talked to Dad about this already. I want this baby, and I know I will be a good mother. Wanda knows too, and she'll be helping me. She's very supportive," she told him with a smile.

Warren looked at her and studied her closely as he tried to figure out how to respond to that.

I didn't think he'd be this hesitant, but he had his reasons to be.

"So you don't know who the father is, I suppose?"

Azula shook her head. "But my midwife, Mona, said that we could find out during my pregnancy. I don't mind finding out."

"You think that's a good idea? The boys don't know yet?"

"No, I haven't told them. And I think knowing would prepare whoever the dad is."

I raised a brow. "Prepare? Baby, that kid will be loved no matter who the dad is, and we'll all take good care of it," I told her.

"Still. I think whoever the father is should know," Azula said, looking at me with determination in her eyes.

I lifted both hands to defend myself, then I got into bed while Warren kept standing there.

"I think that's a good idea," Warren said. "If I'm the dad, I wanna know."

In the end, it would all be up to Azula, but at least Warren took it well and didn't freak out.

"Come here," Azula said, reaching for Warren's hand, and when he grabbed it, he let her pull him onto the bed and under the covers.

"Are you excited?" she asked him as she turned her back to me to face him.

"Still seems surreal, but I'm happy for you, Z. If you're happy, you know that I am too."

I placed my hand on her hip and moved closer to her, pressing my crotch against her.

Just because she's pregnant, didn't mean we couldn't still fuck her. And I knew she wanted it too.

Her back arched, pressing her ass against me.

"It'll all be okay," I whispered, kissing the back of her head and moving my hand into her panties and caressing her soft skin.

"Take this off," I heard Warren say, and Azula quickly took off her shirt before pulling at her panties to get rid of them as well.

Without having to talk about it, we knew exactly what to do, and so I pushed down my boxer briefs to rub my hardening cock and run the tip along her slit from the back.

Whatever Warren was doing, he was making Azula moan and relax making it easy for me to push inside of her asshole with my two fingers to stretch her.

Now that I was inside her, I could feel Warren's fingers pressing against her walls, and as we both fingered her, Azula tilted her head back against my chest.

"So wet. This pregnancy won't stop you from letting us fuck you, hm?" Warren growled.

I hoped the fuck not, because when Bee was pregnant, fucking her during those months was crazy.

"Oh, God!" she cried out, gripping Warren's shoulder with her left hand and reaching back with her right, pushing her fingers into my hair and tugging on it.

"I need you both," she then whispered, moving her hips to meet our finger's thrusts.

When I was certain that I had stretched her enough, I grabbed my dick and pushed the tip against her entrance. "Fuck," I growled, feeling Warren's fingers move inside of her.

Once I pushed into her, he pulled his fingers out as well to then fill her with his own dick, stretching her even more.

"You okay?" I whispered against her head as her body tensed, but she quickly nodded and moved her hand to the crook of my neck.

"I'm more than okay. This feels incredible. Please don't stop," she breathed.

I moved my gaze to Warren's, meeting his eyes as we both moved in and out of Azula slowly.

It wouldn't take long before we'd take this up a notch and make her cry out from pleasure, but sometimes, taking it slow didn't hurt anyone.

thirty-seven

AZULA

Kisses to my cheek woke me the next morning, and I smiled as I felt Warren pull me closer to him.

As I turned to face him, I opened my eyes to look at him. "Morning," I whispered, placing my hand on his chest.

"Morning, baby. Sleep well?" His voice was low and raspy, just what I liked to hear first thing in the morning.

"I did. You?"

He nodded and ran his hand through his hair, then he wrapped his arm around my waist and pulled me closer.

Dad wasn't in bed with us anymore, but I heard him out in the kitchen already making breakfast.

I could also hear voices, which meant my brothers were up as well.

"Are you feeling okay? It was a pretty rough night, huh?" he asked, smirking.

"I'm a little sore," I admitted, but that only meant that they had done their job right last night. "How are you feeling? I know you didn't take the news well."

"I didn't?" he asked, chuckling. "Azula, I'm happy for you. I guess I didn't expect it, although I should have. But I can tell that you want this, and as long as you're sure about it, I'll be supportive."

I looked at him and smiled, thinking that if Warren was excited for me, there was nothing standing between me telling the boys.

"Thank you," I whispered, smiling and placing my hand on his cheek to gently brush my thumb along it.

"Are you nervous?"

"A little, but I know Wanda will help me out a lot. And you have experience raising a child, and so does Dad. I'm sure I can get a lot of tips from the both of you."

"Of course. I bet you've already wondered who the father is. If you could choose, who do you want it to be?"

That was a hard question to answer, so I shook my head and denied him a reply.

"Come on, Z. You must've thought about it."

"I did, but I don't have an answer to that, Ren. Whoever it will be, I'll be happy about it."

He studied me for a while, then he gave me a quick nod and a tight smile. "You're right. That was a stupid thing to ask."

He moved, pushing himself up to lean over me with his face close to mine. "Are you planning on telling the boys?"

"I think I'll tell them at breakfast. I don't wanna hide it any longer, and I think Wesson is already suspicious."

Warren chuckled and brushed the tip of his nose against mine. "Probably. He was acting weird last night."

After kissing my lips gently, he pressed one more to my cheek before pushing himself up and pulling me with him.

"Let's go eat. I can smell bacon," he said with a grin.

I put on the clothes I wore yesterday, not caring if they smelled of smoke from the bonfire.

With my hand in his, Warren and I walked out into the kitchen to find all of them already sitting at the table.

"Good morning," I greeted, placing my other hand on Thane's shoulder and squeezing it gently.

"Morning," they all replied, mostly murmuring the word and sounding tired.

"Come sit," Reuben said, offering me the seat to his right, and once I let go of Warren's hand, I sat down and smiled at my cousin.

"You look happy this morning. Is sleeping with those two old men really that good?" he mocked, but he didn't receive any response from Dad and Warren.

"I slept very well," I stated. "And since we're all together, I need to tell you something."

I looked at Reuben, then Thane, and lastly Wesson who had been watching me closely ever since I stepped into the kitchen.

"Here we go," he muttered.

He definitely was suspicious of something, but I didn't think he'd know about me being pregnant.

I took a deep breath and looked at Dad, getting an encouraging nod from him.

"Be nice," Warren said to the boys, but I knew they would take the news well.

"Shit, now I'm nervous."

I looked at Thane and shook my head to assure him that he didn't have to be.

•

"I told Dad and Warren already, and they've got my back with this. But I'm sure you will too." I stopped and looked at each of their faces, and after taking a deep breath, I announced it. "I'm pregnant."

This was the third time I had said those words, but for some reason, it wasn't as special as the first two times.

Though, each of the guys' reaction was very different from Dad's and Warren's.

"Really?" Thane asked, his eyes wide and smile bright. "Holy shit, Z! That's wonderful!"

"For real?" Reuben asked, his face unsure. But shortly after he realized that I was being serious, he smiled and wrapped his arms around my waist to pull me closer to him.

"You're pregnant!" he announced happily, kissing my temple.

The only one who wasn't celebrating was Wesson, though he wasn't mad at what I had just told him.

"We're gonna be the best babysitters in the world. God, this baby is already so loved," Reuben said, and although I had told Warren that I didn't have a favorite contestant on being the dad, I wanted it to be Reuben in that moment.

Just because he was so damn cute.

I put my arm around Reuben's shoulders and leaned against him as he pulled me into his lap, and while he continued to talk about how excited he was, I looked at Wesson to try and figure out what he was thinking.

He smiled at me, and once Reuben let me get off his lap, I walked around the table to hug Wesson from the back, pressing a kiss to the side of his neck.

"Are you happy?" I whispered.

Wesson placed his hand on my forearm, tapping it lightly and then brushing over it.

"Very. Should've guessed, but I'm happy for you, baby," he told me. Turning his head, he kissed my cheek and then my lips, showing me that even he could be accepting.

There weren't many times he agreed with things or spoke his mind. He often kept quiet and let it all settle in, but this time, he didn't.

A lot of things still had to be figured out, but with them right next to me and with their support, I had no doubt that I'd get through it.

I was prepared and ready to go on this journey, and my excitement grew bigger now that all of them knew.

"I love you," I said, looking at every single one of them. "I love you now and I'll love you forever."

I didn't need a response because I already knew that they felt the same.

thirty-eight

AZULA

SEPTEMBER

Time flies when you're around people who make your life easy.

Each day I spent with the guys was perfect, and even with my belly growing more and more, I couldn't feel better.

I was almost eight months pregnant, and before I would give birth, I had a few more appointments with Mona, and today was one of them.

Since the guys were at work and Bonnie at school, Wanda was the one who came with me.

I dropped out when I was starting to show, which was around three months, and although I had thought the process of leaving school was difficult, it was seamless.

Kids at school speculated a lot and often asked Bonnie why I didn't attend classes anymore, but the amazing best friend she was, she never said a word.

They did see me around town a few times, but I tried to hide my belly as best as possible.

In the end, it wasn't their damn business, and as long as I was content with my life, I didn't need to let people in who would only try to bring me down.

"All right, darling. How have you been since our last checkup?" Mona asked as she walked into the room.

I sat down on the bed and pulled up my shirt to reveal my bump which looked huge.

"Good. I even danced a few nights ago," I told her with a bright smile.

Summer had been rough, not being able to dance because of back pain, but the heavier my baby got, the less pain there was.

It was strange, but then, no woman experienced pregnancies the same as others did.

"That's fun! And have you decided if you wanna know the gender or not? I know it's only a few weeks until you get to meet the baby, but I know how stressful it can be to decide on a name. Unless you have them picked out already."

I hadn't, and finding out the gender stressed me out for some reason.

"I don't know if I wanna know. The guys all want to, but it makes me nervous just thinking about it," I confessed, biting down on my bottom lip.

"Well, I will write it down and put it in an envelope, and whether or not you open it before birth will be up to you," she said.

I nodded and looked at Wanda who smiled at me, accepting every decision I took on this journey.

"Did you feel any cramps lately? Spotted any discharge?" Mona grabbed the gel and squired some onto my belly, then she reached for the transducer and rubbed the gel all over my bump with it.

"Here we go. Have you felt the baby kick lately? Did it move any?"

"Oh, yes. A lot, actually," I said, smiling happily.

Lying in bed and having the guys hold their hands on my belly to feel the baby kick and move was the best part of each day.

I loved watching them go all soft and gentle, but then turn into animals once I had enough of their cooing.

"That's good. And what about sleep? Are you getting enough of that?"

No.

I definitely did not.

But that wasn't because of the baby.

"Kinda."

"I know it can be rough, but it's important that you rest whenever you can. Try sleeping on your side with a pillow between your legs, and if that's not comfortable enough, try sleeping on a recliner. I used to do that when I was pregnant, and I slept better than ever in those things."

Her tips weren't necessary as I had already figured out what position to sleep in with a belly that big, but I couldn't tell her that it wasn't the baby that didn't let me sleep.

"Okay. I'll try that," I told her with a smile.

I didn't look at the screen because I didn't want to speculate about the gender by seeing certain things, although I didn't think I'd ever be able to read those ultrasound pictures.

"Is it still healthy?" I asked, looking at Mona.

"The baby looks pretty healthy to me, and since we got those tests back, we know that there's nothing wrong with this little being. You got lucky."

I did.

I googled too many things throughout the pregnancy which were scary, but right after getting the results back, a heavy weight lifted off my shoulders.

"Last chance. You really don't wanna know the gender?" she asked, raising a brow at me.

"No." My response came quick and made her laugh.

"Okay. I'll still write it down and put it into an envelope. I bet you can't help yourself to find out before birth. You just wait and see."

"That makes me want to prove you wrong," I said, chuckling.

"Wait and see," she repeated, making me unsure of my own decision.

She placed a few paper towels onto my belly for me to clean off the gel, and once I did, I looked at Wanda who was still smiling at me.

"Did you find out Bonnie's gender while you were pregnant?"

"Yes. I desperately wanted to know. And I'm with Mona on this. You will rip that envelope open the second you get home."

If that were the case, I'd be asking about the gender already.

I didn't want to admit it, but now I wanted to know since they basically pressured me into finding out.

I sighed and sat back up, pulling my shirt down to cover my bump. "And how did you come up with Bonnie's name?"

"It's the name I wished I had when I was little. You

know, when Wanda didn't seem to fit me, so I chose the one name I wished I would've been named."

"And how did you come up with it?" I asked.

"Probably while playing with my dolls. I didn't have many friends when I was little, so I made them up," she explained.

"I found all my kid's names in baby name books. They usually have basic names in them, but there are a few gems in there. Or just google baby name lists. There are hundreds out there. I'm sure you'll find the perfect name," Mona said.

I'd have to check the internet then.

When I got up from the bed, Mona had already written down the gender on a piece of paper and then put it in an envelope. "Baby's doing great, and when you come by next week, we'll talk about delivery. We got your due date set, now all that's left to do is for you to be prepared in case your baby decides to come a little earlier."

"Does that happen often?" I asked.

"Definitely. But we'll hope for you to go into labor on the scheduled due date."

I nodded and took a deep breath, then I grabbed the envelope and looked at it. "I don't have to be nervous," I stated, mostly saying those words to myself.

"No, you don't. Everything will be okay. You'll have me right by your side and Wanda too. And once you hold your baby in your arms, you'll see that it will only get better. You'll be filled with so much love and joy. It'll be overwhelming."

I believed that, and I couldn't wait for that moment to come.

***

"You should open it," Thane said.

I should've known they would immediately attack me and force me into opening the envelope, and there I was, standing in front of them sitting on the couch.

They were staring at me with anticipation in their eyes, all five of them, which was slightly intimidating.

"Right now?" I asked, nervously turning the envelope and rubbing my fingers along it.

"Yeah, why not? You know you wanna know. And I'm sick of calling the baby *it* all the time," Reuben said.

"That baby will come out as a clown if we don't find out the gender and give it a name soon," Wesson joked.

I raised a brow at him.

"Because of the movie. It. The clown," he said.

"I got the reference," I muttered, looking down at the envelope. "What do you think?" I then asked, looking at Dad and Warren.

They both shrugged, but I knew they wanted to find out. Maybe even more than the boys did.

"It's your choice," Dad said.

I sighed at his answer and ripped the envelope open without hesitating any longer.

They wanted to know, and I didn't want to be the only one not knowing.

"You're not doing this because we want you to, right?" Warren asked, only now trying to stop me.

It was too late now, and without answering him, I pulled the piece of paper out and looked at it to read the gender Mona had written down.

My eyes watered immediately as I read the word, and I wondered if I would have reacted the same way if the opposite gender would've been written on there.

"So?" Thane nudged, followed by the other's guesses.

"It's a girl," I whispered, covering my mouth with my hand and keeping my eyes on the paper. "I'm having a little girl."

"Oh, baby," Dad said calmly, getting up from the couch and stepping closer to me. "That's wonderful!"

He placed one hand on my belly and the other on my cheek, brushing over it gently with his thumb.

"That's amazing news," Warren then said, and when I looked at him, I wasn't the only one with tears in my eyes anymore.

I leaned against Dad and put my hand over his covering my bump.

No words came out of me while I processed that I would soon be momma to a little girl, so I listened to the boys joke about who was right about the gender.

"This means you'll have to think about a name," Dad whispered closer to my ear, and I smiled up at him.

"I want you guys to think about one too."

"We definitely will," he replied, returning my smile and kissing my temple.

"I think this needs to be celebrated," Wesson suggested, making me laugh and look at him.

"How?" I asked, although I already knew.

"Do you really have to ask that?" His brows were raised and his eyes filled with amusement.

"No, I don't think she does," Dad said. "One last time, and then we'll let her rest until our baby girl is here."

The living room was where they wanted to show me one last time how much they adored me, before giving birth.

I was lying on the couch, breathing heavily as they

took their turns to fuck me, and now that it was Wesson's turn, I knew I had to prepare not only physically for him, but also mentally

Although my bump was huge, it didn't get in the way. They knew exactly how to position me and themselves to make it comfortable for each of us.

"Turn," Wesson ordered as he pulled me onto my left side.

I had my head in Warren's lap, now facing his cock as he rubbed it slowly, and without seeing the other three anymore, I still had them pictured on my mind the way they were standing in front of the couch, stroking their lengths while they watched the fun going down.

Warren brushed back my hair and positioned the tip of his cock at my lips, silently telling me to open up for him.

Once I did, he slid inside my mouth and I started to move my head back and forth.

"Beautiful," he whispered, cupping the back of my head with his right hand and placing his other on my neck.

I let him take control over me slowly, just like I did with Wesson who was rubbing his tip along my slit.

I was wet, and with the others' cum already inside of me, it was easy for Wes to slide into me.

Moaning, I arched my back a little more and closed my eyes to enjoy every single thing I was feeling.

Wesson didn't hold back, as usual, and he started to thrust into me without showing any mercy.

I had told them before that it didn't hurt when they were rough with me, and even while pregnant, I wanted them to treat me the way they always did.

Wesson's groans got louder, and with both his hands he buried his fingers into my ass and hip, continuing to thrust into me.

I cried out in pleasure and wrapped my hand around the base of Warren's shaft, my moans muffled as he made me take him in deeper until I felt his tip at the back of my throat.

"That's it, baby. Make me come in that sweet mouth of yours," he growled.

Their dirty talk always turned me on, and to intensify everything that I was feeling, I reached between my legs to rub my clit and simultaneously circled my hips to meet Wesson's thrusts.

"Make her come," I heard Thane say, surprising me as he had always been the quieter one between the five of them.

I loved how much not only I opened up, but he as well.

I was already close, seeing as the others worked ahead and dragged me close to the edge, but it was up to Wesson to push me over it.

Warren's cock throbbed, and after only a few seconds, I tasted his cum on my tongue.

"Swallow," he ordered, groaning as the orgasm overcame him.

As if it turned him on, Wesson moved faster and slapped my ass hard, growling something inaudible as I crawled closer to the edge.

The taste of Warren's cum lingered on my tongue after he pulled out, and when Wes buried himself deep inside of me to release himself, my body stilled and tensed.

"Fuuuck!" Wesson loved to be the last one to come because he liked to hold back and accumulate all the tension before exploding, and I didn't judge him for that.

After all the fucking we had done in the past few

months, I had slowly gotten used to how tiring it was, and therefore I had also gotten better at staying awake and not passing out.

I loved seeing them all worn out and out of breath, and as always, they couldn't help themselves from showering me in their piss.

The first time they did this I wasn't aware of it and had only found out after Bonnie told me, but ever since I knew about it, I liked being awake during it.

Just seconds after I had that thought, Dad was the first to step closer, and when his warm urine hit my belly, I closed my eyes again to enjoy what most girls wouldn't.

Letting them do this didn't mean I liked being degraded, but it was more of a kink I enjoyed.

I had learned many things about myself during all this time, and I would never go back and change anything that I experienced.

When Thane and Reuben joined in, Warren leaned in to kiss my lips which was a nice contrast to the dirtiness.

His tongue moved into my mouth, tasting himself as I swirled mine around his.

Wesson was still inside of me, but I knew he was staying right there until the others were done.

"Sure this was the last time until the baby's here?" I heard him ask, and Dad quickly replied with a growling undertone.

"She needs to rest."

As much as I hated to admit it, Dad was right, and I had to start focusing on birthing my daughter which would happen sooner than I expected.

thirty-nine

AZULA

OCTOBER

Going into labor two weeks too early wasn't rare, but it made me incredibly nervous as I realized that I was going to have my baby already.

Mentally, I wasn't prepared for it, and when the pain started to get unbearable, I couldn't stop worrying.

Mona had always told me to stay calm and relaxed, but that wasn't possible with all the cramps making it hard for me to move.

It was early in the morning, almost four, and I was sitting on the couch while Dad and Wesson grabbed the hospital bag which I had packed weeks ago with Wanda for this exact moment.

"Breathe, Z. Come on, take a deep breath," Thane said. He was squatting in front of me, holding my hands in my lap and trying to calm me.

"I'm scared," I whispered. "It will hurt."

"It's hurting already, isn't it?" he asked with a crooked grin. "It can only get better from here on, Zula."

As much as I loved Thane, his words didn't really help. "Can you call Wanda?"

"Yeah, I'll do that. Keep breathing, okay? Deep breaths," he told me.

I tried, but the more the cramps hurt, the harder it was to fill my lungs with air.

Mona had prepared me enough for this moment, but this pain was greater than I could've imagined.

I watched as Thane grabbed Dad's phone from the kitchen table, then he dialed Wanda's number and held the phone up to his ear.

His worried eyes met mine again, and only a few minutes later, he was talking to Wanda.

"Did your water break?" Thane then asked, looking at me like he had no idea what he just asked me.

"No, it didn't." But I knew it could happen any time now that the cramps were getting worse.

I was definitely going into labor, and the water breaking was inevitable.

"She said no. Will you come over? Okay, bye." Thane hung up and put the phone back down before he quickly walked down the hallway and into the bathroom.

"What are you doing?" I heard Wesson growl, and when Thane came back, he held a towel in his hand.

"We'll take this with us in case your water breaks in the car. Wanda's coming over right now," he told me.

I nodded, and while my brothers helped me get up, Dad carried the hospital bag outside to the car.

"Can you walk?" Wesson asked, holding me up and steadying me on one side while Thane did the same on the other.

"I think so. It hurts more when I stand," I told him.

We slowly walked out of the trailer, and when we got to the car, Thane sat in the back with me while Dad and Wesson got in the front.

"I'm here," Wanda announced as she reached the car, and when she got inside to sit next to me, Dad immediately started to drive.

"Have you told Warren?" I asked, not wanting to leave him out of this exciting moment.

"Texted him," Dad replied, focusing on the road.

"I let Mona know and she'll be waiting at the hospital. You'll be okay, Azula. You'll soon be holding your little girl," Wanda said with a smile, brushing my hair away from my face.

I was sweating and felt as if I had just run a marathon. "Will it take long?"

"You just relax, okay? You can ask for an epidural to make this a little more bearable," she told me.

"Right when I get there?" I asked.

"Of course. It'll be beautiful, sweetie. Take it slow and let it all happen naturally, all right?"

I nodded and looked down at my bump which had never looked bigger, and as I rubbed it with my hands, I smiled knowing that I would soon meet her.

It would all become reality, me being a first-time momma and having so many people around me who would support me no matter what.

"Does Bonnie know?" I asked, looking at Wanda.

"I let her sleep but I wrote her a note. She'll come by when she wakes up."

Nodding, I let my head fall back against the head rest and closed my eyes, taking a deep breath.

"I don't wanna stress you out, but you still haven't picked out a name," Thane said.

He made me laugh and that's exactly what I needed in that moment. We had all chosen a name we liked, but out of the six names, I had already set my mind on the one I chose.

It was a name that reminded me of the bonfires we spent so many evenings at, and it was a name I had never heard before, liking that my girl's name would be rare.

"She already has a name," I told him.

"Are you gonna tell us?" Dad asked.

"Yes, as soon as she's here."

VIGGO

She had been in there for over five hours now, but none of us intended on leaving the waiting room.

Wanda came out to explain to us how far along Azula was, and every time I wished I could go back in there to be by her side.

She didn't want me in there.

In fact, she didn't want any of us guys in there, and so Wanda and Mona were the only two in the room with the nurses.

"God, I can't wait any longer. Do births always take this long?" Bonnie asked.

I raised a brow and looked at Warren who chuckled as we thought back to the time Reuben was born.

Shayleen had been in labor for too damn long, but I remembered Bee telling me that Shay went into early labor, which could take up to eighteen hours.

Azula wasn't in early labor, and I was positive that we would soon hear our baby girl cry.

"She'll be here soon," I told Bonnie, then I looked at the boys. "You guys wanna go grab something to eat? Don't think that coffee was enough earlier. You have to eat."

"I'm too excited to eat," Thane told me, and Reuben agreed with a nod. "Besides, I have a feeling that the second I leave this room, she'll be here."

"Then leave so we can finally meet her," Wesson mocked, grinning at his brother.

"I'll go grab something," Warren sighed, getting up from the chair he was sitting in, but as he walked toward the open archway, the door to Azula's delivery room on the other side of the hallway opened.

A proud smiling Wanda stepped out with tears in her eyes, and once she nodded, I knew our baby girl was here.

"She's beautiful," was what she said first, and we all got up to step closer to her.

"Can we go in?" Wesson asked, anxious to see the baby.

"They're doing a physical exam to make sure everything's okay. You can meet her in a few," Wanda said.

"How's Z?" I asked, wanting to make sure that she was okay too.

"Azula is doing wonderful. She's exhausted, but she's the happiest Mama. She did great for her first time."

That was the most important part. "Does she need anything? Something to drink?"

"She's got everything in there. I'll come let you know when they're both ready."

I was glad Wanda was around, and I knew that Azula was happy to have her too.

Not having a mother had never been an issue for her, but I knew if Bee was still around, Azula would've wanted her close.

Wanda headed back into the room and closed the door behind her without letting us get a glimpse of Azula or the baby, who still didn't have a name.

We'd give them the time they needed to settle in, and so we all sat back down and waited our turn to meet our new family member.

Another thirty minutes passed, and Wanda finally came back out. This time with a nurse, and none of us got up knowing that we couldn't all go in together.

"You can come meet her now. Maybe only two at a time because Azula's midwife is still in there," the nurse said.

Warren and I were the first to stand up, and leaving the boys and Bonnie in the waiting area, we went into the room to finally see our baby.

"Hi," Azula said, sounding tired but happy as she smiled at us.

She was holding the little bundle of joy in her arms, cooing it gently and close to her chest.

"Oh, sweetheart," I whispered, walking around the bed and sitting down on the edge of it to see her better.

"Isn't she beautiful?" Zula asked, looking down at her daughter with eyes filled with love.

"She's perfect," Warren said, sitting on the other side of her. "How are you feeling?"

"I feel good. Pushing her out wasn't as hard as I thought it would be, but I'm happy she's finally here."

I reached out my hand to cup the side of the baby's face, caressing her soft skin with my thumb and admiring those long, blonde lashes and cute little nose.

She had pouty lips, and the more I looked at her, the more she reminded me of Wesson when he was born.

"And she's healthy. That's most important," Mona said. She was standing at the end of the bed, and we all knew how big of a risk this pregnancy was.

Guess we got lucky.

"What's her name?" Warren asked, placing his hand at the back of Azula's head.

Her smile grew thinking about the name she chose. "Her name is Fiamma. It means flame in Italian, and I'll call her Fia for short."

"Hey, little Fia," Warren whispered, smiling down at her.

"That's a beautiful name," I told her, letting Warren now caress Fia's cheek. "I'm so happy for you," I whispered and leaned in to kiss Zula's head.

"I'm happy too. I can't wait to take her home and spend every single day with her."

I had no doubt that her days would be filled with joy, but having the experience of raising three kids, I knew she'd also have many sleepless nights.

We'd all have them, but we would adjust to ensure that little Fiamma would get all the attention she deserved.

And Azula too, of course.

"The boys and Bonnie are already anxiously awaiting their turn to meet her," I said, implying for Warren and I to leave the room but Mona had other plans.

"Oh, don't worry. I'll leave you guys alone and go get myself some lunch. Once all of you met her, Azula should rest for a little while. Maybe take a quick nap before Fiamma wants to eat for the first time. I have a feeling that she's gonna fall asleep soon, but in case she wants to eat earlier, just call the nurse and she'll help you," Mona said.

Azula nodded and smiled at her before looking back at Fia, and when Mona left the room, Wanda went ahead to call in the others.

"They're gonna fall in love the second they see her," Warren said as he walked around the bed to sit down on one of the chairs.

I did the same to give the others some space, and when they appeared in the door, I couldn't help but chuckle at their wide eyes and stunned faces.

"Oh, my…" Bonnie was beaming, immediately stepping up to the bed to look at Fia. "Z, she's beautiful!"

They boys were quiet but it was clear that they already adored that little girl.

"And you're glowing. Gosh, look at you two." Bonnie was fascinated, and we all let her take a moment before Azula's brothers stepped up to meet their niece.

Or, well…their possible daughter.

It was still strange to think about all of us possibly being the dad, but we'd soon find out after taking a paternity test.

And no matter what, I was ready for the result.

forty

AZULA

"Look at you," I heard Reuben whisper, making me open my eyes. After a long day of short naps, breastfeeding Fia, and having everyone move into a different room to not stay in the room I gave birth, I was finally able to sleep for more than just a few minutes.

It was already dark out, and when I looked at Reuben standing over the little crib Fia was in, I smiled.

"Is she awake?" I asked.

"Yeah, did you get enough rest?"

I nodded and then looked over to the table where Dad was sitting with Warren and Thane.

Bonnie and Wanda had left before I fell asleep and they told me that they'd be back tomorrow, and Mona was still at the hospital but not in my room.

"Where's Wesson?" I asked.

"He went to grab something to eat. Are you hungry?" Dad asked, standing up from this chair and walking over to me while Reuben carefully picked Fia up.

I trusted each and every single one of them with her, and watching them be so protective and loving over her warmed my heart.

"A little bit. Is he getting me something too? I don't like the food they have here," I told Dad.

"Of course. How are you feeling now that you got some sleep?" He sat down next to me on the bed and caressed my head, then we both looked over at Reuben who sat down on my left side, holding Fia close to his chest.

"I'm still tired, but I feel good. Do you guys have to leave soon?"

"In an hour or so. Mona also asked if someone will stay here with you. Told her I'll let you decide who you want to spend the night here with you two," Dad explained.

I nodded, and although that seemed like a difficult decision, I knew I wanted Warren here with me.

I missed being alone with him.

"Would you like to stay, Ren?" I asked, looking over at him.

He smiled and nodded. "Of course."

The door opened and Wesson stepped inside with two plastic bags with the Subway logo on it, and my mouth immediately watered. "You're awake. That's perfect," he said as he looked at me and set the bags on the table, and once he pulled one of the wrapped sandwiches out, he brought them over to me.

"I got the same for everyone," he told us, and I immediately started to get rid of the wrapping to then take a bite.

"Thank you, Wes," I said, my mouth full.

He chuckled. "You're welcome, baby. How's Fia?"

"Sleeping. Look at her. She gets cuter with every hour that passes," Reuben said with admiration in his voice.

I smiled at him and watched as he continued to coo Fia while I ate my sandwich.

"She's so calm. Maybe it'll stay that way when you take her home," Wesson said, sounding optimistic.

"You guys were all calm the first few days, but as soon as we got home you all started to fuss and cry like crazy," Dad told us.

"She's a baby. She's allowed to cry," Thane said, defending Fia and making us all laugh.

I couldn't wait to experience all the things new moms did, and with the help from the others, it would all be okay.

We finished eating our sandwiches and watched Fia wake up later that night, and when Mona came back, I said goodbye to the guys who sadly had to leave for the night.

"We'll be back tomorrow," Dad assured me, kissing the top of my head and then Fiamma's.

I nodded and smiled up at him, then I looked over at Reuben, Thane, and Wesson to say goodbye. "See you tomorrow."

They said goodnight, and once they were gone, I turned to look at Warren who was making the bed he would be sleeping on tonight next to the window.

"Is it comfortable?" I asked, watching him test the mattress by sitting on it.

"Comfortable enough for one night. You can leave tomorrow, right?"

275

I looked at Mona who was cleaning up around the room a little since my family left it in a mess after only a few hours.

"You'll be good to go tomorrow. The nurse will do one last check up on you and the baby, and then you're ready to bring her home," she told me.

Good, because I didn't think I could go one more night at the hospital.

I wanted to see Fiamma in her crib, the one we bought for her, and where she will be surrounded by all her fun toys and books we got from the thrift store.

I didn't want the guys to spend too much money on her, and so we often went to check if there were new things at the thrift store, often finding cute things for Fia.

"That's great. I can't wait," I said, looking back down at my daughter.

I still couldn't believe she was actually mine, but our bond was already so strong and it would only grow from now on.

"I'll see you again soon for your follow-up visits. I'll give you a call so we can schedule a time, but for now, you'll be going home tomorrow and enjoying some time with your daughter."

I smiled at her and tilted my head to the side, showing her how much I appreciated her.

"Thank you for everything, Mona. You made everything so easy," I told her.

She stepped closer to the bed and caressed Fia's arm before doing the same to mine. "That's what I'm here for. And if you do need my help during the night, call me, okay?"

"I will. Thank you," I repeated.

After saying goodbye to Warren, she left the room, leaving us alone.

For a short moment I felt lost, not having someone around who could help in case Fia wouldn't latch on, but then I remembered that there were nurses around who could help, and Warren wasn't so clueless either.

"Wanna try and feed her?" he asked, getting up from the bed and coming over to mine.

I looked at Fia and nodded, hoping she would be hungry and then ready to go back to bed. "Wanna try and eat a little more, baby?" I asked, not expecting an answer from her because, well…she was a newborn.

I pulled down the strap of the long gown I was wearing, one Wanda gave me to wear as she figured it would be the most comfortable thing to have on after giving birth.

It was ideal for breastfeeding, and once I uncovered my left breast, I held Fia close to it, tickling my nipple against her lips softly the way Mona had taught me to.

It all came naturally, and Fiamma was already a pro at this.

Smiling, I caressed her back with my thumb and watched her drink while her eyes were set on Warren.

"I think she likes you," I said quietly, admiring my little girl.

"I think she does," he replied, smiling down at her proudly. "Fiamma…you never mentioned that name before."

"No, I didn't. But I had it on my mind for a while now. It reminds me of the bonfire. All those nights we spend at the beach," I whispered.

"And if her hair turns red, she'll do her name justice," he added. "I'd love a little mini Z running around."

"Dad said she looks like Wesson when he was first born. What do you think?" Hearing that made the possibility of Wes being the father increase a little, but for some reason, I didn't think Fia was his.

"She reminds me of all of you kids when you were little. I guess we'll have to wait and see."

Nodding, I leaned into him and ensured that Fiamma would keep on eating and being comfortable, then I closed my eyes, feeling tired.

I was content with my life and ready for whatever obstacles may come my way, but with them by my side, and Fia in my arms, there was nothing that could scare me.

***

My first night with Fia was slightly nerve-wracking, but with Warren's help, we got her to fall back asleep after every time I fed her again.

She woke up often, fussing but never crying to tell me that she was hungry, and although my eyes barely stayed open, I managed to not fall asleep on her while she ate.

It was early in the morning when I quietly sang to her, with Warren asleep next to me on the bed and his hand cupping Fia's back.

He had lifted her out of her crib just a few minutes ago, but since he wasn't used to waking up almost every two hours, I let him get some rest.

"Are you full already?" I asked in a whisper, smiling at her as she turned her head to look up at me. "God, you're precious. You're gonna make all the boys' heads turn when you're older." But deep down, I hoped that wouldn't be the case.

She was my little girl, and the thought of boys, or even girls, being all over her was a little scary.

When I heard a knock on the door, I looked across the room to see a nurse I hadn't seen before come in.

She smiled at me, closing the door behind her. "Good morning. I'm Jen. I just wanted to come in to see if everything's okay?"

I smiled back and nodded. "Everything's perfect," I told her, looking back at Fia. "She just ate and I think I'll have to burp her."

"Have you had any trouble tonight?" Jen walked over to me, eyeing Fiamma as her eyes glowed.

I trusted her immediately, seeing as some nurses were just working to do their job.

Jen, on the other hand, was passionate about hers which made me feel comfortable around her.

"No, no trouble at all," I replied, carefully lifting Fia to hold her over my shoulder which was covered in a small towel.

"That's perfect. Dad's sleeping, hm? First time being parents?" It wasn't much of a question, and since I didn't wanna tell her about the complicated situation I was in, I simply nodded.

"You'll get used to it. Once you'll settle in at home, things will get easier." She said those words making them sound like she had experience. She was in her mid-twenties, but the way she looked at Fia and spoke with a soft voice I could tell she was a momma too.

"I've been loving the time with her. I think I've already gotten used to it," I said, smiling.

"That's good to hear. I will bring you two breakfast soon, and after that, you're free to go. Do you need anything?" she asked.

"No, thank you."

"Okay. I'll be back soon."

When she left the room, I moved my gaze to Warren and nudged his side to try and wake him, and luckily, it didn't take him long to open his eyes.

"Hey," I whispered, carefully laying Fia back into my arms. "Good morning."

"Morning. Everything okay?" he asked with concern written all over his face.

"Yeah, don't worry. A nurse just came in and said she'll bring breakfast soon. She also said we can leave after that, so we should let Dad know that they don't all have to come by again."

"Okay. I'll send him a text. How's Fia?" He sat up and leaned in closer to get Fiamma's attention who immediately reached for his face.

I knew that babies didn't have perfect vision and focus yet, but I liked to think that she already knew that Warren was someone she could trust.

"You had your breakfast already, huh? Lucky," he murmured as he kissed her neck and cheek.

"I think she'll eat again soon. She didn't have a lot just then."

"That's okay. She'll let you know when she wants more," he assured.

While Warren talked to Fia, I just watched and enjoyed this moment with them before Jen was back with our food.

"Soon we'll be home, and then you'll see your crib, your toys, and all the book we got for you. You'll be the most spoiled little girl in the trailer park," Warren said.

"And she'll be the most loved, too," I added.

That was for sure.

epilogue

AZULA

All five envelopes with each of their paternity test results were on my lap, and ever since I sat down on one of the chairs around the bonfire, I couldn't take my eyes off them.

I was nervous to find out although I had been waiting for this moment ever since I held Fia in my arms for the first time.

I had come down to the beach with her almost an hour ago, and now that Bonnie was here with us, she was holding and cooing her while I kept staring at the envelopes.

"I think it's Warren's. Look at that blond hair she has," Bonnie said.

Looking over at her, I smiled as Fia pulled at her hair. "You think?"

"Based on just her hair, yes. But she does look more like Wesson. I guess the only way to find out is to open those test results."

"I wanna wait for them to come so we can find out together," I explained.

She studied me for a while, then she smiled and tilted her head to the side. "What exactly are you scared of?"

I shrugged.

"Probably the thought of one of them being sad and upset about not being the dad. They're all incredible with her, and knowing only one is her real dad doesn't sit right with me."

"Well, but there can only be one. I don't think that will change the way they are with Fia. She's loved, adored, and all of the guys will keep on loving her no matter what. It's getting to your head, Z. It'll be okay."

I believed her wholeheartedly, but my mind whispered things to me that made me feel unsure and unwell.

"Hey," Bonnie said, sighing and turning to me in her chair. "You know how much I wished I'd be in your position? You have five amazing guys who look after you, who support and love you, and they do and feel the same for your daughter. You two are the luckiest girls on this planet, and you thinking that things would change when you find out is wrong. It's pointless to worry and you know it, so don't let your mind deceive you so much."

I let her words sink in while I looked at my sweet daughter playing with Bonnie's hair.

She was beautiful, and ever since we brought her home from the hospital, I hadn't spent a day without showing her how much I adored her.

I reached out to her and placed my hand on her cheek, gently brushing along it with my thumb and getting her attention back on me.

"I wishe they could all be your daddy," I whispered.

"Well, they can't. Now, stop frowning or you'll scare her. I heard babies can tell when you smile or frown."

I heard that too, and to not upset my baby, I smiled and reached for her to pull her into my arms. "I'm sorry, baby. I bet you won't even care who your real daddy is when you're old enough to understand."

I was sure of that, because when I was little, Warren was like a father to me too.

"So, will they be here soon?" Bonnie asked.

"Yeah. They just went to grab some things at the store. They also said to start the fire, but I don't think I know how," I admitted.

"I don't know either. They can do it when they're here."

I nodded and kept cradling Fia as she stared up at me with wide blue eyes. "Is Wanda coming?"

"Don't think so. She's probably tired from work."

"How's the new job?" I asked, knowing about all the people the country club outside of town hired for the winter season.

Wanda would be helping out in the kitchen, and although I had no idea that country clubs had guests during the fall and winter season, I hoped for her to keep the job for longer than just six months.

"She likes it, actually. And I'm happy to see her working again. It's been a while since she's been motivated to actually do something other than sit around all day."

"That's good."

Almost ten minutes later, Wesson was the first to

arrive by the bonfire, carrying one of the coolers while Thane followed close behind with the other.

I smiled at them, taking them in as they reached us, and when they were close enough, they immediately looked to Fiamma.

Of course, they only had eyes for her.

"Look at that cute face," Thane said.

As if she had understood him, Fia kicked her feet excitedly.

"Let me take her first. You've been cuddling her all morning," Wesson exclaimed, putting the cooler down and stepping in front of me, ready to take Fia from me.

I lifted her carefully and let him take her, and when Reuben appeared with Warren and Dad following him, I grabbed the envelopes again to nervously play with them.

"Relax," Bonnie whispered, but that didn't help any.

"Hey," Reuben said as he stepped up behind me to then lean down to kiss my cheek.

I smiled and turned my head to look at him, and after he placed another kiss to my lips, I let out a heavy sigh.

"You okay? Are you cold?" he asked.

"No, I'm okay," I promised with a smile which didn't meet my eyes.

"She's worried," Bonnie told him.

"Why worried? Because we'll finally find out?" He placed both his hands on my cheeks while still standing behind me, and as he tilted my head back, I had to look into his eyes. "It'll be fun. We had those results for almost a week now, and I be lying if I said that I wasn't close to just snagging and opening them."

I laughed and rolled my eyes at him. "Maybe you

should've so I wouldn't have to go through this torture today."

"Torture? Shit, thought we've put you through worse before," Wesson joked.

Reuben let go of me again to then help Dad with the fire, and I moved my gaze to Warren who was taking out all the meat they got. "Are you nervous?" I asked him.

"Nope. I'm excited. Told you we should've opened those the day we got them."

Great.

That didn't help.

Another heavy sigh escaped me, and I looked at Fia in Wesson's arms for a second before picking a random envelope and reading Thane's name on it.

"Don't you wanna wait until after dinner?" Wesson asked.

"No. It's now or never," I told him, convinced that if I didn't open the first envelope now, I'd throw all five of them into the fire.

"All right then. Go ahead."

As soon as all of them had their eyes on me, I ripped it open and pulled out the result, scanning the piece of paper for the percentage of probability.

"Wait," Reuben said, stopping me from reading any further. "Can those tests even be exact? I mean…we're all related. We all carry some of the same DNA."

His words made sense, but since I had no clue how all that worked, I couldn't add to his statement.

But neither did the others, so I looked back at the piece of paper and found the gray bar with the sentence *probability of paternity: 0%* on it.

"Zero," I said, looking up at Thane. "You're not…"

"That's fine," he said, smiling at me and then at Fia.

"I'm the fun uncle," he added with a smug grin, making us laugh.

"Look at mine next," Reuben told me, and I picked his results out and opened them quickly.

After a quick scan, I found the same sentence on his as I had on Thane's, and once I looked up and shook my head, Reuben waved his hand. "All good. I'll still cuddle her all day long," he told me.

Smiling, I looked at the three left whose test results I hadn't checked yet, and when I picked the next one, Dad's name was written on it.

I ripped it open, unfolded the paper and found the gray bar immediately, but instead of a zero, there was a ninety-nine percent written there.

My heart stopped, and while I kept my eyes on that number, no one around me said anything.

Fiamma was Dad's daughter, and for some reason, I started to feel strange on the inside.

"Whose is it?" Wesson asked, and I was certain that they all knew I had the only positive test results in my hands.

My eyes watered, and although I was in a state of shock, I managed to speak. "Dad's," I croaked out, chewing on my bottom lip.

"Shit," I heard Thane whisper, and when I finally looked up, my eyes went straight to Dad's.

His were filled with tears too, but other than mine, his were definitely happy tears.

"Congrats," Warren said, sincerely sounding happy for us.

But with all of them being okay with this, I couldn't get it into my head properly.

"You're not happy," Dad said as he stepped closer

to then squat down in front of me. He placed his hands on my lap and squeezed my thighs gently, and when I managed to look into his eyes again, I couldn't hold back my tears.

"Hey...baby," he whispered, trying to find the right words to say. "Would you have reacted the same if it wasn't me?"

I shrugged because I honestly didn't know.

Maybe it was the fact that all of them being the father would've overwhelmed me, and maybe I didn't feel this feeling right and was deceived by my own thoughts.

"Fia's healthy. She's a sweet and incredibly happy baby girl, and as long as that stays that way, I won't push these other guys into the background. They'll be Fia's dad and uncle, or whatever they wanna be. She might be mine biologically, but she belongs to all of us. And most importantly, she's yours."

Dad was never this sentimental, but hearing him say those words made my heart beat faster and quickly push away those negative feelings I had when I first read the result.

"Look at her," Warren said, placing his hand on my shoulder and making me look at Fiamma who was still in Wesson's arms. "She's too young to understand, but when she gets older, she'll see that each one of us adores her. She's so loved, and when she sees that you're happy, she will be too."

And I had no doubt that my little girl will love us all the same, despite only having one actual mom and dad.

"Come here," Dad said quietly, pulling me with him as he got up. With no other words needed, he made me get closer to Wesson and I placed my right hand on Fia's tiny body and the other on Wesson's back.

All of the guys moved in closer into a big hug, leaving out Bonnie which for some reason looked funny in my head.

"This is what we're all about, baby. We're family," Dad whispered close to my ear.

"A fucked up family," Reuben muttered amused.

"A beautiful, loving, and strong family," Warren corrected him, making my smile grow even bigger.

I had five amazing men who loved me, who showed me each day how good they were with my daughter, and who would forever be by my side no matter how many ups and downs our lives would put us through.

I lucked out and I wouldn't wanna change a thing about my life.

And in the end, being happy was what mattered the most, and my family was the one thing that made me feel just that.

Happiness.

bonus chapter

AZULA

4 YEARS LATER

"Mommy, look!" Fia's sweet voice called out from the water and I turned to look at her standing on Wesson's shoulders.

He was holding on to her ankles and I was always amazed by how strong and balanced my little girl was.

Her hands were up, reaching for the sky with the biggest grin ever.

"Ready to jump?" I heard Wesson ask her, and when Fia nodded, he pushed her up to get as high as possible before she jumped off into the cold lake.

It was November, but as always, the beach was where we spent our evening.

"Our little monkey's getting more fearless each day. Two weeks ago she wouldn't even stand on his shoulders," Warren said as he sat down on the chair next to me.

I had moved them closer to the water so I could watch Fia and the boys, well…men, enjoy some time with her before she'd have to go to bed.

We had something fun planned for tonight, but Fiamma was too little to be part of it.

Or to ever be a part of it.

"She reminds me of you when you were her age. Same energy and never stands still," he added, smiling at me and placing his hand on my thigh.

"We'll have to sign her up for gymnastics or something. I think that would tire her out," I said, smiling at him and then looking back at Wesson who helped Fia come back up.

She already knew how to swim, thanks to Reuben teaching her, but I liked that they made sure nothing happened to her.

All three of them were so insanely protective over her, and whenever I watched Wes, Thane, and Reuben spend time with Fia, I couldn't stop smiling.

She loved and adored them so much, but no one was greater than Dad.

It took me a while to get over the fact that my dad was also my daughter's dad, but Fia was a healthy kid who already knew that our family was special, so there was nothing I had to be worried about.

We weren't the first daughter and father who conceived, although I wasn't sure if any daughter ever did it consensually.

I let my dad, uncle, brothers, and cousin do things to me I'd never go back and change, and I was still as happy as I was when I was Fia's age.

What we did privately was no one's business, and since the trailer park's community was one we could trust, no one outside of it ever found out about whose daughter Fiamma really was.

There was one occasion where a random kid my age asked me if Fia was a result of incest, and although that was the truth, all I left him with were speculations.

Unless I answered him and told the truth, everything he'd spread around town would be lies and false assumptions.

In the end, we were the only ones who actually knew, and I wanted to keep it that way.

"Did you see? Mommy, I was this high!" Fia called out excitedly as she ran toward me, splashing the water all around her.

When she reached me, I let her jump onto my lap and I hugged her to me, no matter how cold her little body was.

As much as I loved to swim, I could never do it in the middle of November.

"You even jumped higher than that, sweetie," I told her, brushing my hand over her wet hair.

It was darker from the water than the usual blonde she was born with, and now that the sun didn't come out as often anymore, her little freckles across her cheeks and nose were slowly disappearing.

She got those from me, and all her other looks from dad.

She started to look more and more like him, although she was so similar to Wesson when she was a baby.

But then, we were all related, and we got lucky that our baby turned out more beautiful than all of us together.

"Did you have lots of fun today? You've been in the water all afternoon," I said to her, letting Warren place a towel over us to dry Fia up.

"I don't want today to end. Can I go in the water again?" she asked, her eyes wide and sparkling with joy.

When she was still a baby, I needed lots of help from Wanda, Dad, and Warren, seeing as they already raised children of their own, but once I learned more about being a parent, it got easier.

Fia made it easy, being the calm and gentle little girl she was.

"It's late already, but once we're done cleaning up around the trailer and have gone grocery shopping tomorrow, we'll come here again and then you can play in the water for as long as you want, okay?"

"Why not tonight?" she asked, frowning at me now.

"Because monkeys have to sleep too," Warren told her, reaching out a hand to brush back her hair. "When you see us come back home tomorrow, you can run to us and we'll take you here, all right?"

Fia smiled and nodded at Warren, then she looked back at me. "Maybe, when we go to the store, we can go say hi to them at the garage," she suggested.

"I think that's a wonderful idea," I replied with a smile, then I leaned in to lean my forehead against hers and whisper, "We can go by the bakery and bring them all something yummy to eat. What do you think?"

Her eyes widened, and after checking to see if Warren had heard me, she nodded. "Can we get them muffins or donuts?" she asked, her voice filled with excitement.

"We can get them both," I told her with a grin.

Getting pastries was never something we did before

Fiamma was born, but ever since the guys' business started to get more clients, we were able to afford more things.

Sure, we still lived in the trailer park, but even with money that could buy us a house in town, we'd never leave our home.

We were happy here, and I wanted to raise my daughter where I was raised.

Chuckling, I looked over at Warren who was grinning and acting as if he hadn't heard us, and when Thane approached us, he tilted his head with question in his eyes. "What are you guys all grinning about?" he asked, getting Fia's attention who turned her head to look up at him.

"Mommy and I have a secret you don't know," she told him, reaching out her arms so he would pick her up.

Once he did, he laughed softly. "Wouldn't be a secret otherwise, huh? But now I'm intrigued. What's that secret about?"

Fia wrapped her arms and legs around Thane and leaned back to get a better look at him, and with a mischievous little grin, she said, "It's not a secret anymore if I tell you."

"Touché," Thane said with a chuckle. "I think it's time for you to go to bed, huh?"

I turned to look into the direction Thane was looking, seeing Wanda walking our way from across the beach.

Wanda usually made sure Fia was in bed whenever the guys and I wanted to spend some time on our own, and every time we did, Wanda took Fia to her trailer where she'd sleep in Bonnie's bed.

Bonnie wasn't around much, but that was because

of her new boyfriend who lived on the other side of town, and although I was happy for her, I missed all the time we spent together before Fia was born.

Bonnie and I were still best friends, and seeing her with the biggest smile whenever she decided to sleep at home made me just as happy.

"Let us say goodnight to her first," Reuben said as he stopped next to Thane to then kiss Fia's cheek. "Gonna dream of the monster that lives in the lake?"

"Reuben," Warren warned, but instead of being scared, my little girl grinned from ear to ear.

"Mister Lakey is always in my dreams and we always play in the water," Fia explained, holding her little finger up to emphasis her statement. "And in one dream we played who can hold our breath longer."

"I bet you won," Wesson said, standing on the other side of Thane.

"I always win!" Fiamma exclaimed.

"Of course, you do. You're like superwoman. You can do anything," Thane told her.

Seeing my brothers and Reuben treat her so good always melted my heart, and to my luck, they had still enough love left for me.

I got up from the chair and kissed Fia's cheek then rubbed her back gently. "Goodnight, little one. When you wake up in the morning, I'll be right there to hug and kiss you, okay?" I assured her.

She didn't have any issues sleeping away from me or the guys, and at times I wondered if she liked sleeping at Wanda's so much because she let her stay up late to watch recordings of kids' shows.

I didn't want to know if I was right, as long as my sweet girl was happy.

"Goodnight, Mommy," she said, placing her hand on my shoulder and leaning in to kiss my cheek.

"Do I get a goodnight kiss too?" Dad was walking out of the water after he swam back from the floating dock, and when he got to us, Fiamma immediately wiggled out of Thane's arms to get into Dad's.

"Goodnight, Daddy," she told him, hugging him tight and nestling her face into his neck.

"Sleep tight," Dad whispered, kissing the side of her head and holding her tightly against his body.

When Reuben grabbed my hand and pulled me against him, I leaned into him as he wrapped his arm around my neck. "Finally getting some time to ourselves, hm?" he whispered.

I smiled and nodded, placing my right hand on his forearm and brushing along it with my thumb.

"I'll miss her though," I said, knowing that not having her in my arms would wake me multiple times a night.

"She'll be okay. And we can finally give all the love to you for once," he said quietly, exciting me more for the night we'd all have together here at the beach.

"Can I have a hot chocolate before bed?" Fia asked Wanda after Dad put her down.

"Of course," Wanda said with a smile, and after taking Fia's hand and giving me a nod to assure me everything would be okay, they walked off together and left me there with the five men it all started with.

"What's on your mind?" Dad asked as he stepped closer, placing his hand on my cheek and cupping it gently.

I moved my eyes to him and smiled, then I shrugged and whispered, "Just thinking about how lucky I am."

"We all are. Especially when we get to show it off," Dad told me, moving in closer while I was still leaned against Reuben.

Warren had gotten up from his chair and was now walking back to the bonfire where he laid out a few of the towels so the sand wouldn't get anywhere.

We had learned from that after having sex on the sand, and the outcome wasn't always fun.

Dad's lips met mine as he leaned in closer, and I reached out my hand to place it on the side of his neck, keeping him right there while I felt the others move around us.

Reuben's hands moved to my hips and he held on to them as he pushed his hardness against my ass, making me feel all of it.

Sighing into the kiss, I let Dad's tongue move into my mouth and brush along my tongue, and with our tongues dancing with each other, I started to relax and let them take over.

I love being in control at times, but tonight wasn't one of those times because I knew the more control they'd have, the more intense it would be.

"Let's take her over there," Wesson suggested, and sure enough, Dad broke the kiss to then grab my hand and pull me toward the bonfire where Warren was already waiting on us.

When we got to him, I watched as Thane stepped closer to Wesson, placing his hand on his bulge and massaging it over his swim shorts.

Wes and Thane surprisingly enjoyed some time alone, especially when I wasn't up for fun or wanted to enjoy time with Fiamma, but I loved seeing them please each other.

Wesson never denied being into guys, but there was

no need for him to.

It was clear, and I was proud of him for not pushing Thane away.

As they started to kiss, Warren pulled me to him and tugged at my shirt before pulling it off me, leaving me standing there in nothing but my skirt.

I didn't have a bra or panties on unless I needed to go into town.

Here, I could wear whatever I wanted.

To our luck, in the winter months, none of our neighbors ever came to the bonfire, and we knew we never had an uninvited guest around.

It all just fell into place like a puzzle.

Like the universe wanted it to be like that.

"Take that off," Reuben demanded, nodding to my skirt while he pushed down his shorts to reveal his hardness.

I didn't hesitate and reached for his length, rubbing it gently while Warren and Dad took off their shorts, and once all of us were naked, I got down on my knees.

I was surrounded by the five of them, all of them rubbing their cocks as I leaned in to take Reuben's into my mouth.

That wasn't enough though, and when Warren moved closer to him, I wrapped my hand around his base and started to take turns on sucking them.

I had gotten fairly good at these things, but then, I started when I was only sixteen.

Now, at twenty, I had myself under control and passing out as they fucked me hard wasn't happening very often.

"Look at her," Dad muttered, his hand caressing the

back of my head. "Not a thing has changed."

"I still see my baby sister when I look at her," Wesson said, and I could hear him grin.

I hadn't changed much.

I had maybe gotten a little more mature about certain things after becoming a mother, but I still had the same mindset as I had when I was sixteen.

Only goes to show that when you're young, that doesn't mean you're immature.

I could make my own decisions, be the girl I wanted to be, and figure things out along the way.

And if the life I had now was the one I wanted, why try and get me to become a whole different person?

This was who I wanted to be.

Who I've always been.

"But our girl will have to give us all the same attention like she always does," Thane said, hinting on how long I've already had my lips wrapped around Warren's and Reuben's cocks.

I'd never put any of them first but would always treat them the same, unless it was my daughter.

She came first, always, and whatever she desired, I'd let her have it.

I had no idea who Fia would become, but I would let her live her life the way she wanted without bossing her around or restricting her.

I would be patient with her the way Dad and Warren had been with me, and I would be spontaneous the way my brother's and Reuben had always been.

My family meant everything to me, and although it sounded cliché, I had no other way of putting it.

It was simple.

"Who knows," Wesson said. "In a few years we might have another beautiful girl doing all these things to us."

His words didn't make me stop and look up at him with an angry glare.

One day, Fiamma would find out about it all. About who her family really is.

And if she'd one day decide to go down the same path I had, I wouldn't stop her.

We'd have to wait and see.

Until then, I'd enjoy all of their attention.

more by seven rue

All books are age gaps besides RAW
All titles in cursive were banned and are only available on my website!

Reverse Harem
Birdie (Forbidden & Baby Bird in one)
Echo

Student/Teacher
When October Starts (Juno & Ezra #1)
Serendipity (Juno & Ezra #2)

Dad's best friends
Falling for Two #1 (Falling for #1)

Extremely Taboo
Genesis (Niece/Uncle)
RAW (Brother/Sister)

Family Friend
The Way We Get By (The Way We #1)

Single Dad
Undisclosed Desire

follow seven

Instagram
@sevenrue

Reader's Group
Seven Rue's Taboo

Amazon
Seven Rue

Bookbub
Seven Rue

Subscribe to my newsletter!

Authorsevenrue.com